What did I ever do to deserve this?

Charly wondered.

Oh, there was no doubt that he was a magnificent specimen of masculinity—broad of shoulder and narrow of hip, with dark blue eyes, and a chin and jaw that Dudley Doright would envy. In short, Troy was the perfect all-American male.

And he was everything Charly despised. She'd known him ten minutes, and she already knew that he was polite to a fault, greeted people with "Hey" instead of "Hi," and addressed every female over the age of consent as "ma'am." He was, in short, *Southern*. And even if his touch did seem to have affected her like a straight shot of Tennessee bourbon, there was no way in hell she was going to let him get that close to her again. Ever.

But, oh Lordy, hadn't it felt good.

Dear Reader,

Winter's here, so why not curl up by the fire with the new Intimate Moments novels? (Unless you live in a warm climate, in which case you can take your books to the beach!) Start off with our WHOSE CHILD? title, another winner from Paula Detmer Riggs called *A Perfect Hero*. You've heard of the secret baby plot? How about secret *babies*? As in *three* of them! You'll love it, I promise, because Ian MacDougall really *is* just about as perfect as a hero can get.

Kathleen Creighton's *One More Knight* is a warm and wonderful sequel to last year's *One Christmas Knight*, but this fine story stands entirely on its own. Join this award-winning writer for a taste of Southern hospitality—and a whole lot of Southern loving. Lee Magner's *Owen's Touch* is a suspenseful amnesia book and wears our TRY TO REMEMBER flash. This twisty plot will keep you guessing—and the irresistible romance will keep you happy. FAMILIES ARE FOREVER, and *Secondhand Dad*, by Kayla Daniels, is just more evidence of the truth of that statement. Lauren Nichols takes us WAY OUT WEST in *Accidental Hero*, all about the allure of a bad boy. And finally, welcome new author Virginia Kantra, whose debut book, *The Reforming of Matthew Dunn*, is a MEN IN BLUE title. You'll be happy to know that her second novel is already in the works.

So pour yourself a cup of something warm, pull the afghan over yourself and enjoy each and every one of these terrific books. Then come back next month, because the excitement—and the romance—will continue, right here in Silhouette Intimate Moments.

Enjoy!

Leslie Wainger
Executive Senior Editor

Please address questions and book requests to:
Silhouette Reader Service
U.S.: 3010 Walden Ave., P.O. Box 1325, Buffalo, NY 14269
Canadian: P.O. Box 609, Fort Erie, Ont. L2A 5X3

ONE MORE KNIGHT

KATHLEEN CREIGHTON

Silhouette®

INTIMATE™MOMENTS®

Published by Silhouette Books

America's Publisher of Contemporary Romance

SILHOUETTE BOOKS

ISBN 0-373-07890-0

ONE MORE KNIGHT

Books by Kathleen Creighton

Silhouette Intimate Moments

Demon Lover #84
Double Dealings #157
Gypsy Dancer #196
In Defense of Love #216
Rogue's Valley #240
Tiger Dawn #289
Love and Other Surprises #322
Wolf and the Angel #417
A Wanted Man #547
Eyewitness #616
One Good Man #639
Man of Steel #677
Never Trust a Lady #800
One Christmas Knight #825
One More Knight #890

Silhouette Books

Silhouette Christmas Stories 1990
"The Mysterious Gift"

Silhouette Desire

The Heart Mender #584
In from the Cold #654

* Into the Heartland

KATHLEEN CREIGHTON

has roots deep in the California soil but has relocated to South Carolina. As a child, she enjoyed listening to old-timers' tales, and her fascination with the past only deepened as she grew older. Today, she says she is interested in everything—art, music, gardening, zoology, anthropology and history, but people are at the top of her list. She also has a lifelong passion for writing, and now combines her two loves in romance novels.

For Andy...
Thank you for loving me
in spite of all the ways I've let you down.
With all my love,
Mom

Prologue

From the diary of Charlene Elizabeth Phelps Private—*do not read on pain of* death—*this means* you!

April 13, 1978

Dear Diary,

Today I am leaving this God Forsaken place forever. Aunt Dobie says everything that happened to me is the Will Of God, and that He must have something important in mind for me to do and that's why He's testing me so.

Well, if He does, I'm just going to have to do it in California, because that's where I'm going. And if I never set foot in Mourning Spring Alabama again in this lifetime, well, that's all right with me.

Thought for the Day: A place doesn't necessarily have to be ugly to be God Forsaken.

Chapter 1

June 4, 1977

Dear Diary,

This is so dumb, writing to a *book* like it was a real person, but Aunt Dobie gave it to me and she says that's how you're supposed to do, so I guess I have to. Not that anybody will ever know, since it's supposed to be *private*, and it had *better be.*

Anyway, today is my sixteenth birthday, and I'm really tired of people asking me if I've ever been kissed, haha. Like I would tell them! Personally, unless it's John Travolta or his twin, I'm not interested. Tonight Colin and Kelly Grace and I are going to see *Saturday Night Fever* again. I have seen it six times so far. I swear, I could see that movie sixty more times and never get tired of it. That John Travolta is just such a fox.

Aunt Dobie says I should write down some kind of thought for the day every day, so here it is: since there's nobody in Mourning Spring that even comes close to look-

ing like John T., I guess that means if I never get out of
here I will go to my grave unkissed.

The sign caught Charly off guard, since it was half-obscured by
creeping honeysuckle vines that had managed to elude the highway department's mowers. She rounded a bend and there it was:
Mourning Spring City Limit.

A quarter of a mile or so beyond that sign she came to another
that said Scenic Overlook, with an arrow pointing to the right.
She pulled her rented Ford Taurus into the paved, crescent-shaped
parking area and turned off the engine. She had the place to herself; dogwood season was well past and it would be a long,
muggy summer before the leaves turned again in the northern
Alabama hills.

She didn't get out of the car but sat for a few minutes and
stared through the Taurus's windshield at the mountains marching
off toward Tennessee, a soft June mist draped like a feather boa
across their shoulders, and at the town nestled in among the cow
pastures and copses of oaks in the valley at their feet. She could
count five church spires from where she sat.

She'd forgotten how beautiful it was.

"Oh, God, how I hate this place." Those words she breathed
aloud, gripping the steering wheel helplessly while her throat
filled and the tears welled up and ran down her cheeks.

Godforsaken. She'd called it that once, hadn't she? Oh, yes,
she had, long ago, the day she'd left it—she'd thought—forever.

If there was one place on earth Charly Phelps had planned
never to set foot in again, it was Mourning Spring, Alabama. And
as far as she was concerned, the fact that she was here on this
lovely June afternoon was all Mirabella Waskowitz's fault. Last
Christmas her best friend in all the world had lost her mind, not
to mention any sense of taste whatsoever, and had gone and fallen
in love with the redneck Georgia trucker who'd delivered her
baby on a snowbound Texas interstate. So now, if Charly wanted
to be her best friend's maid of honor and godmother to that sweet
little Amy Jo—and she did, in the worst way—then there was

just no getting around it; she had to come back to the South. She wasn't about to call it *home*.

Only thing was, Mirabella's wedding was in Georgia, and a whole week off at that. Charly couldn't as easily explain what had possessed her to book her flight to Atlanta a week early without telling anyone, then rent a car and go driving off west to Alabama.

But then, Charly didn't believe in explaining herself to anybody. Even herself. She'd sworn off that a long time ago.

She sat up straight, wiping her cheeks and checking her eyes and nose in the rearview mirror for telltale signs of her momentary lapse of control. Then she took a deep breath, turned the key in the ignition and pulled slowly out of the scenic overlook and onto the winding highway that, sure as God made little green apples, was going to return her to the town she'd run away from more than twenty years before. Call it Fate, or call it lunacy…she was going back to Mourning Spring.

"Are you *sure?*" Mirabella was asking for the third or fourth time. "I think we should go over it once more just to be on the safe side. Now, I want to make absolutely sure the ceiling fan switch and the lights are on *that* side of the cabinet. The intercom—"

"Marybell, honey." Jimmy Joe's patient drawl drifted up the stairs. "Come on, now, and leave the man alone. Twenty years in the navy, I think he probably knows how to follow orders."

"I am *not* ordering," said Mirabella.

Up on the ladder, her soon-to-be brother-in-law watched in silent appreciation as she bristled the way only a drop-dead-gorgeous redheaded woman can get away with doing.

"I'm just trying to make it clear, that's all. After all, we're not going to be here if he has any questions. I want to be sure—"

Troy grinned and touched his temple in a mocking salute. "Yes, ma'am, and you can be. Swear t' God, it's all up here, and clear as a bell. You two just go on along, have fun in Atlanta, now, y'hear? By the time you get home Sunday night, it's gonna be all taken care of. Nothin' to worry about.'

Mirabella had her hands on her hips and was staring up at him, giving him the look that always reminded him of a little cock robin. He watched it melt into a smile that would have just about knocked him off that ladder if it hadn't been on the face of the woman who was about to make his baby brother the happiest man on earth.

"Troy, you are a lifesaver to be doing this. With the wedding only a week away, and Charly coming, I just *have* to get this nursery project finished. I cannot *believe* that contractor, flaking on me like that. Gets it halfway finished and just...disappears!'

"Well, now, you know, these things happen," said Troy soothingly. Especially, he admitted to himself, in the South.

"Not to me," snapped Mirabella, getting that feisty-robin look again.

Jimmy Joe appeared in the doorway with Amy Jo's carrier seat in one hand and a suitcase in the other, and kind of a harassed look on his face. The look seemed to melt away the moment he set eyes on Mirabella, however, to be replaced by something that could only be described as a glow. It was a phenomenon Troy had observed before, and in a strange way, was beginning to envy.

"Hon, we need to be goin'. J.J.'s out in the car, and Mama's waitin' on us over at the house. We don't want to be hittin' Atlanta at rush hour."

"Coming..." Troy noticed that Mirabella's voice, which was normally California crisp and sort of bossy, had gone all husky and breathless, and that the smile she turned on Jimmy Joe was different from the one she'd dazzled him with. Softer, kind of misty. Then her gaze dropped to the carrier seat where her baby girl, having just recently found out what a terrific source of amusement a tongue could be, was raspberrying merrily away in a puddle of drool. The look on Mirabella's face was a lot like the glow that had just lit up Jimmy Joe's. It was almost embarrassing, Troy thought, watching those three together, as if he was intruding on something intensely private, some rare intimacy he could never share.

He waved them off with the screwdriver he was holding. "Go on—get! I never will get this job done if you keep standing around here jawin' at me. Get out of here, y'all—have a good time. And don't forget to write.''

Jimmy Joe chuckled and gave him a nod rather than a wave, since his hands were full, as he herded his bride-to-be out of the room. Troy could hear her hollering all the way down the stairs.

"...and we'll call you with the number where we can be reached as soon as we get to the hotel. Oh, there's plenty of that chicken left for salad or sandwiches, if you get hungry. *Call if you have any questions...*''

Troy waited where he was, shaking his head and laughing to himself, until he heard the front door, and a minute or two later the slamming of three car doors, one after the other. Then he put down the screwdriver and climbed off the ladder and went down the stairs and onto the front porch, just in time to watch a silver Lexus pull out onto the main road, spittin' gravel. He noticed that Mirabella was driving, which surprised him some even though it was her car. In Troy's experience, professional drivers like his brother Jimmy Joe didn't usually give up that ol' wheel to an amateur if they could help it. But then, most drivers didn't have to deal with Mirabella.

"Bubba," he said to the chocolate Lab who was just coming up the steps onto the porch, wet and stinking of pond muck, "I do believe my baby brother's got his hands full...what do you say, old boy? Huh? What do you think?''

Bubba, who at ninety-five pounds was still a puppy and hadn't figured out yet where he left off and the rest of the world began, was weaving his way ecstatically around and between Troy's legs and leaving them well smeared with whatever it was he'd just been wallowing in. In spite of that, Troy gave him a good rough-house and hug, partly to fill the lonely, empty place that always seemed to open up inside him when he watched his brother and his woman and her baby together.

And sometimes for no reason at all. In fact, he'd been having that feeling a lot in the past six months or so, pretty much ever since he'd made the decision to retire from the navy. It seemed all his SEAL training and experience hadn't done a whole lot to prepare him for what came after that.

"Whoo-ee, you stink," he said to Bubba. And now, of course, so did he. He gave the dog one last rub and went in to wash himself off. He had a nursery to rewire, and he figured if he tried he could probably stretch the job out to take up the whole weekend. Might as well, he thought. He didn't have anything better to do.

Charly drove slowly, trying to take in everything at once and at the same time watch where she was going—not that there was any traffic to worry about; that much hadn't changed. She didn't know which was the greater wonder to her—the things that were different or the things that, even after twenty years, were still exactly as she remembered them.

She noticed that there was now a great big new Winn-Dixie on the outskirts of town, on a spot where there'd been nothing but a whole bunch of trees half buried in kudzu and a curb market that used to sell fresh honey, peanuts boiled or roasted and peaches and tomatoes and watermelons in their proper season. And praise the Lord, fast food had found its way to Mourning Spring! Both a Burger King and a KFC appeared to be flourishing, cunningly planted as they were, across the street from the high school.

But there was B.B.'s Barn, better known in Charly's day as the Beer and Boogie, just as tacky as ever, still standing alone at the edge of town like the village outcast, with only the equally trashy Mourning—or Moanin', as it was locally pronounced, with an implied snicker—Springs Motel across the road for company. And the big old redbrick and white frame Victorian houses on Main Street looked just the same, although Charly noticed that a few now had quaint, handcrafty signs like The Good Mourning Bed And Breakfast, and Mourning Glory Inn planted in beds of geraniums on their front lawns.

The butterflies in her stomach didn't start in earnest, though, until she drove onto the courthouse square. It was still as pretty and quaint as she remembered, like something Norman Rockwell might paint, shaded by big old oak trees, with the white bandstand in the middle looking like something that belonged on the top of a wedding cake. And yes, there was still the blatantly phallic Confederate Memorial, rising out of the flower beds at the far end. And judging from the petunias and day lilies and the baskets of impatiens and ferns cascading from every light pole and street sign, the town's two rival garden clubs were still trying hard to out-green-thumb one another.

Charly considered that pretty amazing. She'd have thought surely most of the old biddies would have died off by now.

Twice she drove past the redbrick courthouse with its imposing white columns, her heart pounding. Would he be there now? she wondered. It was after hours, but he'd often worked late in his office behind the second-floor courtroom, the one with the window that looked out toward the mountains, not down on the square. In the winter when the leaves were off the trees and the darkness came early, she'd been able to look out her own bedroom window and see the light shining in his.

Naw, she told herself, taking a deep, restorative breath. He wouldn't be there. For all she knew, he might even have retired by now.

On her second pass around the square, Charly aimed the Taurus into one of the head-in parking places that faced the park and turned off the engine. Her palms were sweaty and her mouth was dry, and she had an idea that when she tried standing on them, her legs were going to be wobbly.

She was having major second thoughts about this whole thing. She'd been truly crazy to come. It was a bad idea. Foolish, at least.

But she'd done it, she was here and how was she going to face herself in the mirror if she didn't go through with it now? It simply wasn't in her to turn around and drive away without doing what she'd come here to do. Not after all this. She'd come too far, and not just in miles. She had to finish it. She owed herself that much...the closure, at least.

But before she faced him, she had to settle her emotions down. She was going to have to be calm, cool and adult about this. She couldn't let him sense her vulnerability. She knew him. If she did, he'd go straight for the jugular.

Charly got out of the car and locked it after her—a habit born of living her entire adult life in L.A.—and then stood for a moment gazing in bemusement at the restaurant on the corner across the street. The sign above it still said Coffee Shop, in the same two-foot-high red plastic letters she remembered from twenty years ago. But in her day the smaller, hand-painted sign hanging in the big front window had said Dottie's Diner. Now, in the identical style, it said Kelly's Kitchen instead.

No way, Charly thought. *Could it be?* Emotions were tumbling around inside her like old gym shoes in a clothes dryer.

Finally, smiling for the first time since she'd passed that city-limits sign, she crossed the street to the restaurant, pushed the door open and went in.

For a moment or two the sense of déjà vu was so overpowering she felt light-headed. There was the same black-and-white linoleum set in squares, like a checkerboard, and the same Formica-and-chrome tables and counter, the same red plastic seats. Four teenagers—two couples—were crowded into a booth toward the back, boisterously socializing, ignoring an Elton John song playing on the jukebox. In the alcove off to the right near the rest rooms, another teenager was punching and pinging away at a video game. In Charly's day it had been a pinball machine, but everything else was just as she remembered it, including the fact that in spite of the ceiling fans whirling drunkenly overhead, the air was too warm, and heavy with the smell of frying grease.

Behind the counter a pretty woman with poufy blond hair was busy stocking the glass pie cabinet. When she heard Charly come in she turned half around, her face already lit up with an automatic smile of welcome, and sang out, "Hey, there! You just go on and have a seat, hon, and I'll be with you in a sec, okay?"

What happened then made Charly feel as if aliens had taken over her body. All of a sudden she felt herself scrunch down and lean over to one side, as if she were trying to see out from behind an invisible obstacle. Those aliens must have taken over her voice, too, because when she spoke it seemed to have gotten a lot louder and higher pitched than her normal adult speaking voice, with a stronger Alabama accent than she'd heard coming out of her own mouth in almost twenty years. "*Kelly?* Kelly Grace, is that you?"

At that, the blond woman sort of scrunched down herself, and stared at Charly for a second or two. Suddenly her mouth fell open, and she pressed both hands to her chest and gasped, "Oh, my *Lawd,* I don't *believe* it!"

She advanced on Charly with open arms, at the same time cutting loose with a blood-curdling squeal that would have prompted anyone within earshot to immediately dial 911 anywhere in the world, that is, except in the South, where they're used to that sort of carrying on. It was, in fact, completely ignored by the teenage couples in the back booth and the boy playing video games three feet away.

"Charlene Elizabeth Phelps, is that really *you?* Oh, my stars, I swear I'm gon' die. You just come here an' let me look at you—why, you haven't changed a bit, not one little bit. Where in the *world* have you been all these years? Oh, God—my poor heart's just goin' like a freight train. Why didn't you evah *write?* Oh—oh my, I b'lieve I'm just gon' have to sit down 'fore I fall down. Charlene Phelps, I swear I could just *kill* you...."

Although this was all delivered with the accompaniment of laughter, tears and hugs and at a decibel level rivaling that of a factory whistle, and was certainly all the welcome any prodigal son—or daughter—could have asked for and more, Charly didn't let it go to her head. Since Kelly Grace had been her best friend all those years ago and was prone to emotional outbursts even then, it was pretty much what she'd expected.

"It's Charly now," she said when she could get a word in edgewise. "I'm sorry I didn't write...." Well, okay, she couldn't help but be a little choked up.

Kelly Grace waved that away as if it were just an old fly making a nuisance of itself. "Oh, hey, don't you say a thing, not a thing. I know how it is, I really do—I'm terrible about that myself. But you coulda let me know you were comin'!"

"Well," Charly mumbled, "it was kind of on the spur of the moment."

Kelly Grace wiped her own hands on her apron and grabbed

for Charly's. "Well, you just tell me all about everything, *this minute*. Charly, you say? Oh, that's cute, I really do like that— but you *know* I am never goin' be able to call you anything but Charlene. Come on over here and sit. Are you hungry? Can I get you something to drink? How 'bout some sweet tea? Oh, Lord— you used to like cherry Cokes, remember? Do you still drink those things?"

"Maybe if you put a little bourbon in it," Charly said, not entirely facetiously.

Kelly Grace laughed and fanned herself with her hand. "Oh, my, you *haven't* changed a bit." She cocked her head sideways and studied Charly with the frankly critical appraisal permitted lifelong friends. "But look at you, there's not a gray hair on your head!"

"And never will be," declared Charly, "while there's breath left in my body."

Kelly Grace laughed some more. "Well, now, I hear *that*. Let's hear it for Clairol. No, but I swear, you look just the same as you did back in high school."

"So do you," Charly lied as she slid into a booth.

"Go on, I do not. I've put on at *least* twenty pounds since the divorce—"

"Oh, Kelly, I'm sorry."

"Well, yeah, me too. It's been a while, now, though. I'm okay with it—things work out for the best, you know?"

"Did you and...?" Charly made a rotating motion with her hand.

"Bobby Hanratty," Kelly Grace filled in for her, leaning against the opposite bench with her arms folded across her plump waist. Her smile, the dimples, were the ones Charly remembered. It was her eyes that were older—reminiscent and a little sad. She shrugged. "Yeah...you know how it was. We got married right after we graduated. Probably shouldn't have—we were real young and stupid. Had our babies right away, too...." Her eyes suddenly darkened, and she caught herself and blurted, "Oh, God, Charlene, I'm just so sorry. I didn't mean—"

Charly grimaced. "Jeez, Kelly Grace, it's *okay*. It was years and years ago.'' She put a bright smile on her face. "So, you have kids? What kind, how many, tell me all about it."

It was the right thing to say. Kelly Grace was all sparkles and dimples again. "Oh, yeah, got two, one of each. Well, good Lord, they're all grown up by now, though—Bobby Jr.'s graduatin' next week, and Sara Louise is a year behind him."

"No way!"

"I know, doesn't seem possible, does it? Seems like it was just yesterday you and me were in high school, and it was me and Bobby and you and...oh, Lord, there I go again. Charlene, I'm just so sorry, I should keep my big mouth—"

"Hey, I told you, it's okay. It was a long time ago."

"Yeah..." Kelly Grace's eyes rested on her, a slight frown making wrinkles appear in all the places Charly had recently begun to study minutely in her own mirror. This is too weird, she thought. How can my best friend have wrinkles? The last time I saw her we were sixteen. *Sixteen.*

"How 'bout you?" Kelly Grace asked hesitantly, obviously still feeling uneasy about it. "What all have you been doin' with yourself? Did you ever...you know?"

"Get married? Have kids?" That, of course, was the biggy. The ol' sixty-four-thousand-dollar question. "Nope," said Charly cheerfully, "not yet. Guess I just haven't had time."

With that out of the way, Kelly Grace relaxed and settled herself like a nesting hen into the opposite side of the booth, from whence she resumed her artillery barrage of less important questions. "So, what have you been up to? Where've you been? Hey, did you ever get to California? I remember you were always talkin' about goin' out there."

"I did." Charly nodded, her head going up and down like one of those tacky little doggies people used to put in their car windows. "That's where I live now. I'm an attorney, actually."

"No way! *Get out!* You are not!"

"It's true. I'm a lawyer," Charly said, her own laughter feeling like rocks rattling inside her chest. "Swear to God. Who'd a' thought, huh?"

"A lawyer! Oh, my God, the judge musta had a cow when he heard that!"

The laughter died. Charly rested her elbows on the tabletop and pressed interwoven fingers to her lips. After a moment she cleared her throat and said, "He doesn't know."

There was absolute silence. Then Kelly Grace leaned forward and said in a hushed voice, "You mean you haven't..."

"Nope." Charly shook her head. "Haven't seen him, haven't spoken to him. Not in twenty years."

Kelly Grace's eyes went wide. "Then you don't—" She cut herself off and clamped her lips together, while her gaze slipped away and down.

Charly tried laughing it off. "Hey, give me a break, I just got into town. You're the first person I've seen, much less talked to."

"But you're going to, right? I mean, well, for heaven's sake, you are goin' to go see him, aren't you?"

"I guess I'm gonna have to," Charly said dryly. "I'm sure the news will get to him that I'm here." And probably already had, she thought as the door gave its warning ding, and she glanced around nervously to see who had just come in. A couple of teen-agers, nobody she'd know. She shook back her hair, making a conscious effort to unclasp her hands and relax her shoulders. "Actually I was driving around the square trying to get my courage up, and I saw the sign. I wondered if that was you, and I just thought I'd stop in for a minute, say 'Hey,' you know, maybe give my nerves a chance to settle a little... *Damn*, Kelly Grace," she burst out, "this isn't gonna be easy!"

Kelly Grace shifted in uneasy sympathy. "I guess not."

"Hey," said Charly brightly, "I don't suppose you'd happen to have a bottle of Black Jack tucked away someplace?"

Kelly Grace put a hand over her eyes and groaned. "Oh, Lord, does that bring back memories! Remember that Fourth of July... Lord, I thought I was gon' die."

So many memories, Charly thought. So many years. And maybe...not nearly enough. Because if it still seems like yesterday to me, and to her, then it probably does to everyone else, too.

"I should be going," she said, covering an involuntary shiver as she slid out of the booth.

Kelly Grace followed, but when Charly glanced over at her, she saw that her friend had her hand clamped over her mouth and that above the hand her eyes were way too bright. Somehow Charly knew that the brightness wasn't laughter.

A new thought and a terrible fear clutched at her heart. She halted, touched Kelly Grace's arm and said airlessly, "He's okay, isn't he? I mean, he didn't...die or anything?" And tried to laugh, as if it were of no consequence to her one way or the other.

Kelly Grace blinked, then gave a sharp bark of laughter. "The judge? God, no. I guess there was some talk he was goin' to retire a year or so ago, and I b'lieve he has cut back some. But...no, the judge is still—" she shrugged "—the judge."

"And Aunt Dobie, is she...?"

"Aunt...you mean miz—" Once again she stopped herself. She swallowed, nodded, and her eyes slid away. "Oh, yeah, she's still goin' strong."

"The Stewarts?" The word caught, and emerged in a croak.

Kelly Grace's lips twisted in a little half smile of sympathy. "No, hon, they're gone. Mr. Stewart, he passed on a few years back, and Miz Stewart, she sold the old place and moved down to Mobile to be closer to her grandkids. Becky and Royal—the girls, remember them?—they're both married and livin' down there somewheres."

They were at the door. Charly paused, looked over at the woman, now inexplicably middle-aged, who at the age of sixteen had been her best friend in all the world. *Save one.* She searched for something to say. But so many emotions were backed up inside her that she couldn't say anything at all. Kelly Grace seemed to be having the same problem. She wiped away a tear, and they both laughed.

"It was so great seein' you again."

"Yeah, you too."

Sniffling, Kelly Grace said, "Charlene, you come on back here later on, now, y'hear? After you've been to see him. We have catchin' up to do. You just have to meet my kids...come up and see Mama...."

Charly tried clearing her throat, but the ache there obviously meant to stay awhile. "Oh, Kelly, I wish I could, but I can't. I have to get back to Atlanta. I just came to..." She made the mistake of looking at Kelly Grace's face again. She turned away, saying tightly, "You know people in this town aren't going to be exactly thrilled to see me back. I doubt that's changed, even after all this time."

"My Lord, it's been twenty years!"

Charly drew a breath and let it out in a snort of ironic laughter. "Kelly Grace, *fifty* years wouldn't be enough. You haven't forgotten anything that happened, have you? Don't kid yourself—neither has anybody else."

It had been a good many years since Charly Phelps had made a fool of herself in a public place, and here she was, not thirty minutes back in Mourning Spring and trembling on the brink of doing just that. I've got to get out of this town, she thought. Do it, get it over with and get out of here. *God, I hate this place.*

"I'll stop and see you before I go," she finally promised, desperate to escape. She gave Kelly Grace a quick hug and pushed her way through the door.

Looking neither right nor left, she hurried across the street. She unlocked the Taurus, got in, started it up, backed out of the parking space and drove off, all without allowing herself to think even once about what she was about to do. She'd conquered skydiving pretty much the same way, come to think of it. And if I did that, she told herself, teeth clenched with determination, I can do anything. I can do this. *I can.*

Her courage thus bolstered, her resolve fortified, she turned off the courthouse square and onto Hill Street, so named for the residential neighborhood in which it dead-ended. The Hill wasn't much of a hill, as hills go, but it did lend a kind of exclusivity to the cluster of mansions dating back at least to Reconstruction. A few were even said to have actually survived the Yankee invasion. All the homes on the Hill had the same quiet, if rather stuffy elegance, surrounded by brick and wrought iron and shaded by oaks so huge and old they arched over the street and met in the middle, turning it into a sun-dappled tunnel.

Her destination was the second house from the end, a redbrick Victorian monster with a white-columned portico and black shutters. She turned into the semicircular driveway, shut off the engine and sat for a moment, watching dust motes dance in the afternoon's last sunlight where it slanted through the trees. The ache in her throat felt like a betrayal.

Oh, God, I hate this place.

She opened the car door and stepped out, then closed it carefully behind her. Had she ever done anything more difficult?

Oh, yes, once. Twenty years ago.

But this was only one step…still so many more to go.

Her heart pounded and her breath came in soft, quick snatches as she mounted the steps between two concrete urns filled with bright red impatiens and yellow day lilies. She crossed the wood plank porch where white wicker armchairs and rockers sat empty, reminiscent of long, hot summer evenings, tall glasses of cold, sweet tea, and lightnin' bugs blinking on and off in the twilight.

On the doormat she paused, looked down, and from a habit she'd thought long forgotten, carefully wiped her feet. She wiped her hands on the sides of her expensive gray gabardine slacks, wrinkled and creased now from the flight and the long drive from Atlanta. Then she took a deep breath, held it and firmly pressed the doorbell. She could hear the old-fashioned chimes go echoing through the great, high-ceilinged rooms. She bowed her head and waited, counting her own heartbeats.

The door opened without warning, thrown wide to frame the figure of the woman who stood there. She was as straight and regal as in Charly's memory, though she seemed perhaps a little smaller. Her close-cropped hair, once pepper black with only the lightest sprinkle of salt, was snowy white now, but her mahogany skin was still without a wrinkle, stretched taut over the bones of a face that might have graced the walls of an Egyptian pharaoh's tomb.

Her deep-set eyes seemed equally ancient in that eternally

young face, missing nothing. They skewered Charly where she stood, narrowed, then went wide with shock. She lifted her hands, sucked in air and whispered, "Oh, my sweet Jesus..."

It was in no way a blasphemy, but a heartfelt prayer.

Chapter 2

June 10, 1977

Dear Diary,

This is just so unfair! The judge found out about my platform shoes, and did he throw a fit! He says no daughter of his is going to show her face in something so trashy, and besides, I'd probably fall off of them and break an ankle, which is the most ridiculous thing I ever heard of. They're *not* trashy. Everybody's wearing them but me. Colin even says they're bitchin', and he's got the best taste of anybody I know. The judge says they're just a fad, and a waste of money, but I bought them with my birthday money, so I don't see how it's any of his business!

Thought for the Day: It's the absolute pits, having a judge for a father.

Charly lifted her hands, tried a smile that didn't work and finally just said, "Hi."

"Sweet Jesus...sweet Jesus..." Tears had begun to trickle down the woman's cheeks.

In about another second they were going to be flooding down Charly's, too. Desperate not to let that happen, she laughed instead, and said in a shaking voice, "Yes, it's me, Aunt Dobie. It's me, Charlene. How are you?"

One hand rose slowly to touch Charly's cheek. "Charlene Elizabeth...is that you?"

Then the same hand hauled off and smacked her hard on the arm. "That *is* you! Wicked, *wicked* girl! Never called, nor wrote...I thought you was *dead.*"

Trembly with relief, Charly rubbed her arm and said, "Ow!"

Aunt Dobie whacked her again for good measure. "I thought you was dead, and here you stand. Come here and let me look at you. Oh, praise the Lord, praise Jesus. My baby's come home. My baby's come home."

And with that, Charly found herself enveloped in loving arms, familiar arms, and in old, familiar scents—Ivory soap and starched cotton clothes, oil of wintergreen and strong coffee laced with a splash, just a splash, of bourbon whiskey—and in the time and place those scents evoked. Just like that, she was a child again, seeking solace and protection in those same strong arms, while inside, her heart quaked with dread.

Because, of course, she wasn't a child, and had not been in more than twenty years. And not even Dobrina Ralston, the only mother Charly had ever known, was going to make what she'd come to do easier.

"Aunt Dobie," she began, "is he...is my...?" But her voice was betraying her. She drew herself up straight and tall to give it support, and with a good strong breath behind it, tried again. "Is he here?"

"He is. Yes, he is," Dobrina crooned, wiping her face with the big wraparound apron she'd worn for all the years Charly could remember. "You just come in here, child. Come in."

Dobrina backed up into the house, keeping a good firm grip on the arm she was holding as if she thought Charly might be about to bolt and disappear on her for another twenty years. Once she had the door shut solid behind them, she plunged her hand into an apron pocket and pulled out a tissue. She swiped it hastily across her cheeks and nose and then waved it at Charly.

"Stay here, child, you hear me? Stay right here. Don't you move a muscle, now. I'll go fetch the judge." And off she went toward the back of the house, her flat summer shoes slap-slapping down the long hallway. From far away Charly could still hear her muttering "Praise the Lord!" and "Thank you, Jesus!"

In the distance a door closed and the silence settled around her, and suddenly Charly was overwhelmed by feelings, most of which she didn't understand. How, she wondered, could it all seem so familiar, and yet so strange? Everything was exactly as she remembered, including the smells—a mix of lemon furniture polish and old wood and dusty draperies and pipe tobacco. She felt as if she'd been caught up in a time warp and hurled back into her own childhood. Except that, since she was no longer a child, she didn't belong in this time, in this place. She was a stranger here. And standing in the house she'd grown up in, she knew a terrible sense of alienation, and loss.

Panic seized her. Lord, she couldn't face him like this! Not in so vulnerable a state, standing here in the entry hall like a charity case—like somebody come collecting for the heart fund or the March of Dimes!

On the verge of flight, she was suddenly aware of warmth on her cheek, like a kind and comforting touch. Turning, she saw through the open arched doorway on her left that the formal living room—the "front room," Aunt Dobie had always called it, though the judge preferred "the parlor"—was awash with the last golden light from the setting sun. It was that light, slanting into the hallway, that had reached out to Charly where she stood. Like an omen, perhaps? If she believed in such things.

But maybe, she thought, her panicked heartbeat slowing and her breathing becoming calmer, that *would* be better. She could confront him there, with her back to the windows so her face would be in shadow, his in the light. Basic interviewer's strategy. That way *he'd* be the one at a disadvantage.

She walked through the archway and instantly felt a sense of safety, inspired, perhaps, by the almost awesome gentility of the room. This was too lovely and formal a setting for angry words and recriminations. No memories here of emotional scenes and bitter confrontations.

She turned slowly, taking in the elegance of the high ceilings and wood moldings, the warmth of the beautiful old mantelpiece and hardwood floors, the graciousness of stunning antiques perfectly set against a backdrop of soft spring colors, cream and green and mauve. Here, too, it seemed that nothing had changed, except that maybe now she had a better appreciation for the beauty of it.

But then the arrangement of photographs on the mantelpiece caught her eye. At last here was something that was different. She remembered the candles in their silver candlesticks, and the clock that used to mark the quarter hours with advancing phrases of the Westminster chimes, with the complete chime on each hour following by the tolling. And fresh flowers in the cut crystal vase, picked by Aunt Dobie from whatever the yard and the season had to offer. But in Charly's memory there had been only one photograph there, the formal portrait, framed in silver and black velvet, of her mother, Elizabeth, who had died the week after Charly was born.

But now there were other pictures there, too. Curious, since she'd never known the judge to be sentimental, she went to take a closer look. The photographs all seemed to be of a boy, the same boy at different ages and stages: a laughing toddler with golden curls, posed with his favorite toy, a lop-eared, black-and-white-spotted dog, clutched to his heart; a gap-toothed Little Leaguer in his uniform, holding a glove almost as big as he was; a proud and handsome high-school graduate in cap and gown, the golden curls shorn and darkened to a sandy brown.

How odd, Charly thought. She stared at the pictures. Who is this? I don't know this person.

But her world had gone strange and still, like the quiet that precedes a violent storm. She felt it shift, and put out a hand to steady herself, but didn't feel the mantelpiece beneath her fingers.

But I do. I know this child. I know...

Her body was cold...so cold. She didn't recognize that phenomenon yet for the symptom of shock it was but only felt pleased that she could be so calm, pleased that she wasn't falling apart, that her hands were steady, that she felt no pain. She felt nothing at all, in fact. Just that strange, all-consuming, all-enveloping cold.

She must have heard something—some sound, a faint gasp, an indrawn breath. She felt herself turn within that cold, silent cocoon to face the man who had come to stand in the arched doorway. Some part of her mind must have recorded the fact that he was heavier than when she'd last seen him, that his hair was whiter, that there were jowls and eye pouches and a slight stoop to his shoulders that hadn't been there before. That he'd grown old. But none of that registered then. Her world, her perspective, had narrowed to a single laserlike beam, from her eyes to his—eyes that, though she'd always hated to acknowledge the fact, were so very much like her own.

She'd tried not to plan what she would say to him, knowing that the first words out of *his* mouth would send it all flying out the window anyway. As it turned out, it wouldn't have mattered if she'd written a speech and tattooed crib notes on the palms of her hands. Now nothing mattered. Except...

The words came quietly from her mouth, but in more than a whisper. Almost a growl. "Who is this?"

She realized only then that she was clutching the graduation portrait in both hands, holding it before her like a shield.

Judge Charles Phelps drew himself up, breathing in through his nostrils in a way she'd seen him do so many times before when he was about to deliver a pronouncement—a broadside, an edict, an ultimatum, a sentence. Though he was wearing no jacket or tie, just shirtsleeves and suspenders on this warm June evening, she could almost see his judicial robes.

For once the old intimidation tactic failed to have its intended effect on her. Still focused with that laserlike intensity on one thing, and one thing only, she repeated it. *"Who is this?"*

His eyebrows bunched and lowered, but he didn't answer her question. So she tried once more, her voice a guttural croak, forced between tightly clenched teeth. "Is...this...my...son? Tell me. I have a right—"

The judge's voice boomed out then, as shocking in that sun-washed room as thunder on a cloudless day. "You have no right!" The next words came like its rumbling echoes, slow and measured, the handing down of a sentence. "None whatsoever. Any right you may have had, you signed away twenty years ago."

Charly flinched, then braced herself. "Is this my s—?"

"You have no right, and you have no son!" His voice bludgeoned hers to silence. "You gave up the one when you gave away the other!"

"Gave up? *Gave up?*" How long had she been crying? Her face was wet, and her throat felt raw, as if she'd been screaming. "You *made* me! You took him away from me." She swiped a hand across her eyes and then could see, with the shimmering edges of her vision, that Dobrina was crying, too, standing behind the judge with both hands pressed to her mouth, folded as if in prayer.

"I wanted to keep him," Charly whispered, trying so hard to suppress sobs, her eyes clinging desperately to the face of the man she had once both feared and idolized. With every ounce of her strength and will she searched for some, for any sign of softening, wanting to believe that, just this once, she could make him hear. "You know that. I would have kept him if you'd let me."

With a single bark of laughter the judge's demeanor changed from an almost Biblical wrath to icy disdain. "Kept him? How did you propose to do that? You were a selfish, irresponsible—"

"I was sixteen!"

"You were not fit to raise a child then, and to all appearances, you have not changed. And now, if you have any decency—" His voice suddenly faded, and he turned away.

In despair Charly shot out a hand and clutched at his arm. "I want to see him."

The judge's eyes flicked downward, then slowly rose to her face. Chilled to the bone, she snatched her hand away.

"Young woman," he said, in the quiet, impersonal voice of a

trial judge, a voice with the cutting power of steel, "I would be obliged if you would leave my house."

That, finally, was too much for Dobrina. With an anguished cry she threw up her hands and fled. Unable to believe what she was hearing, Charly shook her head and whispered, "My God. I'm your *daughter.*"

"*I have no daughter!*" On the last word the powerful voice broke, and once more, this time with finality, he turned away.

She saw then the signs of weakness she'd been hoping for— the trembling hands and bowed shoulders, a tinge of gray pallor— but instead of triumph it was fear she felt, a little girl's fear, fear that struck her like a blow to the belly, taking her breath away. She held out a hand like an abandoned child and heard herself whisper, "Daddy..."

But he continued on down the hallway as if she hadn't spoken. As if she wasn't even there.

She had no way of knowing how long she stood there frozen and trembling. It was a small thud followed by the tinkle of broken glass that shocked her into motion and some degree of awareness, if not reality. *Not reality.* She told herself it couldn't be real, that it wasn't happening. Somehow she'd gotten caught in her worst nightmare, and now she couldn't seem to wake up.

The graduation portrait had slipped from her fingers and lay ruined at her feet. She thought there must be a kind of symbolism in the handsome young face smiling confidently up at her through a crisscross of glass shards, but the pain that engulfed her in the same moment was so overpowering she couldn't grasp it. She found herself kneeling on the floor, trying to gather up all the broken pieces. Except that she was crying so hard she couldn't see them. And then she was outside, running as if wild dogs were chasing her, across the porch and down the steps.

Through a blur of tears she saw Dobrina waiting for her beside her rental car. She looked like an ancient goddess, Charly thought, standing straight and tall and proud with her arms folded under her apron. Except that, although the bright colors of June were drowning in sunset shadows, Charly could still see the shine of tears on the woman's cheeks.

She held out one imploring hand. "Baby...oh, baby, please don't be goin'—he doesn't mean what he says. You know he doesn't mean it—"

Charly had both of her hands out, too, and was holding them up as if to ward the other woman off. The car keys were already in her hand—another Los Angeles habit. She fumbled for the door handle, muttering, "No...no...I have to get...out of here."

Dobrina's fingers closed around hers. "Where you think you're goin', child?"

"Anywhere," Charly growled with a prolonged sniff, "as long as it isn't here."

"You're in no condition to be drivin'!"

"I'm *fine*. At least I will be. Aunt Dobie..." But her voice gave way. She turned in a rush and clutched the other woman in her arms, whispering into the downy softness of her close-cropped hair, "I'm sorry, Aunt Dobie. I'm so sorry...I'm so sorry. I shouldn't have come. This was a mistake. I'm sorry."

Oh, God, the tears had started again. Somehow she managed to get the car door open and herself inside. She kept trying futilely to stem the flow with the back of her hand, blotting her streaming eyes with her sleeves so she could see to get the key in the ignition and locate the headlights.

As she put the car in gear and drove away, the last thing she saw in the rearview mirror was a shimmery image of Dobrina, still standing in the driveway, straight and tall as a pillar with her arms once again folded beneath her apron, the very image of dignity in the midst of overwhelming grief.

That was when the pain really hit her. It woke and grew inside her like a living thing. But all she cared about at that moment was getting away, as far away from Mourning Spring as it was possible to get, and as fast as she could possibly get there. Then maybe, she told herself, just maybe, the pain would go away....

Of course it would. Just as it had before. Once before, so many years ago.

Oh, yes, she knew this pain, these tears. Knew them very well, like old friends—or enemies. And she knew what was causing them. They were the natural consequence of a broken heart. Once, long ago, this town, these people had broken hers. But what she was finding out only now was that in all those years, it had never really mended.

And she thought she'd done so well! She'd been proud of the way she'd healed, not without scars, but like a tree re-forming its bark around an old wound and growing up tall and strong and spreading its branches in spite of it. Now she wondered how she could actually have thought she could come back here and face down the town, these people, her father on equal terms, as the successful adult she'd become. What a fool she'd been. Two hours in this place, and it was as if she'd never left. Just like that, in the blink of an eye she was sixteen again, terrified, heartbroken, and alone....

Okay, not quite alone. Those headlights in her rearview mirror were awfully close. Too close.

Damn redneck drivers, Charly thought, dashing furiously at her tears and hating all things Southern with a passion that would have astounded her closest friends. Good old laid-back Charly— she knew that's what they thought of her. Charly the cool one, the sophisticated one, renowned for her dry and often acerbic wit. That's what they all thought—even Mirabella.

What would Bella think if she could see her now?

She reached up and, with a flourish of defiance and a few choice swear words, flipped the mirror's dimmer switch.

Then she glanced down at the speedometer and muttered, "Oh, hell," under her breath. All right, so it seemed she'd been toddling down the highway at just under forty miles per hour. When had she left the town behind? For that matter where *was* she? Dusk had deepened into darkness while she wasn't watching, and suddenly nothing looked familiar.

Plus she was still crying like a baby—couldn't seem to stop. Could barely even see. And those damn headlights were *still* right on her tail. Why didn't they just pass, for God's sake?

Charly was never sure exactly what happened next. One minute she was looking in the mirror at the shimmering lights, and the next minute she was looking ahead into the path of her own headlamps and seeing nothing but trees. Her heart jumped into her throat, and she jerked the wheel hard to the left—too hard; she was used to her own car, a nice, solid eight-year-old Mercedes. The lighter rented Ford responded to such brutal handling by careening wildly back and forth across the highway, while behind her the headlights suddenly seemed to break up and began to flash rainbow colors.

Something in Charly's mind—the answer to a silently screamed prayer, perhaps—told her to tromp on the brakes. This she did, but too late. The Taurus was already tilting and lurching, bucking and banging its way down an embankment. Somehow she managed to keep her foot on the brake and hold on to the steering wheel—there wasn't much else she could do, except maybe pray, and she was sure it was way too late for that, as well.

She heard things snapping and crashing all around her, and the sound of glass breaking, and then the air bag blew up and hit her in the face.

And there was darkness. Stillness. Silence.

She heard herself whimpering, "Oh God, oh God, oh God." Which she told herself wasn't actually praying, no matter what it sounded like.

Then she heard more rustlings and crashings and thumpings. Something rapped against the car window barely inches from her head. She jumped when a flashlight stabbed at her through the glass.

A voice, strangely muffled, called out, "Ma'am? Hey, you okay in there?"

Charly shook her head, but not in response to the question. She didn't know if she was okay or not. She *felt* as though she was—nothing hurt or anything—but then she'd heard stories about people in shock running around on broken legs, having horrendous injuries and not even knowing.

The door beside her was wrenched open. The light slapped across her eyes, making her wince again, then moved on. Hands touched her, not gently. Quickly and efficiently exploring.

A voice, young and male, said, "Okay, ma'am, you just sit tight now, y'hear? We'll have you out of there in a jiffy." She heard the click of her seat-belt buckle, and felt the release of pressure. "You hurt anywhere?"

"I don't think so," Charly said, rubbing her chest. It did hurt where the seat-belt strap had crossed it, but since it was probably what had saved her life, it didn't seem like something she should complain about.

"Can you tell me your name?" That was a different voice, also male, also young.

"Charly...uh..." Damn.

"Ma'am?"

She ground her teeth silently, but there was no help for it. "Charly...Phelps."

She'd hoped that might get past them, but she could see it wasn't going to. The first young man, hunkered down in the open doorway, exchanged a look with the second young man, who was peering over his shoulder.

'Phelps, huh? Charlie, you say?" He slanted a look back at Charly. "You know, we got a judge in this town by the name of Charles Phelps—now, how's that for a coincidence?"

"Wow," said Charly weakly.

"Ma'am, you know where you are?" It was the second young man again, the one with all the questions.

"Yeah...Mourning Spring, Alabama." She sighed and closed her eyes. Because it had just registered that both of the young men giving her aid and comfort were wearing uniforms—law-enforcement uniforms, complete with thick belts and guns and things that creaked and clanked when they moved. And that the colorful flashing lights on the edges of her vision were not some sort of residual effect from the accident or her recent crying jag, but the lights on top of a patrol car.

Under her breath she muttered softly, "*Damn*, I hate this place."

"Ma'am, I'm gonna need to see your license and registration."

"Oh—yeah, sure." She pawed at the deflated air bag until she got it out of the way and reached for her purse with shaking hands—at least for the place where it should have been, just across the center console, on the passenger seat. Then she realized that of course, everything would most likely have been thrown onto the floor during the accident. Mumbling "Just a minute," she leaned over as far as she could and groped for it on the floor.

A strong odor, one she recognized instantly, filled her nostrils. She registered the thought, But that's impossible.

"Ouch!"

"Ma'am?"

"Nothing—I cut myself. I think...there's something...broken down here." Cautiously now, she got a hand on it and pulled it out. Sat holding it, staring at it, winking in the beam of the young patrolman's flashlight—a squarish bottle minus its neck and its contents, wearing a black label with Jack Daniel's Old No. 7 boldly printed on it in white.

"But," said Charly firmly, "that's impossible."

The two patrolmen exchanged another long look; they had to have gotten a whiff of the whiskey by this time. One of them took the bottle gingerly from her hands. The other said politely, "Ma'am, if you can, I'm gonna have to ask you to step out of the car."

"I don't know where that came from," Charly said. "It isn't mine."

Neither of the patrolmen seemed to feel that required an answer.

The one not holding the bottle put his hand under her elbow and thoughtfully murmured, "Watch your head," as he helped her from the car.

"I'm telling you, that bottle is not mine," Charly insisted. "Look, if you'll just let me..." She closed her eyes and took a deep breath. Okay, she thought, I can't believe I'm about to do this, but... "That judge you mentioned—Charles Phelps?" She let the breath out in a rush. "Okay, you're not going to believe this, but I'm his daughter. I just left his house. Somebody there will vouch for me. If you'll just—"

The two patrolmen were looking at each other again. The one holding on to Charly's arm was kind of scratching at the back of his head. The other one hitched at his belt and shifted his feet, cleared his throat and said, "Well now, ma'am, there's just one problem with that. I've lived in this town for most of my life, and far as I know, Judge Phelps hasn't even got a daughter. Kenny, you know anything about Judge Phelps havin' a daughter?''

"First I've heard of it," said Kenny.

Sizing up the two officers, Charly decided she wasn't all that surprised. She figured they'd both had to have been barely out of diapers when she'd left town. This town. Why, oh, why, had she ever come back? This town had tried once before to eat her alive; maybe that was meant to be her destiny.

She tried again, but with a growing sense of futility; her story sounded far-fetched even to her. "Look, I've been away. For a long time, actually. I live in California now. If you'll just let me get my purse—''

"We'll take care of that, ma'am." Patrolman Kenny already had his head and shoulders inside the Taurus and was shining his flashlight around, looking in the glove box, in the back, under the seats. He paused to give Charly a look over his shoulder. "Sure don't see a purse in here anywhere. You sure you had one with you?''

"Of course I had one with me," Charly said, pleased that she'd had the presence of mind not to actually add the words *you nitwit*, even if her tone clearly implied them. "Look, it has to be there. It was right there on the seat. Maybe it—'' She stopped.

But *had* it been? She'd been pretty upset. Too upset to notice? She was sure she'd had it when she'd left Kelly's. Could she have taken it into the house with her? She didn't remember. But she might have—reaching for her purse when getting out of a car was something she usually did automatically.

Okay, she must have. The purse wasn't here. Therefore, she *must* have taken it someplace with her and left it. And after Kelly's she'd only been to one place.

"Wait," she said, breathing through her nose and trying not to panic. "Okay. I know where it must be. I must have left it at the judge's—I was just there. If you could just...I don't know, take me back there, or let me call, or something...''

The two patrolmen were flanking her now, half facing her with arms folded ominously on their chests, grave, official looks on their peach-fuzz faces. Charly's heart began to pound; she thought she knew how a cornered rabbit feels.

"Well now, ma'am," said the one not named Kenny, "we've got a little situation here."

"What...situation?" asked Charly. She suddenly felt air starved. *You in a heap a' trouble, girl.*

"Have you had anything to drink this evening, ma'am?" Kenny was the speaker again; it was getting to be almost like a comedy routine, Charly thought, the way these two passed the conversational ball back and forth.

"D-drink?" She shifted uncomfortably, remembering that she needed to go to the bathroom and wondering how he knew. Then the full meaning of the question hit her and she gasped, "No! Of course not!"

"You sure about that?" Kenny sort of hefted the Jack Daniel's bottle.

"No, I swear. Look, I can explain—"

Not-Kenny leaned over until his face was close to Charly's and said in his nice, soft, polite Southern voice, "Ma'am, I'm sure you can, and we're gonna give you a chance to do that. There's just a couple problems we need to get cleared up first, okay?"

"P-problems?" Charly resisted an urge to cringe; she'd been in worse situations, she supposed, but none quite so embarrassing. She was a lawyer, for God's sake—she knew how bad this looked.

"Yes, ma'am. Now, first off there's the little matter of this bottle. I found the neck underneath the seat, and see here, the seal's broken? Which means it looks to me like you had an open bottle of whiskey in your car, ma'am. And along with the way you were drivin'—"

"You were tailgating me! Your lights were in my eyes!"

Kenny held up a warning hand. "Ma'am, we followed you quite a ways at well under the speed limit, and you were weavin' back and forth across the road. Then you lose control of your car for no good reason that I could see, and we find an open whiskey bottle in your car—now, you tell me, what are we supposed to think? And then you give us this story about bein' Judge Phelps's daughter, when everybody knows the judge don't even *have* a daughter, and you got no driver's license, no identification, no registration on this car you're drivin'—and that's another little problem. Well, a big one, actually.'' He nodded at his partner, offering him the punch line.

Which his partner—whom she was unable to identify, since by this time Charly had lost track again of who was Kenny and who wasn't—was delighted to deliver. "You see, ma'am, the reason we were following you in the first place is because this-here vehicle was reported stolen—''

"*What?*"

"Yes, ma'am. Brown Ford Taurus, Georgia plates...'' He took a notebook out of his shirt pocket, read the number off, then tucked the notebook away again and jerked his head toward the car now resting lopsidedly with its front end mashed up against a tree. "Look's to me like that's this car right here, ma'am.''

"This is a mistake,'' Charly muttered. A terrible mistake.

"Yes, ma'am. But right now what I'm gon' do is, I'm placin' you under arrest, and then we're gonna take you on over to the hospital and make sure you're okay, and while we're at it, we'll get this alcohol question settled, okay? And then you're gonna have all the time you need to get things straightened out. Now, you have the right to remain silent...''

Charly just closed her eyes.

Chapter 3

July 1, 1977

Dear Diary,

Guess what! I think Richie Wilcox likes me. He told Bobby Hanratty he did, and Bobby told Kelly Grace, and Kelly Grace told me. I don't know if I should tell Kelly Grace to tell Bobby to tell Richie that I like him back or not. I don't want to be too forward. On the other hand, the Fourth of July picnic is coming up. Maybe Richie will ask me and Bobby will ask Kelly Grace, and then we can double-date! Yowza!

Thought for the Day: I think Richie does look just a *little* like J.T.

Troy was in the nursery putting the last screw in a four-switch plate when he heard the phone ring. Since he was pretty sure he knew who it was, he finished up what he was doing before he went across the hall to the master bedroom to answer it. He got there just before the machine picked up.

"Hey," he said, without bothering with formalities, "'bout time you guys checked in. You must be havin' fun."

All he got in response to that were some breathing sounds, which gave him a hint that it probably wasn't his brother or Mirabella on the line after all. But before he could apologize and start all over again, a woman's voice inquired in an ominous tone, "Is this the Starr residence?"

"Sure is," said Troy cheerfully. "Sorry about that—thought you were somebody else. What can I do for you?"

"May I speak to Mirabella, please?"

"Ah, shoot—I'm sorry, she's not here right now. Can I—?"

"Is this...Jimmy Joe?"

"Naw, this is his brother Troy. Neither one of 'em's here, ma'am. Gone to Atlanta for the weekend." The silence on the other end of the line had a hollow sound to it, Troy thought, as if the person there had just run out of options. "Hey," he said, trying to be helpful, "I'd be glad to give 'em a message for you, if you want."

He heard more breath sounds, a quick in and out, the kind of breath people take to bolster their courage when they're looking at the end of their rope. "Do you have a number where they can be reached?"

"Uh, sure don't. I'm expectin' to hear from 'em any minute, though. Thought that was who it was when you called, matter of fact. Tell you what, why don't you give me a number where you can be reached, and I'll have Mirabella give you a call? How's that sound, ma'am?"

This time he got a high, muffled sound, about halfway between a snort of irony and a squeak of frustration, which made him more than ever suspicious that the person on the other end of the line might be just a little too tightly wound. His "Beg pardon?" was cautious.

A chuckle reassured him somewhat, and so did the dry humor in the voice when it replied, "Nothing—I've just about been *ma'am*ed to death lately, is all."

At least, he thought, whatever her problem was, the lady appeared to have some fight left in her. He ventured, "Well, ma'am, if you want to give me a name, I'd be glad to call you that instead."

There was a moment's hesitation, as if it was classified information he'd asked her for. Then she replied with an almost inaudible sigh, "It's Charly. Charly Phelps. Mirabella's friend— from California?"

The light dawned. "Oh, yeah—the maid of honor, right? You're comin' in next week?" Then another light dawned, and he thought maybe he had the whole thing figured out. "Oh, Lord, it *is* next week, isn't it? Don't tell me. We haven't got that wrong, have we? Where in the hell are you?" If she was sitting in Atlanta at the airport waiting for somebody to pick her up, it would explain a lot.

There was a pause before the answer came, in a curiously hollow tone. "I'm in Mourning Spring, Alabama."

"Alabama! Well, what in the hell are you doin' in Alabama?" And why did she say it like some sort of doomsday curse? "You *lost?*"

This time there wasn't anything equivocal about the sound she made. It was definitely a snort. "You could say that. Listen, when you hear from Mirabella, just give her a message for me, okay? Tell her—"

"Wait, let me get something to write this down on."

"Never mind. I don't even know the number. Look, will you just tell her I'm in jail?"

"Jail? Wait, did you say *jail?* What—hold on, don't... hang...up...." But he was talking to himself.

He thumbed the phone's disconnect button and put it down, then ran a hand over his hair, which was still trying to grow out of its military cut. "Oh, *man*," he muttered. "Oh, Lord."

Mirabella was going to love this. Just when she and Jimmy Joe had finally managed to get away for some R an' R, too. Troy hadn't been around long enough to get to know his about-to-be sister-in-law all that well, but it seemed to him she might've had about all the stress and strain she could handle lately, even for somebody as capable and efficient as she liked to think she was. First having the baby the way she had, then quitting her job in L.A. and moving all the way to Georgia, lock, stock and barrel. And now planning this wedding and trying to remodel the house to make a nursery for Amy Jo on top of it. Suffice to say, he was *not* looking forward to breaking the news to her that her maid of honor had gotten herself thrown in the pokey somewhere in Alabama.

However, if there was one thing Troy *did* know well, it was how to take control of a situation in crisis. And it didn't take much for him to conclude that this was probably one he was better equipped to handle right now than either Mirabella or his brother.

Far better, he reasoned as he shaved and showered and packed his overnight bag with the efficiency born of long years of practice, if he just hopped on over to Alabama and took care of matters himself. That way he wouldn't have to bother the happy couple with it, mess up their weekend in Atlanta and all. Shoot, the way he saw it, as his brother's best man, it was no more than his duty.

And it would be a whole lot easier facing Mirabella with the news *after* the fact, when everything had already been straightened out.

So where in the hell was Mourning Spring?

He decided what he needed was a road atlas, which he was sure his brother would have in his truck, the big blue Kenworth tractor-trailer rig that was parked on its gravel turnaround out beside the house. Jimmy Joe kept it locked up tight when he wasn't driving, mainly to keep young J.J. from playing in it, but that was no problem, either. Living where they did, in a small community where everybody knew everybody else, and Jimmy Joe being a trusting soul by nature, Troy figured he'd keep the keys in the handiest and most obvious place. And that's where he found them—in the top drawer of the oak rolltop desk in his brother's tiny, cluttered office, just off the kitchen.

He got the atlas out of the truck and took it into the kitchen where the light was good, where, with the help of a magnifying glass, he located Mourning Spring way up in the northeast corner of Alabama, near Tennessee. After that, all he had to do was put in a call to his mama's house to let her know he was going to be gone for a while and to leave a message for Mirabella and Jimmy Joe, and then one last check of the house and his wallet and he was out the door.

Except that he'd forgotten about Bubba, who naturally had gotten wind that something was up, dogs having a natural sixth sense about things like that. All the way down the steps and across the front lawn, the pup did his best to get on all four sides of Troy at once, weaving himself around and between his legs and whumping him with his tail and slobbering all over him in his eagerness to be included in whatever that something might be. So when Troy opened up the back door of his brand-new Jeep Grand Cherokee and said, "Let's go," he almost got his legs knocked out from under him. Bubba shoved right through him and clambered up on the back seat, big tongue lolling and dripping, happy as a pig in petunias.

Troy was grinning himself as he backed the Jeep around and drove down the driveway and turned onto the main road. It felt good to be heading out on a warm summer night. It had been a long time since he'd had a mission—a place to go and somebody needing him. Okay, as missions went it wasn't much, fetching a maid of honor out of a small-town Alabama jail, but it did beat the hell out of installing light fixtures and intercoms. If there was anything the past few weeks had taught him, it was that he wasn't cut out to be a handyman.

Not that he had a clue what he *was* cut out for. To tell the truth, he'd never thought much about it. His life had been focused on training and conditioning, keeping himself in a constant state of readiness as a member of the most elite and effective strike force in the world. On missions the focus became the job, and survival—his own and that of the other members of the team—in that order. He'd learned not to think too far beyond that, nor to form emotional ties or acquire too many responsibilities.

Now he was learning that he was highly trained for a lot of things, most of which had very little application in a peaceful world. And that having few responsibilities and emotional ties was a sure-fire recipe for loneliness.

To drown out that thought, he tuned the radio to a golden-oldies station out of Atlanta and opened the windows and let the car fill with the soft June night and the sweet smell of honeysuckle. He rolled down the back windows, too, so Bubba could stick his nose out and feel the wind tearing past his ears, which he thought might be a dog's idea of heaven. Troy understood that. He felt a little bit the same way himself.

He picked up an hour at the Alabama state line, so it was only about eleven o'clock local time—2300 hours by the way he was used to reckoning—when he rolled past the Mourning Spring city-limits sign. Though by the time he'd driven another two miles without coming to anything resembling a city, he thought the sign was maybe a little bit optimistic.

Then, just when he was beginning to wonder if he'd missed it somehow, he drove past a sign that said Mourning Springs Motel. It was attached to one of those places that always seemed to him to belong to the same era as convertibles and drive-in movies, a row of dismal little one-story units painted a sickly green with doors that opened directly onto an asphalt parking lot. He was glad to see, though, that the Vacancy sign was lit up.

Even more encouraging, B.B.'s Barn, which occupied a cinder-block building across the street, appeared to be doing a booming business on this Friday night, and one of the two gas stations on the next corner was still open. He didn't stop to ask directions to the jail; like most men, Troy liked to do his own reconnaissance.

Which didn't prove to be too difficult. The main road into the town, which was empty of both cars and people, led him right to the town's hub, a brick-paved traffic circle built around a nice little park and lit up with modern street lamps to a bleached and ghostly emptiness. He drove once around the square, past a stately brick courthouse and old-fashioned stores that had once housed banks and hardware and department and drugstores, and a five-and-dime or two. Now the signs in the windows mostly peddled antiques and real estate and insurance and flowers. There were a couple of restaurants, one of the basic-diner variety, the other a pizza place—both closed and dark even on a Friday night. Mourning Spring was definitely a town that rolled up its sidewalks soon after the sun went down.

On his second time around the square, alerted by a sign that said Police and an arrow pointing the way, Troy turned down one of the streets. A block farther on, slowing for the flashing yellow caution light over the street in front of the Mourning Spring Fire Department, he discovered that the police department evidently occupied the same building, with an entrance in the rear.

He parked in the brightly lit and almost empty parking lot, ran Bubba's window down far enough for him to get his nose out and told him to stay. Bubba's reply was a whine, followed by a heart-rending howl that followed Troy all the way to the door marked Mourning Spring Police Dept., Ring Bell For Admittance.

Troy pushed on the buzzer once and then tried the door, and since it was unlocked, he went on in. That put him in a little tiny vestibule with doors on both sides and a window straight ahead, behind which he could see a dispatcher sitting at a desk surrounded by muttering radios and glowing computer screens. The dispatcher had one hand cupped over the ear part of his headset and his elbow propped on the desk, and since whatever he was listening to didn't appear to have him too excited, Troy went ahead and tapped on the glass to get his attention.

The dispatcher, who appeared to be the only officer on the premises, glanced up, nodded once and went on with his business. When he had it taken care of, he swiveled his chair around and got out of it, ambled over to the glass and said, "Yes, sir, can I help you?" The voice came through the glass muffled, sounding a mile away.

"Well, now, I hope so," Troy said, raising his voice but smiling in a comradely way. He hadn't quite figured out yet how he was going to play this, but the way he saw it, it was always a smart move to get on the good side of whoever was in charge. "What I'm lookin' for is your jail."

The officer, who, according to the pin on his pocket, was named Baylor, did not smile back. He had meaty-looking jowls and a buzz haircut and was built like the back end of a truck—

sort of reminded Troy of Sergeant Carter on the old *Gomer Pyle* TV show. "Which jail would that be, sir?"

Troy scratched his head. "Lord, I don't know. You got more'n one?"

"We got the county jail, down on Court Street, but I'm afraid you'll have to wait for visitin' hours tomorrow, sir. Unless you're lookin' for somebody in holding."

"Holding?" Even though he'd been raised by people who would have skinned him alive if he'd ever been stupid enough to get himself arrested, and consequently his personal experience with such things was limited, Troy did know what "holding" was. He was just feeling his way.

And the dumb-and-innocent approach did seem to be working; at least Officer Baylor finally cracked a smile. "Drunk tank. Mostly."

"Ah." Troy thought about it. Hard as it was to imagine a friend of Mirabella's occupying a drunk tank, it seemed even less likely that one could have done anything to warrant actual jail time. "Damned if I know. Person I'm lookin' for is named Phelps. Charly. That's a woman." He took a wild guess and added, "About mid-thirties."

"Oh, yeah, sure—she's back there." Officer Baylor relaxed some more and jerked his head toward the door on Troy's right. "Already been processed. I'm just waitin' on confirmation of her ID. Should be gettin' that from the California DMV any minute now. Then she's free to go. She's gonna need a ride, though. Her car's not goin' anywhere."

"Oh, yeah?" said Troy uneasily, more than ever sure he was about to have an inebriated woman on his hands and looking forward to it less and less. "Why's that?"

"Tried her best to climb a tree with it, is what I understand."

"Oh, boy." It wasn't difficult to look shocked at *that* bit of news. "Is she okay?"

"Oh, yeah, just a little shaken up. She's seen a doctor, everything checks out okay. But, uh..." He paused. "Turns out there's a stolen-vehicle report out on the car."

"Oh, man." Oh, Lord, thought Troy, this was getting better

and better by the minute. What in the hell had he gotten himself into?

Officer Baylor, who seemed to have become downright chatty now that he'd unbent, put up a hand to reassure him. "That's lookin' like just some sort of a misunderstanding. Turns out there were papers in the glove box. It's a rental."

"Well, that's good." A drunk, he thought, but at least not a felon.

"So," the officer went on, "if she turns out to be who she says she is, she's clear on that. Don't think we'd be lettin' her go if she wasn't."

"I...see," said Troy, who wasn't at all sure he did. "If...she's who she says she is? You got some reason to think she *isn't*?"

Baylor shrugged. "She didn't have any ID on her."

"No ID. You mean—"

"No license, no wallet, no pocketbook."

"But how—?"

"Sir," the officer said, looking stern, "unless you're her lawyer, I really can't tell you any more'n I already have."

Which struck Troy as being kind of like locking the barn door after giving the horse away.

"Well, hell," he said, deciding that the whole thing was just too damn weird not to see it through to the end. And besides, no matter what kind of fruitcake this Charly Phelps turned out to be, there was still Mirabella to contend with. "I can vouch for her, if that's all you need."

After he said that, he decided it was the truth, which was always his first choice, if at all possible. Even if he'd never personally set eyes on the lady, when she needed help, she'd called on Mirabella, hadn't she? The way he saw it, a person would have to be a close relative or a very good friend to do that. Plus, he'd been listening to Mirabella talk about her best friend Charly for weeks now. So he almost felt as if he knew her.

"And you are...?" Officer Baylor was still minding his p's and q's.

"Family friend. My name's Troy Starr." He got out his wallet and held it up to the glass so the man could get a good look at the military ID next to his Georgia driver's license.

Officer Baylor did so, then glanced up at Troy, trying not to look too impressed. "Navy, huh?"

"Yes, sir—retired." He folded up his wallet and shoved it back in his hip pocket, then gave the officer a wry grin. "As of a couple months ago. Still gettin' used to bein' a civilian again."

"I hear ya," Officer Baylor said, slipping enough to grin back. Then he put on his policeman's deadpan expression again. "Okay, sir, if you wanna step through that door there on your right? You can wait there at the counter, and I'll bring Miz Phelps right out. Oh—" he started off, hand going for his belt, then turned back "—she's gonna need somebody to pay her bail. You prepared to do that?"

"Let me guess—no money, either?"

"Not a dime."

Troy heaved a sigh, and he and Baylor exchanged a "Women—what are you gonna do with 'em?" kind of look.

"Yeah, sure," Troy said, "I'll pay it." He watched the officer disappear through another door, shuffling keys.

The door on his right opened into a long hallway with a counter partitioning off the dispatch room on the left. While he waited there, leaning his elbows on the countertop and listening to the radios burp static and unintelligible mumbles, he told himself it wasn't any of his business what kind of crazy, screwed-up lady this Charly Phelps was. His job—his mission—was to get her out of this jail and this town and deliver her safely to Mirabella in time for her wedding. Period.

It wouldn't be the first time he'd rescued somebody whose character wasn't exactly stellar, or whose politics he didn't agree with.

He didn't have to wait long; it couldn't have been more than a few minutes before he heard a door swish open down at the other end of the hallway. He turned his head that way, then slowly straightened up and watched them come toward him—Baylor and the woman he was holding by the arm.

He couldn't be sure what it was he was feeling right then, just that it wasn't anything he could recall ever feeling before. Later, when he tried to take it apart and put it back together in a way that made sense to him—he still thought of it as "debriefing" himself—he was astounded to recall that his first reaction had been a gut-level antagonism, an almost possessive resentment, and that it seemed to be centered around the officer's meaty masculine hand encircling the woman's bare arm. The kind of thing where, if he'd been in a bar and already a few too many beers to the good and possessed of a lot less self-control than he was, he might be inclined to grab the guy by the collar and snarl, "Hey, get your filthy hands off of her, bub!"

Then he thought about it some more, and that's when it really got interesting. *Possessive?* How could that be? How could another man touching a woman he'd never laid eyes on before make him seethe with a kind of primal, caveman jealousy that to the best of his knowledge wasn't even in his nature to begin with?

It sure couldn't be anything sexual; in Troy's judgment, Charly Phelps wasn't a sight to arouse a man's lust, at least not right then. In fact, if you asked him, she looked like hell warmed over.

Her hair, which was black or close to it, was mostly straight and came just about to her shoulders, and it was pretty obvious it hadn't seen a comb or brush in a good long while. And her clothes...well, he was no expert, but hers—gray slacks and a peach-colored knitted top with no sleeves—looked like they might have been expensive, maybe even silk. Which was a shame, because it looked to him that they were going to be hard to salvage. He'd seen people on the losing end of a barroom brawl in better shape.

Though there wasn't anything wrong with the body underneath all the dirt and wrinkles, now that he thought about it. Taller and a little less cuddly than he liked, personally, but rounded out in the right places without being obvious about it. And he liked the way she carried herself—head up, shoulders back and a sassy bounce in her step, which was not exactly what he'd expected from somebody who'd just spent several hours in a drunk tank.

Oh, yeah, Troy thought, she was trying. But it was her face that gave her away, especially her eyes. Even though he could see the burn of anger and defiance there above the dark thumb-prints of exhaustion, even though the vulnerable softness of her mouth was more than offset by a certain go-to-hell feistiness to the set of her chin, he'd seen enough of the real thing to know that hers was mostly bravado. Whatever had happened to the lady, it hadn't got her beat, not yet. But she was holding on with sheer guts and willpower.

And when he got around to figuring it all out, he thought maybe that explained all those possessive and protective impulses. He'd always been a sucker for underdogs. It was as simple as that.

She didn't say a word as she came closer to him. Mindful of the fact that underdogs are apt to bite, Troy limited himself to a casual nod and a wary and all-purpose "Hey."

She didn't reply to that, either, just nodded while she watched him with a sideways look that had some resentment in it, but maybe a touch of curiosity, too. Up close he could see that her eyes were what people generally call hazel, for want of a better way to describe eyes that change color depending on the mood and the light. Right now hers were mostly brown, with just enough green in them to make him think of deep woods and soft, sweet-smelling earth.

"I'm Troy," he said genially. "We spoke on the phone...?"

"Okay, ma'am, I'm gonna need you to sign some things." Officer Baylor was spreading some papers out on the countertop. He nodded in Troy's direction. "This gentleman here is postin' your bail. This here's your order to appear. You might want to get yourself a lawyer 'tween now and then. Make sure you read and understand everything before you sign."

"Where?" Her voice sounded rusty, but she didn't bother to do anything about it.

"Right there, ma'am. And initial it here, and here."

"You take a check?" Troy asked, reaching for his hip pocket.

Officer Baylor glanced at him. "No, sir, we do not."

He'd been pretty sure of that answer, and was already assessing the contents of his wallet. "How much we talkin' about?"

The officer told him. He had enough to cover it but figured he was going to have to be looking for an ATM soon. He counted out bills and handed them over, took the receipt the officer handed him, folded it and tucked it where they'd been. And all the while Charly stood in silence beside him. Not stony, though—it seemed to him he could almost *feel* her seething.

"That do it?"

Officer Baylor nodded. "Yes, sir. Ma'am, you're free to go."

As soon as he said that, she turned on her heel. She made it through two doors before Troy had a chance to open one for her. Once outside, though, she stopped so suddenly he ran into her, muttering blasphemy under her breath as an eerie howl floated toward them out of the artificial twilight. He could hardly blame her; it was enough to raise the hair on the back of Troy's neck, and *he* knew what it was.

"What in the *hell*," she croaked, breathing hard, "is that?"

He'd taken hold of her upper arms to steady them both. He could feel tension vibrating through her muscles, just under skin as soft as...he didn't know what. But it felt nice. He got a sudden reprise of the image of Officer Baylor's big ol' beefy hand on that skin, and the feeling it had aroused in him. The night got warmer.

"That's just my dog, ma'am. Sorry about that. He cries when I leave 'im."

She angled a look at him across her shoulder and said evenly, "Next person to call me *ma'am* is going to become a homicide statistic."

He let go of her arms and backed away in mock alarm, holding up a placating hand. "Sorry, ma'am—won't happen again."

Her only reply was a snort, a sound he remembered from the telephone, as she headed off across the parking lot, taking her reckoning from the racket Bubba was making. He lengthened his stride and as he pulled up alongside her, she was shaking her head and muttering something along the lines of, "Of *course* he'd bring his dog...."

Troy didn't bother to answer that; the way he saw it, he hadn't had much choice in the matter. And in case she'd forgotten, neither did she.

They'd reached the truck. Charly pulled up short and said,

"Good G—" while Troy was singing out, "Hey, ol' Bub—" They both got no further because by that time Troy had gotten the door open and Bubba was doing his best to leap out into his arms.

Charly was backing away, muttering the kinds of things they teach you in Sunday School not to say if you want to stay out of hell. "That's not a dog, that's a lion!"

"Ah, no...Bubba's just a great big ol' baby," Troy purred. "Aren't you, boy? You miss me? Yeah...I know."

He gave the dog a wrestle to pacify him and managed to get a grip on his collar before he could turn his attention to the lady, who was obviously intending to make Bubba's acquaintance from a considerable distance. Not out of fear, though—Troy was pretty sure of that. He just wasn't sure *what* to make of the expression on her face. He tried to ease things by explaining to her that ol' Bubba was still just a puppy and hadn't even got his growth yet, but he could see she wasn't going to be soft-soaped.

She said, "He's got yellow eyes," in a tone somewhere between revulsion, disbelief and awe.

"Well, sure," said Troy, "he's a chocolate Lab. They have eyes like that."

"And of course his name would be Bubba."

Troy heard the soft hiss of an exhalation, and then a muttered something he couldn't quite hear. But he didn't miss the note of sarcasm in it. He glanced up at her, but she was gazing off into the trees, looking as if she hoped a taxi was going to happen along any minute, or at the very least, a Greyhound bus.

Now, he was generally a patient and easygoing soul by nature, and he was certainly mindful of the fact that she'd had a few things happen recently that might upset her. But she was starting to get to him—kind of like a rock in his shoe; he was willing to overlook the aggravation for just so long.

"If you don't mind," he said carefully, "I think maybe I ought to take ol' Bubba for a walk. He's been in the car awhile."

"By all means. I'll wait."

While Troy was getting the leash out of the back of the Jeep, she went around to the front passenger's seat and got in. He looked back once before Bubba hauled him out of range, and saw her sitting there staring straight ahead through the windshield, her face pale as marble. Kind of made him wish he hadn't looked. He thought he'd never seen anybody so alone. Made it kind of hard for him to stay ticked off at her.

In the warm, gray stillness that smelled of equal parts new car and young dog, Charly was fighting for control with every ounce of strength she had left in her. Her belly jumped with every pulse beat; tremors vibrated through her muscles and resonated inside her chest. She wanted to scream and kick and tear things. She wanted to cry—great racking sobs, the kind that felt like they would turn her whole body wrong side out. But she wasn't going to. She'd already done that. She'd cried in front of *him* today; she was never going to forgive herself, or him, for that. And she'd cry no more. Not for anybody. Ever again.

Oh, but I'd give almost anything to make this pain go away.

There had been a moment…just a moment…when it had dampened some. When the volume of the pain had seemed to diminish at least to a bearable level—something like what happens when you stick your fingers in your ears to shut out noise.

It had happened in her first moment of freedom, when she'd burst out into the soft June night and heard that god-awful howl and stopped dead in her tracks. And he—Troy—hadn't been able to stop, and had run into her, and suddenly she'd felt his body, solid against hers, and his hands, strong and sure on her arms. Then for a moment, just a moment, as his masculine heat and smell had enveloped her, she'd felt a flash of warmth and comfort, an instant's surcease of pain.

Then she'd made some smart-ass remark and he'd removed his hands from her arms and stepped away from her, and the moment was gone.

She thought about that moment as she sat watching the man-shape and the dog-shape playing hide-and-seek with the shadows of the woods at the edge of the parking lot. She remembered the way he smelled of warm male and clean clothes and soap and aftershave—she wasn't up on masculine scents enough to know the name—and just enough of a hint of dog to call to mind the way he'd looked, tussling with that golden-eyed monster. The way the muscles pulled taut across his back and shoulders and rippled down his arms, bunching beneath smooth, tanned skin.

And this was Troy Starr. Mirabella's about-to-be brother-in-law. Jimmy Joe's big brother. Perfect...just perfect.

What, she thought, did I ever do to deserve this?

Oh, there was no doubt that he was a magnificent specimen of masculinity—broad of shoulder and narrow of hip and with pecs and abs that were, as she could personally attest, as closely akin to steel as you'd ever want human flesh to be. He had dark blue eyes with both squint lines *and* thick lashes, a jaw and chin Dudley Do-Right would envy and a mouth with a long upper lip that turned up at the corners, as if it enjoyed smiling. His hair, right now roughly the colour of those famous amber waves of grain, would probably have golden highlights if he ever let it grow out to a decent length. And to lend just the right touch of character and maturity to what might otherwise have been too much perfection, his hairline appeared to be receding just a bit, while his nose looked as if it had been broken, probably more than once.

In short, he was the all-American male, clean-cut and wholesome as grits, the recruitment poster boy for *A Few Good Men*.

And he was everything Charly despised. She'd known him ten minutes, and already she knew that he was polite to a fault, greeted people with "hey" instead of "hi," and addressed every female over the age of consent as "ma'am." He had a dog named Bubba that went everywhere he did—probably slept with him— and he drove an American-made 4×4 that she was certain was lacking a gun rack only because it was so new he hadn't got around to installing it yet. He was, in short, *Southern*. And even if his touch did seem to have affected her like a straight shot of Tennessee bourbon, there was no way in hell she was going to let him get that close to her again. Ever.

But, oh Lordy, hadn't it felt good.

Chapter 4

July 2, 1977

Dear Diary,

I can't believe it! This has been just the best day. First it was kind of scary, you know, because I decided I was going to let Richie know I like him, and I was really nervous about it. I mean, what if I made a total fool of myself, right? So anyway, Kelly Grace and I were down at Dottie's having a coke, and he and Bobby came in together. So I just sort of flirted with him—more than usual, you know—like I brushed up against him accidentally-on-purpose, so that my breast touched his arm. Oh, God, I thought I would die when that happened. It was like I got this weird, tingly feeling all over, and my skin felt all hot, and I couldn't get my breath. Anyway, then he said he'd walk me home, and...you guessed it, he did it. He asked me to go to the Fourth of July picnic with him! Of course I said yes. But I made him wait awhile before I did—I'm not a complete dufus.

Thought for the Day: I don't think it's a good idea to let boys get too sure of themselves, do you?

After Bubba had taken care of business and run off some of his excess enthusiasm, Troy took him back to the truck. This time, since it was clear his new passenger wasn't likely to enjoy having a great big ol' pup licking and slobbering down the back of her neck, he put the dog in the cargo compartment and tied his leash to the rear door handle.

She—the passenger—didn't have a word to say to him when he climbed into the driver's seat and stuck the key in the ignition. Since he'd given himself a pretty good talking to, out there in the darkness, reminding himself of all the reasons why he ought to cut her a little slack, he waited a moment and then put both hands on the steering wheel and said, "Okay, where to...?" He only just remembered not to add "ma'am."

He heard her pull in a breath—sort of priming the pump—and then the words came in a rush, if still a little gruff and crusty. "Hey, listen, I really do appreciate this. You coming all this way. I didn't want—didn't expect anybody to do that. And it was nice of you to pay my bail. I want you to know I'll pay you back."

He kept his face deadpan. "I was countin' on that."

"No." She stopped to clear her throat. "I mean I'll pay you back right away. Now. I just have to get my purse."

Troy had been reaching for the ignition key again; now he let go of it and turned his head to look at her. "You know where it is? From what the man said—"

"I have a pretty good idea." She was staring straight ahead so he couldn't see her expression, but her voice had the same hollow note he'd heard earlier on the phone when she'd said the words, "Mourning Spring."

He tapped his fingers on the wheel and waited for her to explain, telling himself he didn't need to know any more about her business than she cared to tell him, and he sure as hell wasn't going to pry. But at the same time, he had a normal store of curiosity, which had been building up inside him for a while, and damn if he was going to sit in this parking lot all night waiting for her to clue him in. So, when it was obvious she wasn't going to, he didn't think it would hurt to give her a little nudge.

He looked over at her once more and said with exaggerated patience, "So, you want to go get it now? Say the word."

"I don't think that's a very good idea, do you?" He could see the corner of her mouth turn upward, more with irony than amusement. "At this time of night? People turn in pretty early around here."

"I noticed that." He gave her a similar smile in return, which was wasted effort since she still wasn't willing to look at him. He waited another moment or two, then prodded some more. "Okay, so what do you want to do? You hungry? Want to go get somethin' to eat?" There were some eager whimpers from the back of the Cherokee at that, the words *hungry* and *eat* being of major importance in Bubba's command of human language.

Charly's profile tilted and took on a look of surprise. "I am kind of hungry, actually." She glanced down at the place on her arm where her watch should have been, realized it was in the manila envelope she was holding and frowned. "What time is it, anyway?"

"Gettin' on toward midnight."

"Jeez...all right, well—" she took a deep breath "—the only place that's going to be open is B.B.'s, out on the highway."

"I saw it on the way in," Troy said, giving the key a turn. "They have food there?"

"Just the basics—hamburgers, hot dogs. Maybe steaks. At least, they used to."

"Sounds good to me." He put the Cherokee in gear and drove out of the lot, turning left toward the town square. He looked over at Charly. "You know this town pretty well?"

She didn't answer that. Instead she cleared her throat and said, in a voice that was still a little rusty, "You know, you don't need to stay here. If you need to get back—" He stopped her with a snort and a shake of his head just to politely let her know how dumb that was, but she plowed on anyway. "I mean it. It was

nice of you to get me out of jail, but there's no reason you should
have to wait around while I get all this straightened out.''

Troy let a minute or two go by. Then he said, in a quiet tone
not very many people ever heard and fewer cared to argue with,
"Look, ma'am, it's late. I'm not goin' anywhere tonight, and
neither are you. Now, what I figured I'd do is, I'll get us a couple
rooms at that motel I saw comin' into town—''

"You mean the Moanin' Springs?"

That surprised him. He gave a bark of laughter. "You know
the place?"

"By reputation only, I assure you." She glanced at him briefly,
then away again. But she was looking more relaxed. Maybe even
like she'd remembered her sense of humor.

Troy grinned his appreciation and drove awhile in silence. It
wasn't a comfortable one; for some reason it seemed to him to
have grown stuffy in the car. Downright sultry, even with the air
conditioning going. He rolled down the window.

Charly leaned over and reached for the radio, cocking her head
toward him to ask belatedly, "May I?"

"Be my guest."

But when she turned it on, there was only a rush of static, so
Troy, being helpful, punched in the tape he'd been listening to
since he'd lost the golden-oldies station out of Atlanta. It was a
seventies greatest-hits collection, and he'd had it turned up pretty
loud, so the theme from *Saturday Night Fever* suddenly pulsed
through the car like jungle drums: "...huh, huh, huh, huh, stayin'
alive, stayin' alive..."

Charly swore like a hissing cat. Her hand shot out and silence
fell, so suddenly that for a minute or two it seemed as loud as
the music it had just eclipsed. Troy held on to his surprise and
threw her a mildly questioning look, but she just sat dead still
and stared straight ahead, and there wasn't much he could tell
about what was going on with her from that frozen profile.

Then suddenly she laughed, a light, false-sounding ripple, pure
Alabama belle. "My, my, you are full of surprises. I'd have taken
you for a country boy, for sure."

"Hell, I like country," Troy said, keeping it light, too, since that seemed to be the way she wanted it. Keeping it easy. "Don't know anybody that doesn't—exceptin' maybe Mirabella, and she's comin' around. But this—" he made a smacking sound with his lips and waved a hand at the now silent tape deck "—this is the music of my youth."

She exhaled softly, all traces of lightness gone. "Yeah, mine, too."

"Brings back a lot of memories, though, doesn't it?"

He could feel her turn her head toward him, but she didn't speak. And when he looked over at her a moment later, she'd turned away and was staring out the window again.

He thought about pursuing the conversation anyway but didn't. He was starting to get an inkling that maybe it was memories that were the crux of her problem.

As late as it was, B.B.'s Barn was still jumping, judging from the number of cars and pickup trucks and assorted characters gathered around and the country beat pumping out into the parking lot. Which, according to some signs plastered on the front of the building was Live! on Friday and Saturday nights. A hand-lettered sign tacked up on the door identified tonight's featured attraction as Mudcat Casey's Band, The Pride Of Chattanooga!

"We use to call this place the Beer an' Boogie," Charly said out of the side of her mouth as she passed under the arm Troy was using to hold the door with. "Doesn't look like it's changed all that much."

He arched an eyebrow. "You knew the place well, did you?"

She made that snorting sound again, and he suddenly realized it must be her version of laughter. "You kidding? I was underage. Plus, my father would have skinned me alive."

Which confirmed what he'd already guessed—she'd spent at least part of her growing-up years in this town. At the same time, one thing she'd said did surprise him. He thought Charly Phelps might be the first Southern-raised woman he'd ever met that didn't refer to her male parent as "Daddy."

Strange, Charly thought as she crossed the dimly lighted vestibule, listening to the music thumping out a country two-step and breathing in the smell of tobacco smoke, beer and sweat. In all the years she'd lived in this town, after all the talk, the jokes, the rumors and wild stories about this place, it was the first time she'd ever been inside. B.B.'s had been the forbidden zone, the hangout of the "fast" crowd, the sort of no-account trash no daughter of Judge Charles Phelps would ever be caught dead associating with. Which was probably why, in the years since she'd left Mourning Spring, she'd seen the inside of a lot of places just like it. It had a familiar feel to it, even though it had been years now since those troubled, searching times. There was something womblike about the warm, smoky darkness, the throbbing beat of the music, the crush of bodies, the muffled voices and laughter.

Quite a few people were up and dancing, making it hard to tell which tables were occupied and which weren't, but Charly spotted a small one that hadn't yet acquired an overflowing ashtray and a collection of beer bottles. She made for it, leaving her all-American Boy Scout rescuer to follow if he chose to.

He was getting on her nerves in ways she couldn't quite figure out. For instance, as soon as she dropped into a chair she found herself immediately twisting and turning, making a big deal out of looking for a waitress, just because she didn't want to have to watch the man pull out the chair across from her and lower himself into it. Because he was too damn good to watch, and in the reckless mood she was in, she didn't trust herself.

She was feeling too damn strange. As if all the wires in her system were crossed, hissing and spitting and in imminent danger of short-circuiting. And maybe she wouldn't care all that much if they did.

"Hey, how you folks doin' this evenin'? My name's Lori. What can I getcha?"

A cocktail waitress wearing skin tight Levi's and a tank top had appeared at Troy's elbow, balancing her tray on one perky hip. She had frizzy blond hair pulled up in a stubby little ponytail and was chewing gum. Charly squinted at her for a moment but decided she was too young to be anybody she ought to know.

"Well, Lori, tell you what, we're kind of hungry. You got anything left back there to eat?" Troy was smiling up at the waitress, Charly thought, as if his teeth had been set with diamonds and he was offering them for sale.

And she was obviously ready to buy. Charly watched in a restless state somewhere between amusement and annoyance as Lori stuck out her hip even more, making sure it brushed up against Troy's arm. "Kitchen's closed." She cracked her gum, lowered her eyelashes to half-mast and smiled. "But I think we still got hot dogs and nachos."

"Okay, why don't you bring me a couple of those hot dogs?" Troy looked at Charly, who shrugged. "Make that two more over there."

Lori took time out from flirting just long enough to spare Charly a speculative glance. "That be all the way?"

All the way. Oh, my. It had been twenty years since Charly had heard those words in that context, which in the South meant the works, including onions and the brown glop they called chili.

"All the way," Troy confirmed, beaming.

Charly seconded it, which was a waste of time since Lori had already taken Troy's answer for both of them. "Okay," she chirped, cracking gum, "that's four all the way. Now, what can I get y'all to drink?"

"Black Jack on the rocks," Charly snapped.

Lori looked as if she thought she might be in the company of aliens—at least one. She edged a little closer to Troy, if that were possible, and said, "I'm sorry, ma'am, but this here's a dry county."

"You're kidding."

"No, ma'am. We're only allowed to serve beer."

Good ol' Troy cheerfully ordered a light beer. Charly moodily seconded it, and waited until the waitress had given her cute little wiggle and departed before she shook her head and muttered, "I can't believe this town."

Troy leaned back in his chair and drawled, "Ah, hell, that's not too unusual. There's lots of dry counties in the South."

Charly all but ground her teeth. "Tell me about it. And right now I'd about give my left—" she could see by the anticipatory glint in his eyes that he knew exactly which part of her anatomy

she was about to barter, and just to aggravate him, changed it at
the last second "—*toe* for a shot of good old Tennessee bourbon."

For a minute there it looked like he might go ahead and smile.
Then he looked down at his hands, folded together on the tabletop, and his eyes vanished behind lashes any woman would pay
money for. "Maybe it's none of my business, but isn't that what
got you into this mess in the first place?" The lashes rose suddenly, his blue-eyed gaze skewering her like spear points.

She stared back at him, bitterness and resentment building inside her until she could feel its vibration in her teeth. She clamped
them together and said softly, "What gave you that idea?"

"Oh, I don't know, maybe it seemed like the most likely ex-
planation for why somebody'd be in the drunk tank after runnin'
a car into a tree, instead of, say, in a hospital." Now his smile
was friendly, designed to disarm.

She resisted it with every ounce of her strength, and offered a
stony, unforgiving stare. "Yeah, that's what the cops thought, too.
You're probably not going to believe me, either, but the last drop
of alcohol I had was in a strawberry margarita at Acapulco's in
Brentwood, California. That was...Tuesday. The blood test they
gave me at the hospital confirmed it—you can read the arrest
report if you don't believe me."

"Hell, I believe you." He said it in that same annoyingly easygoing way, but his eyes remained intent and thanks to those damn
lashes, impossible to read.

He really did have beautiful eyes.

The beat of the music was faster now, a rockabilly tune popular
with the younger crowd. Charly listened with her eyes half-closed,
letting her body move to it. Shutting out the eyes. Closing off
thought.

"So, what *did* they arrest you for?"

Unfortunately Lori the waitress arrived with their drinks just in
time to catch that. She gave Charly a nervous look as she set two
sweating long-necks on the tabletop, accepted the bills Troy gave
her without dallying, for once, and hurriedly scooted away.

Charly waited until she was out of earshot, then lifted her bottle, tilted it toward his in a mock toast and recited with lip-smacking relish, "Reckless driving, operating a motor vehicle without a license and open-container violation."

He paused in the process of tucking his wallet away to give a low whistle. "All that without even bein' drunk?"

"That's right."

He was shaking his head as he picked up his beer. "Sounds like you might be needin' a lawyer."

"I am a lawyer."

The bottle halted just short of his lips, and his eyes leaped to hers. "No kiddin'?"

She couldn't seem to shift her gaze away from his mouth. Hers had gone dry as dust. She drank some beer and licked her lips. "It's the truth."

There was a long pause, and then they were both laughing—real laughter, husky and mellow. Troy didn't know which felt better in his belly, that or the beer.

"You feel like telling me what *did* happen?"

"It's a long story." Her eyes stared straight into his, a dark, lost look he took as a personal challenge.

"I'm not goin' anywhere," he murmured. And knew right then and there that he wouldn't be. For better or worse, he was committed to this mission.

Granted, his life had been pretty tame lately, but right now he was feeling more keyed up and alive than he had in months. This woman was turning out to be a real surprise, as full of tension and secrets as a Baghdad bazaar. Intriguing and tantalizing as a pair of beautiful eyes beckoning above a veil. He was developing a real curiosity about her, a growing itch to *know*. He wanted to see what was behind that damn veil.

But it was obvious she wasn't going to show him, not yet. She frowned, suddenly edgy as a caged wolf, and said, "Hey, you don't happen to have a cigarette on you, do you?"

"Hell, no." He said it in surprise; he hadn't pegged her as a smoker. "Those things'll kill you."

She was out of her chair before he'd finished it, heading for the bar. He didn't try to stop her, just picked up his beer and lazily drank while he watched her edge her way in between a couple of guys who were sitting there nursing their Bud Lights and puffing away like chimneys. He could feel his jaw muscles tense as he watched her: the supple bend and sway of her body as she spoke to the two men; the way her hair brushed her neck when she tilted her head and smiled; the way her head fell back and her breasts pushed forward when she laughed.

He watched her take a cigarette from a proffered pack, tap it once on the bar and then put it between her lips, watched a flame sprout and her head dip close to a masculine hand. She lifted her head, her lips pouting around the cigarette as she shook back her hair. Her hand touched a masculine shirtsleeve.

He had to remind himself to breathe as his gaze followed the slender line of her hand and wrist, down her forearm, past the bend of her elbow and upward to the gentle curve of her biceps. He had a sudden, vivid image of Officer Baylor's thick fingers wrapped around that smooth, naked arm.

His mouth had gone bone-dry. His eyes burned in their sockets. He shook himself and drank, but the beer tasted like ground glass going down.

"Ah, that's better," Charly said with a breathless laugh as she dropped into the chair across from him. She picked up her beer and took a swig, then a quick drag from the cigarette. And erupted in a fit of coughing.

Troy watched her struggle for a while, then silently reached over and took the cigarette from her fingers and stubbed it out in the ashtray.

She glared at him in outrage. "What'd you do that for?"

"Come on, you don't want to be doin' that."

For a moment or two he could see she was thinking about arguing the point. Then she propped an elbow on the tabletop, rubbed wearily at her forehead and closed her eyes. "I haven't smoked in years," she said in a soft, tense voice. "It's this damn town. Look at me—I'm here what, six hours? Seven? And it's like I've lost twenty years of my life. I might as well be sixteen again."

Troy got to his feet and kicked back his chair. Her eyes and mouth opened simultaneously, but before she could ask the questions he could see forming in her eyes, he reached across the table and wrapped his fingers around her upper arm. He'd prepared himself in advance for the jolt, but there was still a growl in his voice when he said, "Come on, let's you and me dance."

It was a reckless thing to do, and he knew it. And he had an idea, from the way she was looking at him, that she knew it, too. Her eyes locked on to his, darkened and held as she lifted her head in full acceptance of the challenge he'd thrown at her. Then she rose without a word. The muscles in her arm quivered and pulsed beneath his fingers as he guided her around the table. And beneath his belt buckle, his belly did likewise.

Their bodies brushed and bumped together as they wove their way through the tables to the crowded dance floor. To Charly it seemed like part of the dance...his hand on her waist, her shoulder against his chest, his body heat merging with hers. She could feel his breath in her hair, feel her own pulse beat in her throat and belly and wherever he touched her. And then they were on the dance floor, surrounded by music and moving bodies and gentle darkness, and with one slow turn, he gathered her into his arms.

Gathered her in. Yes, that was what it felt like. So gentle and sure. She felt enfolded, surrounded, cocooned and protected; never had she felt so utterly and completely possessed. She wondered why such a notion didn't terrify her, why instead she should feel a sense of safety and happiness like nothing she had ever known. As if she *belonged* here. Right here, in this stranger's arms, on this murky little dance floor, in this noisy bar that reeked of cigarettes and stale beer and sweat and sawdust. She never wanted to leave.

She couldn't feel her feet. Didn't know any longer what song was playing, what the beat was, what steps they were using. And didn't care. He filled her senses—all of them—with his body, his hands, his heat, his smell. When she swallowed, she could taste him. With her eyes closed she could see the smooth flesh beneath her fingers. Her skin tingled, prickled and caught fire, as if with a raging fever. And yet she shivered.

He murmured something she couldn't hear as his arms shifted

subtly, further enfolding her. Everywhere they touched, she could feel his heat flowing into her...and hers into him. It's only dancing, she thought. But her heart hammered, drowning thought. Her throat moved convulsively. She felt parched...famished. The warm, moist hollow at the base of his throat tasted like manna from heaven; the tapping of his pulse against her lips was like the patter of raindrops on her thirsty soul....

Troy felt her lips move on his throat, and his stomach clenched. The muscles in his back tightened as he arched, drawing her body into his. She lifted her arms and slid her hands upward to meet behind his neck, kneading and stroking the taut cords, inviting them subtly to relax...let go. He could feel her breasts pillow against his chest, feel the pebbly brush of the nipples as if there were nothing but sweat between them. His thoughts began to flicker like a malfunctioning fuse.

With one of the last flares of lucidity before reason deserted him completely, he realized that his fingers were tugging at the silky knit fabric of her top, unconsciously seeking a way to the greater softness that lay beneath. His hands tightened, then grew still. He thought, What am I doing? What in the hell am I doing?

The inside of his chest felt as if an avalanche were taking place there. He cleared his throat and rumbled, "Looks like our food's...uh, maybe we'd better go eat before it gets cold."

There was a pause, during which he thought about saying, "The hell with it," and walking out of there with his arm wrapped possessively around her and her body plastered up against his side, and not stopping until they were locked inside one of the rooms at the Moanin' Springs Motel. He thought about it, with all the healthy male impulses in his body yelling "Yeah!" and egging him on.

It was hard saying no to those impulses, especially since they hadn't had much to yell about lately. He wasn't sure he'd have been able to, either, if just then she hadn't let her breath out in a long, slow sigh and pulled back from him just enough so he could look down and see the fall of dark hair across her pale forehead, the blackbird's-wing arch of her eyebrows, the shadows her lashes cast across her cheeks. Just enough to remind him who it was he was holding in his arms. Who it was he'd been on the verge of making love to in the middle of a crowded dance floor. Enough to make him feel dishonorable and ashamed. Hell, he was supposed to be rescuing this woman, not seducing her.

They walked back to their table in awkward silence. Charly felt intensely aware of her body's shape, its every nerve, fiber and flaw, its every movement, pulse beat and tremor. She was certain he must be, too, certain he could see how wobbly her legs were, how flushed her cheeks, how quick her breaths, how jerky and uncoordinated her hands.

And I don't care, she thought. I don't care!

She felt angry and thwarted, like a child who'd just had a much desired toy cruelly snatched from her hands. For a few moments, out there on that dance floor, she'd felt safe, happy...*oblivious.* For those few minutes in Troy's arms, she'd felt no pain. Felt nothing except the most elemental impulses of hunger, sexual need, desire. She wanted to go back to that place where the universe consisted of his body and hers and thought was an enemy, banished to the remote edges of consciousness. She wanted to go back there and, if at all possible, stay forever.

"Looks good," Troy commented, pulling back his chair. Obviously such thoughts and desires were far from *his* mind.

Damn Boy Scout, Charly thought as she gazed with disgust at the plastic basket before her, at the hot dogs nested there in waxed paper, smothered in onions and that noxious chili. She resented them—and him—with a passion that made her stomach burn. I can't eat this, she thought. I can't. She sat down and instead picked up her half-empty bottle of beer and drank.

Naturally Troy was already tucking into his hot dogs with good-ol'-boy gusto. It was such a revolting sight she couldn't tear her gaze from him. Avidly she watched his supple fingers cradle and manipulate the bun and lift it gently to his mouth...watched his lips open and his teeth come down...watched his lips come together and the tip of his tongue appear to steal a morsel of chili that had stayed behind, leaving them glazed for a tantalizing moment before he touched them fastidiously with his napkin. And she thought about how they would feel...his lips, his teeth, his tongue. How they would feel on *her* lips. How they would taste on *her* tongue.

"Better eat up," Troy urged between mouthfuls.

She pushed the basket away with a shudder. "I'm not hungry."

He shook his head. "Come on, now, you've had a long day. You need your strength."

Having already dispatched his first hot dog, he wiped his mouth with his napkin, then his fingers, dropped the balled-up napkin into his basket and pushed it aside. Then he reached over and picked up one of her hot dogs and held it toward her, cradled in both of his hands. "Okay, now, open up." His eyes smiled into hers.

He really does have the most beautiful eyes. It was Charly's only thought as she gazed into them, lips parted, barely breathing. She could have sworn he wasn't touching her, and yet everything she'd felt on that dance floor came flooding back—the heat and heaviness, the pounding pulses and shimmering nerves—as if she were still in his arms. She opened her mouth slowly, half-mesmerized, and took a bite and chewed without tasting. A lump formed in her throat that had nothing to do with hot dogs.

Something warm oozed down her chin. He caught it with the back of his finger, then wiped the spot clean with the ball of his thumb, laughing softly, intimately. And she laughed, too. How could she not?

"Good girl...ready for another? Yeah..." The words came from the back of his throat, like something erotic crooned in humid darkness amid tumbled sheets. Her own chuckle was a husky counterpoint, part of the same duet.

She put her hand on his to help steady the dripping hot dog and leaned forward to take a bite, while he braced his elbows on the tabletop and bent his head toward hers. It was a small table; his face was very close to hers, so close she could feel his warm, moist breath when he laughed. It was strange, she tasted nothing, her chest felt tight and crowded, her belly coiled and pulsed as if aliens had taken up residence there. And yet when the last bite of the hot dog had been swallowed and the last dribble of chili dabbed from her lips, she was sorry.

"There, now," said Troy, leaning back and reaching for his own basket once more, "that wasn't so bad, was it?"

She shook her head and groped for her bottle of beer, lifted it unsteadily and drained the few swallows that were left. Troy asked her if she wanted another, but she shook her head. He told her she should eat her other hot dog. She muttered, "No, thanks, I've had plenty." Plenty...and not nearly enough.

What in the hell was wrong with her? It seemed that when he was close to her, touching her, she was fine—more than fine. She was every dopey cliché you could think of—higher than a kite, drunk as a skunk, dizzy as a baby on a swing. And the minute he left her she felt...like this. Lousy. Like a baby, all right, a baby woken up too soon, wobbly and cranky and ready to cry at the drop of a hat. *I don't know how much more of this I can take,* she thought.

She watched while Troy polished off the last bite of his second hot dog and washed it down with what was left of his beer. When he said, "Well, if you're not gonna eat that, you ready to go?" she nodded. He pushed back his chair and stood up, and she noticed that he didn't try to help her with hers, or take her arm, or anything that might have brought him into close contact with her again. Miserable and disappointed, she wondered if he was deliberately avoiding it.

He noticed that she was looking around for a rest-room sign, and leaned over and murmured, "I think I saw them up front, when we came in."

She muttered, "Thanks," and pushed ahead of him through the maze of tables.

The women's rest room was deserted, but reeked of cigarette smoke. The glimpse Charly caught of herself as she slipped into a stall was something of an eye-opener to her. She looked like pure hell—bloodshot eyes in a pale, bloated face, hair hanging in lifeless strings, clothes that looked as if they'd been slept in—no wonder Troy didn't care to get close to her. Who could blame him? She probably didn't smell all that great, either.

It felt good to wash her face and hands. Of course, there wasn't much she could do about her hair—or anything else, for that matter. Her purse had vanished, and she supposed all her luggage was still in the trunk of the rental car, wherever *that* was. She would have to see about that tomorrow. *Tomorrow.* There were a lot of things she was going to have to see about…tomorrow. Like that other famous Southern belle before her, she pushed the thought ruthlessly aside.

It was while she was mopping herself dry with paper towels that she noticed the vending machine on the wall—the kind that dispensed tampons and condoms. She knew most public rest rooms had them nowadays, but she'd never paid any attention to them before. This one she couldn't seem to take her eyes from.

Forget it, she told herself. *I said, forget it.* And her heart beat faster.

Besides…well, of course, she had no purse. And therefore, no money.

Which, she told herself, was just as well.

Chapter 5

July 3, 1977

Dear Diary,

I can't believe what's happened. My father is such a *jerk*. He never listens to me. He must really think he's God. I mean, who does he think he is, telling me who I should go out with? It's not his life!

Okay. Here's what happened. I told him I was going to the Fourth of July picnic and fireworks with Richie, right? And he tells me I can't go with Richie, because we're going with the Stewarts, like we always do. So I tried to tell him I'm too old for that family stuff. I mean, I'm sixteen now, and this is like, a *date*. And he says, so what's the matter with Colin? He'll be your date.

Colin? Yuck! I mean, don't get me wrong, I love Colin. He's practically my best friend in the whole world. I tell him stuff I can't even tell Kelly Grace. We've been best friends since we were babies—he's like my brother! I can't even imagine kissing Colin. The very idea makes me feel sort of sick.

The judge just doesn't understand. And as usual he won't even listen to me. He doesn't care what I want. You know what? I think he has his heart set on Colin and me getting together so I can be a Stewart, which in this town is the equivalent of royalty. Is that the dumbest thing you ever heard, or what?

Thought for the Day: I don't think it should matter if a person is new money or old money, or how blue their blood is, or their skin, for that matter. The only thing that should count is how they feel in their heart.

Troy was waiting for her when she came out of the rest room. He said, "Ready?" and when she nodded, held the door open for her without saying another word.

Outside, the air was muggy and warm. The sky flickered like a silent-movie screen, and off to the west, thunder grumbled. A breeze gusted fitfully, stirring the trees and lifting Charly's hair from her shoulders.

"Thunderstorm," she murmured, breathing in the smell of rain. Oh, Lord, she'd forgotten what it was like, rain in the summertime.

Troy came beside her, glanced at her and then at the sky. There was electricity in the air, all right, but it seemed to him more of it was coming from her than from up there. "Yeah," he said, "looks like it's comin' our way. Got your umbrella?"

"You're joking, right?" She gave that miserly snort of laughter. "Where I come from, nobody even knows what an umbrella is for."

"I kind of thought you were from around here."

"Yeah, well..." She slanted a look at him, then caught a quick breath, let it go in a hiccup of laughter and, as she moved on, murmured in a thick Alabama drawl, "That is somethin' I try daily to foh-get."

And not succeeding all that well, darlin', Troy thought as he unlocked the passenger's side of the Cherokee.

He opened the door and out of habit, held it for her, then went around to his side, pausing on the way to give Bubba's ears a tug. The dog had his head hanging out the opening in the window as far as he could get it and was whining and looking as if the rest of him wanted to follow it pretty bad. But at least he wasn't howling.

Troy bumped out of B.B.'s parking lot, across the highway and into the driveway of the Mourning Springs Motel, which still had its Vacancy sign on. Once he'd roused the night desk clerk, he had no trouble at all getting two rooms, except that the clerk seemed to be a little hard of hearing. He kept saying "Two rooms? *Two?*" as though he couldn't quite believe it.

"Probably a first for this place," Charly commented when he told her about it.

He handed her one of the keys. "They are adjoining—that okay with you?"

"That's fine." Her voice was low, expressionless.

"Why don't you go on and make yourself at home?" he said as he started around to the back of the Cherokee. "I think maybe I better take ol' Bubba for a walk first."

The wind was picking up, and the thunder was a lot closer, doing some cracking and booming now instead of just mumbling and grumbling. He opened up the door and untied Bubba's leash and got a good grip on it, Bubba being none too fond of thunderstorms. He looked over at Charly, who was still standing there turning her key over and over in her hands. "I think this storm's about to cut loose. I'll be right ba—" About which time Bubba lifted his leg and cut loose all over the Cherokee's rear tire.

"Guess that takes care of that," said Charly, deadpan.

Cussing and muttering, under his breath, Troy got his overnight bag out of the truck and locked it up, then hauled Bubba away from Charly's legs and over to the door of number 10, which was the number on the key in his hand.

He had just unlocked the door and pushed it open when a flash of lightning lit up the whole place like broad daylight. The thunder crack that followed a moment later propelled Bubba through the door like a rifle shot. With his mouth open and one hand on the light switch, Troy watched as his pup made straight for the bed and tried his best to crawl under it and, when that didn't work, wallowed across the top of it and down into the space between the bed and the wall on the other side.

Still speechless, he turned to look at Charly. She'd unlocked her door and opened it partway, but hadn't gone inside yet, and since she'd just been an eyewitness to his dog's cowardice, he figured he'd see a big grin on her face at the very least, maybe even some laughter and cute remarks. But she was just standing there looking at him as if her mind was on something else.

He started to speak, but for some reason, didn't. Lightning flickered briefly, giving her features the translucent look of marble. The wind whipped her hair, casting strands like shadows across her face.

"What is it?" he asked her. But something in him must have known. Deep in his belly, a pulse began to pound.

She shook her head, reaching up to pull the strands of hair away from her face. Her lips parted, but whatever she said got lost in the growl of thunder. He leaned closer.

But it wasn't words he heard. It was something else, something he couldn't even put a name to, something a lot more primitive than language and a whole lot easier to understand. He knew that words can lie and mislead and throw up all sorts of barriers; this was a direct link between his soul and hers, bypassing all those confusing things like logic, conscience, morality, ethics, rules, customs...all those things he'd had pounded into him by parents and Sunday-school teachers and drill instructors and that he believed in devoutly and under normal circumstances, tried his darnedest to live by. And it was as impossible to deny as a lightning bolt bent on connecting with the ground.

As he hovered there, his face close to hers, he heard the hiss of an indrawn breath—his own. He felt the first raindrops splatter on his scalp, his shoulders, his back, saw them glisten on her cheeks and forehead...and ignored them. As did she. Her eyes gazed into his as if she'd been hypnotized. Electricity ran through his veins.

And then, without his knowing quite how it had come to be there, his mouth was on her mouth, and her lips were melting into his like butter on a hot griddle.

He felt pressure building in his chest and throat and belly. Lightning flashed against his eyelids, and in the second of silence that followed he heard her whimper. He opened his mouth, and she did, too, just as the thunder crashed in on top of them. It drove them together, a collision of lips and teeth and tongues and bodies. His arms were wrapped around her, holding her closer, and closer yet, while her arms coiled around his neck, urging his head lower.

The sky opened up and let loose the rain; it pounded on his head and pummeled his shoulders like a demon taking out its pent-up fury. For all Troy knew or cared, it could have been the Johnstown Flood. He was caught up in a natural disaster of a different kind.

They broke apart, gasping and drenched, to stare at one another for an incredulous, immeasurable time. Then, as if the spell that enchanted them both had suddenly broken, they turned and plunged through the open door together. Troy kicked the door shut behind them and reached for her in the sudden darkness. But the space around him was empty—he could feel its emptiness with every revved-up nerve and sense in his body.

A light came on—the lamp above the bed. Charly was poised in a half crouch beside it, looking like a wild thing pinioned in a car's headlights, eyes wide and luminous, dangerous and alluring as a bayou on a moonlit night.

Cocked and wary, breath coming shallow and quick, he held up a calming hand. "Look—" But she held up a hand, too, and stopped him right there.

"I'm sorry," she said in a low, urgent growl. "I'm sorry. I know what you're thinking of me. But I can't do this. I can't. I'm sorry."

"No problem," Troy drawled with a calm he was a long way from feeling, folding his arms across his hammering heart. Outside, the thunder cracked and grumbled, and the rain roared like a whole herd of demons, and it was nothing like what was going on inside him. "I understand."

She shook her head with controlled fury, hugging herself as if to keep from coming apart. "No, you don't. I want to—I do. Lord knows, I'm crazy, but...I do. All right, so I'm out of my mind. But I'm not stupid, okay? I'm not stupid. We can't...do this."

And all at once Troy was pretty sure he *did* understand. Taking the kind of heart-stopping, gut-tightening gamble he thought he'd left behind him for good, he reached into his jeans pocket, took out a small foil-wrapped package and tossed it onto the bed. "This what you're worried about?"

Her startled glance flicked at it, then at him. She caught a breath, and some of the fight and fury went out of her eyes and was replaced with laughter. Husky and breathless with it, she murmured, "I should have known. You *were* a Boy Scout, right?"

"What? Oh, Be Prepared, you mean?" He shook his head, half-smiling. "No, ma'am—navy. SEAL." He paused, then said stiffly, "I want you to know, just because I believe in being ready for any and all contingencies, doesn't mean I expect those contingencies to take place. You understand? What happened out there just now—maybe we both got a little bit carried away, okay? You want it to end right here, you say the word and I'm gone. No questions, no blame."

She heard him out, lips slightly parted, eyes never leaving his. And when he'd finished she went on like that, just staring at him, while ropes of tension coiled and tightened around his chest.

Finally, unable to stand the torture any longer, he growled, "Well? What's it gonna be?"

She shook her head and said slowly, "I can think of about a hundred reasons why you should go...and only one reason why you should stay."

"And that is?"

"Because—" the growl in her voice became a purr, a vibration he could almost feel in his bones "—I want you to."

She came toward him, one slow step, then another, her eyes catching fire the way hazel eyes can, sometimes, when the light's just right. "Because," she whispered, "I've just had one of the worst days of my life." She stopped right square in front of him. "And I don't feel like sleepin' alone."

He let out a breath, lifted his hands to her upper arms and brushed his fingers back and forth over the smooth, cool skin, and still felt as if the fire in her eyes were consuming him alive. "You don't have to do that," he mumbled, his throat dry and scratchy as kindling. "If that's all you want..."

"Don't be stupid."

He laughed then, a soft hissing like the sound rain makes when it falls on live coals. He tightened his hands on her arms, and she swayed toward him, leaning against their support. "Lady," he growled, "your clothes are soakin' wet."

"So are yours."

"Maybe we'd best get out of 'em—"

"—before we catch our death."

Their laughter tumbled giddily together with shivers as he skimmed his hands down her sides, gathered in the damp, limp fabric of her top, drew it from her waistband, peeled it up and over her head. Her bra was the kind that closed in the back; he reached around her and unhooked it with the kind of practiced ease he could feel grateful for without being proud of. Some things about his life he'd learned it was best not to agonize over, or regret too much, but just to accept as part of what it had taken to bring him to where he was.

And, he thought, where he was now was just about the last place he'd ever thought he'd be when he'd gotten out of bed that morning. Life could be full of surprises.

He flattened his hands and splayed his fingers across her back, then moved them slowly upward, watching her eyes as he hooked his fingers under the straps of her bra, willing now, since he knew it was okay, to let the fire take him.

Slowly he drew the straps over her shoulders and down her arms, lightly grazing her skin with his fingernails so that every tiny follicle sprang erect in a rash of goose bumps. So that when he let it fall, the bra brushed over nipples so hard and sensitive she had to gasp with the exquisite shock of it. Then and only then did he let his gaze leave hers, and set it free to explore what he'd uncovered.

He felt like a kid, opening up his own special box of treasures. Her breasts were small but round and full, the nipples tight and pert, the exact pinky brown of certain seashells. He could almost taste them, cold and sweet on his tongue, feel them warm and swell and soften in his mouth....

His body's response to that notion nearly made him groan aloud. Tight and airless with self-control, he managed an edgy laugh. "You're freezin' to death."

Her response was immediate, if bumpy. "Then warm me."

Her hands were on his sides, already entangled in his rain-damp shirt. He meant to let go of her just long enough to haul it up his back and over his head and toss it aside. But now her hands were tugging at his belt buckle, and it seemed like a smart idea to dispose of that obstacle, too. And then there was her belt. And her hands under his waistband, sliding over the slick, sensitive places just below. And his hands inside her trousers, inside her underpants, pushing them over the swell of her hips so that they fell in a pool around her feet, leaving his hands free to touch, to savor and explore...

His hands stirred over Charly's cold-prickled flesh like a magician's wands, leaving behind showers of sparkly shivers; electricity skated up and down her legs, generating heat that turned her insides to melted honey. Her body grew heavy; pulses throbbed in her belly and between her legs. She leaned against him, lightning flickering around the edges of her consciousness, weak with wanting, so tightly strung with need that every muscle and fiber and sinew in her body quivered, like a tuning fork that hadn't yet found the right overtone. She would know it when she found it, that moment when all the vibrations meshed into one perfect harmony that would drown the dissonances inside her head—the rage and sorrow and pain and regret. The loss and betrayal. The guilt.

For that, she needed...this. Needed *him*. Needed him kissing her until she couldn't breathe, needed to feel the weight of his body crushing down and his fire and force deep inside her. Needed *more*.

She cried out with wordless affirmation when she felt his hands cupping her buttocks, lifting her into him. She laughed when she felt his back muscles harden beneath her palms as his head came down and his mouth found hers.

Yes! she thought as she lifted and opened to him. Come inside me! Kidnap my soul! Take it away and hide it from me. Then maybe I won't have to think or feel or remember.

In all his life Troy couldn't remember ever experiencing anything like this. He'd never had a woman respond to him like this, with all need unmasked, all passion unbridled. He found it irresistible. Impossible not to get caught up in it, like being in the path of a flash flood. What else could he do but go with it, let it sweep him away, ride the crest for as long as he could, wherever it took him?

At the same time there was a part of him that knew and acknowledged that, for all the thrill and intensity of it, what was happening between them wasn't the real thing. That in a way it was more like an amusement-park thrill ride than a force of nature. That the thrills were temporary, and barring some weird catastrophe or some really stupid lapse on his part, the consequences minimal. This was fantasy. *Fun*. It had nothing to do with love. And nothing to do with the rest of his life.

He recognized, too, that there was a darkness in this woman's passion, a kind of desperation in the way she kissed him. He did. And God help him, he ignored it. Maybe he didn't have time to think about it then; maybe he simply didn't want to.

She kicked off her sandals, and he plucked her out of the pile of sodden clothing, carried her, cradling her bottom and riding her soft places against his hard ones while she wrapped her arms and legs around him, threw back her head and laughed out loud. He threw away his thoughts as he laid her on the bed and followed her down, holding himself away from her with his arms while his head swooped down to capture her mouth. She lunged forward to meet him, nipping and tugging hungrily at his lips, raking his

back with her fingernails, inflaming him almost beyond the limits
of his endurance.

Dimly aware that things were moving a lot faster than he
wanted them to, he tried to get his brain to order his body to back
off, ease up, slow down. He might as well have tried to stop a
cyclone. Still kissing her mindlessly, his tongue deep in her
mouth, he felt for the condom he'd tossed on the bedspread.
Found it, and bracing himself with one hand, tore his mouth from
hers and ripped open the packet with his teeth. He heard her
approving chuckle, felt her hands helping him...a silky coolness,
more agony than assistance. And then he was sheathed, first in
latex and then...at last, blessedly...in her warmth and softness.

He was conscious first of a most exquisite sense of relief—and
then of surprise. For all its swiftness, the penetration had not been
easy. He'd felt her body arch and tense in involuntary protest,
heard the gasp she'd so quickly stifled. He wanted to believe he
could have stopped even then, if she'd asked him to, or at least
had the self-control to gentle them both. But she wouldn't have
it. Her legs wound around him; her body tightened and pulsed,
further enfolding him. She lifted her head and shoulders, surging
upward to meet him. Her breath came in gasps.

Thought, reason and control slipped away from him like the
last willow branch in the flood. Instead it was her arms he
grasped, sliding his hands along their smooth, slender length until
he found her hands. She clutched at him, then laced her fingers
through his and glared fiercely up at him when he pinned them
to the mattress. Her mouth opened in invitation—no, demand. He
plunged down and poured himself into the kiss, his body tensing
like an archer's bow as he drove more deeply into hers. And
again, deeper still.

Pressure hammered inside his chest, screamed through his head,
turned his muscles to iron. He heard her whimper and thought,
Oh, no, I must be hurting her. Please...don't let me hurt her.

And then he began to realize that the whimpers were mixed
with laughter, and that her body was already shivering and pulsing
and rippling around him. That her breaths were coming in gasps,
bumping breasts soft as powder puffs against his chest.

His own relief came with the violence of an earthquake. His body rocked with it; a groan seemed ripped from deep inside him. He'd lived through quakes before, including one in Turkey that had killed people, but nothing had ever shaken him as profoundly as this. Nothing. In its aftermath he felt as if a building must have fallen on him. He wondered if he would ever move again.

Little by little he became aware of the woman who lay beneath him, first of the moist warmth of her breath on his cheek, then all the places they still touched—the slick union of bellies, the tangle of legs, the gentle abrasion of her hair against his forehead. He lifted his head and looked down at her, not at her face yet, but at their still-clasped hands, and saw the white imprints her now slack fingers had made on the backs of his.

His gaze shifted almost fearfully to her face. Her eyes were closed now, the lashes wet and spiky, the darkness beneath them like bruises on her pale skin.

Awash with remorse and other feelings less easy to define, he had an urge to touch his lips to each eyelid, to gently smooth back the damp strands of hair from her forehead and maybe kiss her there, too. But suddenly he wasn't sure he had the right to do that, or whether that sort of tenderness was even appropriate under the circumstances. He barely knew this woman. Who in the hell was she?

What had he been thinking of?

Her eyes were open, studying his face with a dark, smoky look he couldn't begin to read.

"Hey," he said huskily.

Her lips moved in and out, moistening themselves. He watched them, wondering how, after what had just happened to him, he could still be thinking about doing that for her, with his own tongue.

"Hey yourself." Her gaze slid past him. "Sounds like the storm's past."

He made a soft, rueful sound. "Think it went by a few minutes ago."

Her lips twisted as she pulled her fingers from his and covered her eyes with her hand. "I was afraid of that. How much noise did we make?"

"Nobody over there to hear except Bubba," Troy said, nodding toward the head of the bed and the wall beyond. He eased himself to one side, propping his weight on one elbow. "Besides, I expect that's why they call it the Moanin' Springs Motel, don't you?"

She gave her special snort of laughter. Troy grinned and leaned down, limiting himself to one quick, hard kiss, one he figured was ambiguous enough that she could take it just about any way she wanted to. Then he gently separated himself from her and headed for the bathroom.

Charly got herself raised up on her elbows just in time to catch a glimpse of his sculpted back and rock-hard buttocks before the door closed, blocking them from view. For a few more minutes she stayed right there, while her heart slowed its hammering and her body awoke to the reality of aches and throbbings in a dozen places, and her lips tingled with the memory of that last kiss. Then she slowly sat up, peeled back the thin covers and crawled between the tightly tucked motel sheets.

She lay in the quiet, listening to the rain drip from the eaves outside, her mind a blessed blankness. She didn't think about the pile of sodden, dirty clothes lying in the middle of the threadbare carpet, or where her suitcases full of clean ones might be or what she was going to do about all of that tomorrow. She was simply too numb and too tired. Too tired to think about the stranger in the bathroom.

Troy. His name is Troy.

Oh, please, God, she prayed, don't let me think about him.

Don't let me think.

She could hear water running. She devoutly hoped he wasn't going to be long; she needed the bathroom pretty badly herself. She needed a shower, too—probably a lot worse than he did.

Then she heard a new sound, this one coming through the paper-thin wall from the room next door. A heartbreaking, whimpering sound.

Oh, Lord, she thought, this is all I need.

She stood about a minute of it, then bounced out of bed, pulling the bedspread with her and wrapping it around her like a toga. Okay, she thought, now where in the hell did he leave the key?

It wasn't on the dresser or on top of the TV. Pocket, maybe? Trying not to think about the intimacy of what she was doing, she snatched up Troy's pants from the pile on the floor and plunged her hands into the pockets, one by one. Intimacy? The irony of that made her lips curl, but she didn't feel like laughing.

The motel-room key turned up on the second try. Swearing and muttering and dragging the bedspread behind her, she threw open the door and swept through it into the muggy, dripping night.

When she opened the door to number 10, Bubba was there to greet her. A much chastened and humbled Bubba, wiggling and squirming and so glad to see her it was pathetic. And damn if she was going to hug and pet and sweet-talk the yellow-eyed beast the way Troy did.

"Well, all right," she snapped, "don't just stand there."

Bubba didn't need to be told twice.

When Troy came out of the bathroom a few minutes later, a meager motel towel knotted around his hips, there was his dog, lying right in the middle of the floor with his paws pillowed on Troy's blue jeans and his muzzle pillowed on his paws, sound asleep. And in the bed next to him there was Charly, propped up on the pillows with her arms folded across her chest and the bedspread in a pile.

"'Bout time you got out of there," she said, glaring at him with her whiskey eyes.

"Sorry," he breathed. It was about all he could manage just then. He waved a hand at Bubba, who opened up his eyes just long enough to flick his eyebrows at him, give a great big sigh and close them again. "What—?"

"He was making noises," she snapped. "Crying, for God's sake. What was I supposed to do?"

Troy shook his head. He was trying hard not to smile, but it wasn't easy when there was a big ol' ball of something warm and sweet oozing like Southern molasses all through his insides. He wasn't sure what it was, but he sure did know what had put it there. It was the challenge in her eyes, that belligerent thrust to her chin, and that rusty, go-to-hell voice that had done it. Because for the first time he saw those things clearly for the camouflage they were.

"Told you," he said as he started toward her, letting the warmth he felt inside come into his voice and his smile. "He does cry when I leave 'im."

She watched him come closer, and he could see the confusion building in her eyes, saw them darken as she fought to hold on to the belligerence.

"Yeah, well...I figured I might as well let him in, since you were taking so long in the shower."

"Sorry," he murmured again, sitting on the edge of the bed. "It's all yours now, if you want it."

"Thanks." She stiffened, drawing the balled-up bedspread closer, fierce and battle ready as a rooster. "Look, just because I brought him in here, I don't want you to think you have to stay."

"You want me to go?" He reached out and touched away a strand of dark hair that had fallen across an even darker eyebrow. Her indrawn breath made a small, sucking sound. He let the backs of his fingers brush lightly downward, following the contours of her temple and cheekbone and jaw. Her skin felt warm and soft, like powder.

She lifted one shoulder, but except for that, held herself rigid and still. As if, he thought, part of her wanted him to stop touching her and the rest of her was afraid he might. She cleared her throat and said gruffly, "Just don't want you to feel obligated."

Obligated? He didn't know whether to laugh or shake her. So what he did was tuck a knuckle under that belligerent chin of hers and lean over and kiss her. Just lightly, letting his mouth brush hers, like feathers over satin.

"Ol' Bubba looks pretty comfortable to me," he murmured as he drew away. "Maybe I better leave him be, if that's okay with you."

"Okay, sure." Her breath flowed across his lips.

So he kissed her again, this time slow and sultry, pouring into her like warm molasses, savoring the sweetness of it. He hadn't planned to take it any further than that—he swore he hadn't, even though his belly was already curling and his body heating and tightening, stirring against the towel.

But he felt her arms relax and ease up on the bedspread she'd been clutching to her chest like a shrinking maiden, and it seemed a natural thing to slide his hand on down there and check the situation out. And then her breast was filling his hand so perfectly, the nipple was hardening under his thumb's circular stroking and her hand was a sliding warmth, creeping up his thigh. With all that, it didn't really surprise him that the kiss should take on a life and rhythm of its own. Nor did it surprise him, when he finally ended the kiss, to find that he wasn't wearing the towel anymore.

The only thing that did surprise him was when he pulled away from her. For the first time since he'd known Charly, he thought he saw fear in her eyes.

His heart stumbled and started again with a new and unfamiliar cadence. "I just want you to know," he said, "if I stay...no obligation." His voice, even his breathing, seemed bumpy and strange to him.

There was a pause—a long one. And then she slowly pulled her hand out of the tumbled folds of the bedspread and held it toward him, the fingers uncurling like flower petals to reveal the small foil packet in its palm.

"I found it," she said in a hushed and stifled voice, "in your pocket. When I was looking for the room key."

Again her eyes took on a whiskey glow. Troy, laughing low in his chest, leaned over to kiss her. It was easy, then, to convince himself that he'd imagined the fear.

Chapter 6

July 4/5, 1977

Dear Diary,

It's almost morning. So much has happened, but I don't want to write about it. I just can't right now. Maybe tomorrow. Right now I can't even see straight, let alone think.

Thought for the Day: If you ask me, thinking is highly overrated.

Troy woke up in a state he could only think of as confused well-being. He couldn't figure out how he could have behaved so badly and feel so good about it.

Here he was in a sleazy Alabama motel room, listening to the shower running in the bathroom and a woman banging around in there and dropping things, a woman he barely knew but had driven all the way from Georgia yesterday to bail out of jail and wound up spending what was probably one of—if not *the* most—

incredible nights he'd ever spent in the company of a woman in his life. If that wasn't reprehensible conduct, he didn't know what was.

He just wished he could stop grinning whenever he thought about it.

About then Bubba, who'd been sitting at attention over by the door, happened to notice he was awake and came ambling over to give him a good-morning lick. And since Bubba hadn't exactly been raised to be a house dog, Troy figured the first order of the day was going to be to take him out for a walk.

He was pulling on his pants when he heard the water shut off, and a moment later the bathroom door opened and there stood Charly with a little bitty towel knotted around her waist. She was holding another towel across her breasts and squeezing water from the ends of her hair with the end of it. Water droplets spangled her shoulders and arms and the fronts of her thighs. He hadn't really had a chance to notice last night, but now he saw that her legs were long and looked as if she either walked a lot or worked out regularly. It was a sight to put a hitch in his breathing.

"Oh, good," she snapped, "you're up. I was startin' to worry about that dog of yours. I was going to take him for a walk myself, but I thought the shock of seeing a naked woman running down the road with a bear on a leash might be too much for this town to handle." Her voice was scratchy and sardonic. He found it stimulating as burlap on his auditory nerves.

He walked toward her, grinning and thinking about how good it was going to feel to kiss her, all fresh and wet from the shower. But the look she gave him made him change his mind about that. He could read all sorts of things in her eyes, most of which added up to one thing: the Charly Phelps who had woken up in his bed this morning was prepared to deny any and all knowledge of the wanton stranger who'd taken over her body last night. Which didn't really surprise him. If he'd given it much thought, he probably would have expected it.

She dipped her head toward his bag, which was sitting on the dresser. "I don't suppose you might have something in there that I could put on?"

He scooped up the bag, opened it and held it out to her. "Help yourself. How 'bout boxers and a T-shirt?"

"It's a start." She peered warily into the bag as if she thought it might have an unpleasant surprise hidden in it, then took it from him and backed up into the bathroom and shut the door.

Troy stood there and looked at the place where she'd been for a minute or two, then huffed out a breath. "Well, okay. You're welcome, darlin'." He pivoted, clapped his hands and said briskly, "Hey, ol' Bubba, whaddaya say you and me go take us a little walk?"

Okay, he wasn't surprised. But he couldn't help feeling a little disappointed.

In the bathroom Charly propped Troy's overnight bag on the sink and peered over it at the faceless blur in the steamed-up mirror. She reached toward the glass with the towel she'd been holding across her breasts...then slowly withdrew her hand without wiping away the fog. The prospect of looking herself in the eye didn't hold much appeal this morning.

Selfish...irresponsible. She heard the words again, in her father's cold, unfeeling voice, along with another word she'd last heard more than twenty years ago. *Shameless.*

It was true. She was all of those things, and more.

A cold, hard knot took shape in her chest, and a cold, hard voice whispered in her ear things she'd tried for twenty years not to hear. *Selfish, irresponsible...shameless. You don't deserve...*

A pair of eyes took shape in the mirror's foggy blur—not her own ambiguous hazel, but darker ones, blue, with heavy lashes and laugh creases—kind, compassionate eyes. Nice eyes. Beautiful eyes. Troy's eyes. When they'd looked into hers, she hadn't felt shameless, or selfish, or undeserving. She'd felt beautiful, sexy, desired.

And *I used him.*

She closed her eyes on the vision and rocked herself slowly, dizzy with shame and remorse. It was true. Like some use drugs or alcohol, she'd used Troy, as something to dull her own pain, to help her forget, to get her through the night. Jack Daniel's would have been a better choice—at least she'd only have a hangover to worry about this morning. But—oh, God, this was a *person*. A human being, and a pretty decent one, as far as she could tell. What was she going to do about him now? How was she ever going to get them back onto a casual footing?

Especially, a hard, practical inner voice reminded her, when she still needed him. There were still some things she had to have his help in order to do.

The fogged mirror was clearing. It was her own eyes that stared back at her now, bloodshot and puffy, but determined. Oh, yes, there was still something she had to do. And she was sorry— truly sorry—but she was going to have to go on using that nice, decent man for a little while longer. There was simply no one else she could turn to.

But no more of what happened last night, she told herself firmly. *That* was unforgivable. I won't let that happen again.

As if in denial, a shiver coursed through her. Her nipples pouted. Her body's secret places throbbed and tingled, mocking her.

Jimmy Joe cradled the phone and looked over at his beloved, who was standing at the window watching traffic flow by on the Atlanta Beltway far below. He could tell just by looking at her that she was ticked off. "Well, that was Mama," he said. "She just heard from Troy."

"So I gathered," said Mirabella stiffly.

He walked over to her, put his arms around her from behind and pulled her back against him. "Is all that freeway traffic makin' you homesick for L.A.?"

"Huh? Not a chance."

"Look," he said in a cajoling tone, rocking her, "I know you're disappointed with Troy for runnin' off like he did and leavin' the nursery job half-finished—" he paused when she snorted "—but I think maybe you're gonna forgive him when you hear what he's doin' instead."

"He told your mom he was going to Alabama."

"Yeah, but you're never gonna guess who he's *with* in Alabama."

She turned in his arms, scowling suspiciously. "Who?"

"Your friend Charly."

Mirabella's mouth dropped open. "Charly! But that's—*Charly?* What's she doing here? What's she doing in *Alabama?*"

Jimmy Joe didn't even try to stop himself from grinning; it wasn't often he got to see his beloved dumbfounded. "Mama didn't say. What she told me was, Troy said to tell you that your friend Charly was in Alabama, and that she was havin' some problems over there and he was gonna stay on awhile and help her out."

"But—but what kind of trouble? And why—?"

"And that's *all* she told me," Jimmy Joe said gently but firmly. "Marybell, honey, I'm as much in the dark as you are."

She twisted out of his arms and sat down dazedly on the bed, "Charly...and Troy? I don't believe it."

Jimmy Joe was still grinning. "Sort of interestin', though, ain't it?"

Still confounded, Mirabella said, "Mmm..." then did a double take and flashed him one of her looks. "Oh, no—no way. That's impossible. Out of the question. Charly and Troy? Never in a million years."

It was her most stubborn, know-everything look. He could see she was primed for a good argument, which was fine with him. Arguing with Mirabella had a stimulating effect on him.

He went and sat down on the bed beside her and said, "Come on, now. Why not? You've met Troy, and from everything you've told me about Charly, seems to me they might just hit it off pretty good."

"Well," said Mirabella, thoughtfully chewing her lip, "for starters, he's Southern."

"Well, hell—"

She shook her head. "I'm sorry, but there's just no way in the world Charly would ever let herself get mixed up with somebody from the South. No way."

"I know somebody else woulda said that about six months ago," Jimmy Joe said mildly; it wasn't in his nature to take offense.

Which was something he knew Mirabella was still getting used to. So he wasn't surprised that she had to look into his eyes for a long measuring moment to find the reassurance she was searching for before she went on, flushed and earnest, "No, you don't understand. Charly hates everything about the South. She grew up in Alabama, in some little tiny town—she actually ran away from home when she was sixteen. She swears she'd sooner die than ever go back."

"The South's not all country roads and rednecks," Jimmy Joe argued. "You know that. Troy's seen more of the world than most people. He knows his way around."

Mirabella was quiet for a moment. Then she let out a breath and shook her head. "It's not just that. I mean, I love Charly— she's a wonderful person. She's funny and smart and has a heart of pure mush—"

"Sounds like somebody else I know."

She laughed softly, and for a minute or two he thought she might be ready to call it quits on this particular discussion. But there was still more she wanted to say, and after too short an interlude, she gave him a gentle push and went determinedly on, "but the point is, she does a good job of keeping that fact a secret." She paused. "Charly...protects herself. She has fun, she dates a lot of guys, but she never lets it get too serious, you know? She never lets herself care too much. Never lets herself..."

"Love?"

"Well...yeah." She was looking into his eyes, and Jimmy Joe could see that she was thinking about how close she'd come to being in that same condition herself, and feeling the wonder and awe of her own miracle all over again. It was something he had no trouble understanding, since it was his miracle, too.

She gave her head a shake, pulling herself away from her own scary thoughts. "What I think is, something happened to Charly when she was young, and that's why she ran away. I think she must have gotten hurt somehow. I don't mean just some broken love affair—I mean really *hurt*, you know? So badly that I don't think she's ever gotten over it. I think she's just made up her mind she's not ever going to let herself get hurt again.''

''Minds can be unmade,'' Jimmy Joe reminded her, dipping his head until his lips found the sweet, fragrant softness of her neck.

''Mmm...never happen...'' Her words grew slurred; she moved her head slowly back and forth. ''Charly's pretty stubborn.''

Jimmy Joe chuckled. He could feel her begin to tremble as he laid her gently back against the cushion of his arm and whispered against her lips, ''Never underestimate the power of a Starr.''

''Breakfast first,'' said Troy as he backed the Cherokee out of the Mourning Springs Motel parking lot. ''And a gallon of coffee. *Then* the car.'' It wasn't the first time he'd said it; Charly had been all for going out and chasing down her rental car first thing, and it was taking some doing to dissuade her. He couldn't blame her for wanting to get her suitcases back, but he also knew what blood sugar could do to a body when it bottomed out.

''Jeez...'' She gave in with poor grace, muttering and swearing, and with conditions of her own. ''All right, here's a Burger King—we can go through the drive-through.''

''You kiddin'?'' Troy glanced in the rearview mirror at Bubba, who he knew was going to be panting and drooling all down the back of the middle seat at the mere mention of Burger King. ''That fast-food stuff'll kill you, don't you know that? Naw, what we need is some real food.''

Her snort was ripe with sarcasm. ''By which, being Southern, I imagine you mean grits.''

He smiled good-naturedly but didn't say anything for a second or two, not being exactly sure which she was feeling sarcastic about—the South, or the grits. Then, squinting into the morning sun, he said, ''Okay, then, you bein' Southern—''

''*Ex!*''

He could have told her there was no such thing, that it was almost a scientifically proved fact that you could take the girl out of the South, but no way in hell you could ever take the South out of the girl. But the mood she was in, he thought maybe he'd best make that point some other time. So he nodded and conceded, "*Ex*-Southern. So what do you eat with your eggs, California? Quiche?"

"Hash browns," she snapped, and threw him a bitter look, like a disappointed child. "Preferably those little greasy stuck-together patties they give you at fast-food places." He laughed. She studied him for a while, then said, "No smoking, no fast food—so, I suppose you're some kind of a health nut, too."

"Too?"

"Mirabella." She sat back with a resigned sigh. "She's always getting after me about my eating habits."

And that was something that just about boggled Troy's mind. He kept trying to imagine those two headstrong, feisty women—the Mirabella he knew and the Charly he'd just met—being best friends. He decided such a volatile combination would have to be either highly entertaining or highly hazardous to a person's health. Either that, or there were facets to both women he hadn't discovered yet. The more he thought about it, the more he decided he'd like to. Especially after last night.

"Way I see it," he drawled, "you only get one body. I try not to abuse mine, is all."

He could feel her studying him again. It gave him a pleasurable little tingle to think she might be wondering about some of his undiscovered facets. He thought to himself, Darlin', if you'll show me yours, I'll show you mine....

After a moment she said, "So, is it true? You're a SEAL?"

"Used to be." He glanced over at her, but she had turned her head and was staring out the window, gazing at the buildings they were just passing.

"Mourning Spring High School," he said, reading the letters on the sign at the base of the flagpole as it flashed by. "That where you went to school?"

"For a while." Her voice seemed faraway, and had that hollowness he'd heard before. "Never graduated."

"Never graduated?" He frowned, thinking she probably hadn't meant it just that way. "How come?"

"Moved." Her voice had a new, bright edge, an artificial lightness. She turned her head toward him again, giving her hair a little flip that made him think of his own high-school days, of bands playing Queen's "We Are the Champions" and cheerleaders flirting.

"Hey, I bet you were a jock—football player, right? Hell, I'll bet you were the quarterback."

"Shows how wrong you are." Troy grinned, still riding on those memories, allowing himself to strut a little. "Wide receiver. All-conference, junior and senior year—voted best hands in the state."

"That I can believe."

He thought she probably hadn't meant to say it like that, with her voice going husky and a catch in her breathing. But suddenly there was silence, except for Bubba's panting, which sounded too much like heavy breathing and didn't help matters. And if she hadn't meant to say it like that, she sure knew right away that she had. She put her head back against the seat and whispered under her breath—most likely swear words, if he knew her. And he thought he was beginning to, a little.

At first he thought the best thing would be to ignore it. But the silence kept getting thicker and heavier, and his mind, looking for ways to fill the vacuum, kept wanting to give him reminders of the very things he was trying to forget. He found himself growing light-headed.

So he finally said, "Hey, look—it happened. It's not like it's gonna go away if we don't talk about it."

Her body jerked slightly, and she turned her head to give him an angry glare. "I hope you don't think I do—"

He held up a hand and stopped her right there, then shook his head and growled, "I can't believe you'd even say that."

"Well, I wouldn't blame you if you did think it," she countered in an edgy voice. There was a pause, and then she gave a tight, high laugh. "I mean, God, I wish I could say it was because I'd had too much to drink. But I don't think one light beer would do it, do you?"

"You had too much of somethin'," Troy muttered, narrowing

his eyes and staring straight ahead through the windshield. Like trouble, stress and heartache, maybe.

And the worst of it, as far as he was concerned, was that he still didn't know why, or what in the hell it was all about. He wished to God he had it in him to just come right out and ask, but he kept telling himself it was her business, not his.

He let out a breath through his nose, calling on all his patience and self-control. "And I...took advantage of the situation. That's not something I'm proud of. But on the other hand I don't feel particularly inclined to apologize for it, either. Unless you feel like I ought to." He looked over at her, issuing the challenge. "You want me to?"

"What?"

"Apologize."

"No!" She threw him a furious look, then put her head back against the headrest and finished it on a soft exhalation. "Of course not. It wasn't your fault."

"Yeah, well, it wasn't yours, either."

"Okay," she snarled, "so it wasn't anybody's fault. It just happened."

"Yeah, it did. And you want to tell me why we're sitting here tryin' to attach fault to something that felt so damn good?"

They were just coming into the town square, on a Saturday morning as bright and blue and sunshiny as an Alabama June day knows how to be. Out there in the park, people were going about their business, kids playing ball, old folks sitting in the sun. And inside the Cherokee where they were sitting the atmosphere was as charged and sultry as it had been in the night with the lightning flickering and the thunder growling and one hell of a storm coming on.

Some of the growling was coming from Troy's stomach, and it wasn't all from hunger—at least, not the bacon-an'-eggs kind. Out of the corner of his eye, he saw Charly shake her head, then look down at her hands, which were all knotted up in her lap. But she couldn't find anything more to say, and neither could he.

Troy found a shady parking place on the square across from Kelly's and pulled into it. While he was rolling down windows and explaining the program to Bubba, and trying to get him to understand that all that howling and carrying on wasn't going to change things one bit, Charly sat and stared through the windshield at the sign that said Kelly's Kitchen.

She told herself she was behaving like a child. More accurately like the emotionally racked teenager she'd once been. It was time she remembered that that girl, Charlene Elizabeth, didn't exist anymore. It was time she remembered who she was now—C. E. Phelps, Attorney-At-Law, according to the brass letters on the door of her plush-carpeted offices on the twentieth floor of a downtown L.A. high-rise. And time she started demonstrating some of the character that had gotten her to that place.

She knew that the first thing she was going to have to do was come to some kind of understanding with Troy. And that in order to do that, she was going to have to level with him—at least up to a point. She owed him that much. Okay. She knew it was the right thing to do, and she'd made up her mind to do it. She just hadn't realized how hard it would be to work up the courage and self-control to make it possible.

By the time Troy had finished sweet-talking his dog and was giving her an "Are we getting out or what?" look, she was ready. Or thought she was.

"I..." It was a false start, but enough to stop him in the act of reaching for the door handle. She cleared her throat and tried again, in a voice still too raspy for the calm, in-control image she was trying for. "I'm the one who should apologize."

He gave a faint "Here we go again" sigh. "What for?"

She could feel his eyes on her, but couldn't bring herself to meet them. Instead she went on looking at the Kelly's Kitchen sign. "Please understand—I'm not making excuses. I'm just trying to explain."

"No need—"

"Yeah, there is. I shouldn't..." She tried to take a deep breath and was surprised by the pain—physical pain, this time. She'd forgotten the seat-belt bruise. Because of it, her voice was an air-starved whisper. "I had some things...happen yesterday."

"I kinda got that idea," Troy said dryly.

She held up a hand. "But that's no excuse. It's my problem. I shouldn't...have dragged you into it."

He gave a soft huff of laughter. "I don't recall doin' any kickin' and screamin'." He paused, then added, "Well, maybe a *little* screamin'."

Ah, damn. She didn't want to smile. She bowed her head and looked at her hands and tried her best to hide it, but his chuckle was like a sensual massage along her auditory nerves. And then she felt his hand on her shoulder, pushing upward to nudge under her hair and his fingers gently probing the tense places in her neck. Heat crept up into her throat and cheeks, and oozed down into her stomach and pooled in the sensitized places that still remembered that touch....

"Feel like talking about it?"

She wanted to. She really did. She'd intended to. She'd thought she was ready to tell him, that she'd talked herself into it. But now... Maybe it was his hand, the way he touched her, the incredible gentleness of it, but suddenly there was a dangerous ache all through her, and a useless lump where her voice should be. She knew if she talked about the past in this fragile, vulnerable state, she would almost certainly cry. And that was something she had promised herself she would never do again. Ever.

There was only the softest whisper of an exhalation to betray Troy's frustration when she firmly shook her head. And she was sorry, truly sorry.

"Let's get some breakfast," was all he said, and gave her neck a gentle squeeze before he took his hand away.

Charly had been half hoping Kelly Grace wouldn't be there for the breakfast shift. There was a lot she didn't feel like explaining this morning, not the least of which was her companion. But no such luck. They'd just gotten themselves seated in a booth and were looking over menus when Kelly came out of the kitchen and spotted them.

She yelled out, "Charlene! I was hopin' t' see you this mornin'!" and intercepted the teenage waitress who was headed their way, coffeepot in hand. "Here, April honey, I'll take that—this here's an old friend a' mine. Hey, how're y'all doin' this mornin'? How'd it go yesterday? I sure have been thinkin' about you...."

And of course, all the time she was talking away a blue streak to Charly, her eyes were about to eat Troy alive.

Resigned to the inevitable, Charly muttered introductions.

"Hey, Troy." Kelly Grace offered him her Miss America smile along with the hand that wasn't full of the coffeepot, oozing Southern femininity from every pore. One thing Charly had forgotten about was how that girl could flirt.

And like any true son of the South, Troy was naturally eating it up, taking her hand like it was the Lady Guinevere's and he was Sir Lancelot.

Then all of a sudden he got very still. He stayed that way for a second or two, then looked over at Charly and muttered, "Kelly...Grace. You're kiddin', right?"

Charly picked up her coffee cup and dipped her head to hide her smile, but Kelly Grace squealed with delight and slapped Troy playfully on the arm.

"No, sir, she is not! Isn't it just *awful?* You have to understand, my mama is a strange person. She claims she didn't plan it that way at all, says she never even made the connection until she saw it written down on my birth certificate, and by then it was too late."

She plunked the coffeepot down and shifted gears. "Where you from, Troy? I *know* I haven't seen you around here before."

Troy told her he was from Georgia, and she echoed it in a tone of pure amazement, as if she thought he must be talking about the one in Russia.

"He's helping me out," Charly reluctantly explained. "I had a little accident last night—"

"An accident!" Kelly Grace's mouth fell open. "Oh, my *Lord,* was that *you?* A couple of the troopers were in here this mornin', talkin' about some woman goin' off the highway last night, up by the spring, but I never dreamed— My Lord, Charlene, are you all right? You're not hurt, or anything...."

"I'm fine." Charly gave her chest a reflexive rub. "Just a seat-belt bruise."

At that, there was a faint, strangled sound from Troy. She threw him an inquiring glance, and found that his eyes were riveted on her chest, his face pale and a muscle working in his jaw, looking as horrified as if she'd just sprouted a third breast. And it dawned on her that what he must be feeling was guilt—for not having thought to ask, in all the time they'd been together, if she might be injured. For all the things they'd done and all the ways he'd touched her. For forgetting to be gentle.

Pictures flashed through her mind; sensations reprised themselves all over and through her body. A strange warmth flooded through her, totally unexpected and indefinably tender. She wanted to tell him it was okay, that she hadn't thought about it, either, that he hadn't hurt her—far from it. But in present company all she could do was gaze at him, and hope he would read those things in her eyes and take it no further.

"My Lord, Charlene, why didn't you *call* me? I would've been glad to help. Or you could have called..." Kelly Grace stopped suddenly, looking confused.

"Kelly, I didn't know your number," Charly reminded her, regretfully tearing her eyes away from Troy's.

"Oh, my Lord, that's right! I should have given it to you yesterday. Don't know why I didn't—I surely meant to. Charlene and I go way back," she explained to Troy, giving him a companionable nudge. "We were best friends back in high school. Oh, that reminds me...I was hopin' I'd see you again. Brought these with me, just in case." She plunged her hand into a pocket of the denim skirt she was wearing, brought out several snapshots and dropped them on the tabletop. "Got to lookin' at 'em last night. Sure does bring back memories."

Then she hesitated, coffeepot in hand, while her natural effervescence seemed to go flat. She tried to pick it up again in her usual friendly way, but it sounded forced now, and uncertain. "Well, listen, I got pies in the oven—guess I better let you alone, hadn't I? Let you get you some breakfast. Let me see if I can get April to come take your order, okay? I'll be seein' y'all later."

She hurried away, and it seemed to Troy as if she was fleeing from the memories she'd left behind on the table.

He sipped his coffee in silence as he watched Charly reach for
the photographs and slowly, almost as if it was against her will,
spread them out in front of her. He couldn't see her eyes; she
was looking down so that her lashes shielded them like curtains.
But it seemed to him her face was unnaturally still, and a lot paler
than a California girl's should be.

He watched, and waited, while questions backed up in his
throat, and his manners and upbringing choked them off like a
too tight collar.

The little waitress—a high-school kid, by the looks of her—
came to take their order and refill their coffee cups. When she'd
gone away again, Troy reached over and casually picked up one
of the snapshots. "Who's this?" he said, "Charlie's Angels?"

She acknowledged that with a crooked grin. "Hey, it was the
seventies—what can I say?"

"You're the dark one, right?"

"Naturally."

"And the Farrah Fawcett blonde is...?"

"That's Kelly Grace."

"Uh-huh. And the two jocks in the football jerseys?"

She hesitated, then reached across the table and pointed.
"That's...Bobby Hanratty. He and Kelly got married. She says
they're divorced now—have two kids. And that's Richie. I went
out with him for a while. This was the homecoming dance. We
were juniors—Kelly Grace was junior-class princess that year."
Her voice seemed oddly flat, Troy thought, for somebody remi-
niscing over her happy youth. And she kept her eyes downcast.
He wondered if it was to keep him from seeing the sadness in
them.

He bared his teeth in a smile. "Yeah? Princess, huh? Why does
that not surprise me? And the next year—queen, I presume?"

She shrugged and her voice went from flat to edgy. "I wouldn't
know. I wasn't here then."

"So," he probed, unable to stop himself, "that's when you
moved away?"

"Right."

He waited, his pulse tapping like an impatient foot, but there was nothing more. So he touched the photograph once more. "Who's the fifth wheel? The guy in the band uniform?"

There was a long pause, and it seemed to him that she had to unstick the words from her throat before she could say them. "That's Colin." She reached across the table and took the snapshot from him, tucking it under the rest as she made a small neat pile of them and set them aside. "He was...a friend. He lived next door. We...grew up together." And suddenly her voice had gone soft, with a kind of tenderness in it that for some reason made something twist and knot up under Troy's belt buckle.

"Where is he now?" he asked her, trying hard to keep it casual.

Her eyes met his, shadowed and deep as the woods in summer. "He died."

"Aw, hell," said Troy softly, "I'm sorry to hear that."

She lifted a shoulder, and her eyes shifted downward once more. "It was a long time ago."

He nodded, though he knew how little that mattered. He'd lost friends himself, a few under circumstances that had given him reason to know how it was to wake up in the middle of the night, cold with self-doubt and self-blame. And how sometimes the smallest thing could send him back there, to the place where the guilt and second-guessing waited in ambush.

"How did it happen?" he prodded gently.

"An accident." The words made a small sticking sound.

And he understood that, too. He knew how hard it could be to talk about. And how important it was to do it anyway.

But before he could encourage her further along those lines, little April, the waitress, was there at his elbow, saying nervously, "Excuse me, sir, but is that your dog that's doin' all that howlin' out there?"

So then he had to go out and try to bribe poor ol' Bubba with the promise of a double cheeseburger if he'd calm down and let them eat their breakfast in peace. By the time he got back, their food had arrived. And naturally Charly jumped on that distraction like a duck on a june bug, energetically critiquing the selection of jellies, the doneness of her eggs, the temperature of the toast, the size of the holes in the pepper shaker as if those details were the most important things in the world to her.

And maybe, Troy thought, in a way, just then they were. Because what they were, it looked like to him, were sandbags she was using in a last, desperate fight to hold back the flood of memories she was scared to death was going to drown her.

Chapter 7

July 5, 1977

Dear Diary,

I'm so confused, I don't even know how I feel.

Richie's been calling all day, but I don't want to talk to him. I don't know what to say to him. What if he wants to go out with me again? I am so ashamed, I don't think I can even look at him. Colin says I shouldn't be ashamed. He came over a little while ago. I told him I didn't want to talk to him, either, but he climbed up the back porch and came in my window, like he used to when we were kids. He was so sweet. We sat on my bed and he put his arms around me. I cried. He said it wasn't anybody's fault, that we'd both just had too much to drink, and that it was okay, nothing has changed, and as far as he is concerned we are still friends. He said we should consider it our secret, and go on as if it never happened.

But it did happen, and it seems like nothing is ever going to be the same again. I even keep looking in the mirror to see if it shows, but I can't see any difference on the outside. I guess that's a good thing.

Thought for the Day: I always thought losing my virginity would be something...I don't know, special. So how come I feel like something the dog left on the lawn?

It was going to be a hot day, a typical June day in the South, already beginning to build toward the afternoon crescendo of thunderstorms. Charly thought she should have been prepared for it, but after twenty years in the land of sun worshipers, endless beaches and backyard swimming pools, she'd forgotten what humidity was like—the way it made the air feel heavy as wet cloth, and the softness of it, like a gentle mist on her skin. Southern California heat had the harshness of the desert in it, a burning dryness that baked the skin to delicious brownness, and then before you knew it, to old leather. In California people played in the sun. In the South they knew better. On days like this, Southerners sat in the shade and drank iced tea and fanned themselves. Those with any sense.

Which obviously didn't include Troy. Charly, watching him from a shady spot on the steps of the bandstand in the middle of Courthouse Square Park, was ready to conclude that the man had not a lick of sense. There he was, gamboling in the heat with that incredible dog of his, playing tag and chase and fetch and wrestling around like a kid, showing off like some kind of grown-up Tom Sawyer. Just because he was—what?—in his mid-thirties, at least, and had a body like...

Oh, God, he did have a beautiful body, even fully clothed in basic polo shirt and blue jeans. Charly had just come from the land of beautiful bodies, and she'd never seen one that made her heart pound and her throat close up the way his did. And what a picture they made—beautiful man, beautiful dog, performing their own special ballet just for her, on a soft summer morning in the dappled shade of big old oak trees.

Watching them, she felt a strange sort of yearning welling up inside, one that succeeded in smothering temporarily the sharper pain that had already taken up residence there. This was a gentler ache, rather like homesickness. A misty prickling that almost—*almost*—made her want to smile. And deep within, the slightest warming, the beginnings of softening in the icy knot of rage she carried, now, in her heart.

Oh, no, you don't! Charly, get a hold of yourself. She leaned forward and let her forehead rest on her knees. It's this place, she thought, laughing silently, feeling not the least bit amused. It's the South. I really think it must be a sickness, like malaria.

"Somethin' funny?"

She lifted her head and watched them come toward her, both dog and master panting and grinning and looking vastly pleased with themselves. Bubba was once more attached to his leash, and Troy was carefully tying a knot in the top of a plastic bag, which he dropped into a trash can as he approached.

"What?" He hooked an arm over the bandstand's wooden handrail beside her and leaned against it, just slightly out of breath, his face flushed and spangled with sweat, his grin tentative. Like a little boy, Charly thought, who knows he has mud on his shoes.

She looked away, keeping her ironies private for a moment longer, then shook her head and gave up a small huff of laughter. "You."

"Me?" He looked around in exaggerated puzzlement. "What'd I do?"

What did you do? It was a question that was beginning to occur to her, and one she was afraid she wasn't going to want to hear the answers to.

She tilted her head toward the trash can. "That something they teach you in the navy?"

His eyebrows rose. "What? You mean, pickin' up after myself? Ah, hell no. I learned that a long time before I joined the navy." He ran a hand over his short-cropped hair, his smile becoming wry. "My mama made the U.S. Navy look like summer camp."

"That right?"

"Oh, yeah." He glanced at Bubba, who was pulling against

his leash, responding to some invisible siren scent, then straightened and held out a hand to Charly. She found herself taking it without a thought. She let him pull her to her feet, and they began to walk together slowly, aimlessly, not talking, letting Bubba sniff and ramble to his doggy heart's content.

After a bit Troy went on in a voice rusty with reminiscence. "Yeah, my mama ran a tight ship. Had to, I guess. There were seven of us, and my dad was a trucker, so he was gone most a' the time."

"Seven," Charly murmured, breathing a silent whistle. She'd heard most of this already, from Mirabella.

He laughed. "It didn't seem like so many, growin' up. Just every few years or so there'd be a new baby in the house, is all."

"Are you the oldest?"

"Second. I'm the oldest boy—got one older sister. The rest are younger."

"Well," Charly said dryly, "then I guess you've done your share of baby-sitting." *Don't think about it. Don't think at all.*

"I have that." His laughter came so naturally. She was surprised at how much she was beginning to like hearing it, and how much she envied him the easiness of it. "Diapered, bathed, read to and done homework with more kids than most fathers ever do, I guess."

Diapered, bathed, read to... His voice seemed to retreat into distance, to be overtaken by a child's laughter, and the image of a boy...a bright, beautiful little boy with golden curls....

She stumbled, and Troy's hand was instantly there, a band of support around her arm.

"Anyway," he said, going on as if there'd been no interruption, "Mama was a schoolteacher, so she was pretty much used to handling a bunch of rowdy kids. Lord, though, I can tell you it was tough growin' up a teacher's kid in a small town. Only thing worse I can imagine is maybe bein' a preacher's kid."

"Or a judge's..." She muttered it under her breath, and instantly wished she hadn't. She could feel his head turn toward her like a sonar beam, and imagine the curiosity and speculation in his eyes.

God, there was so much he didn't know about her. So much she hadn't told him. And after the night they'd just spent together...God only knew what he must be thinking. It surprised her to realize she actually cared about that, cared what this man thought of her. She wasn't in the habit of explaining herself, not to anyone, and she'd never told anyone the whole story about her past, not even Mirabella. But she found herself thinking about telling Troy. And wondering what she would say if he were to ask.

But he didn't ask. All he said was, "Yeah, I guess you probably know what it's like..." And he paused to let Bubba give a nearby tree his undivided attention, watching the dog now, his eyes in a thoughtful squint that fanned the creases at their corners. "Growin' up in a small town like this, where everybody knows you, and your folks and everybody else's business besides."

"Somehow I don't think my growing up was very much like yours," Charly drawled, kicking at a gnarled tree root while she waited for him. Her chest felt tight, stifled.

"No? Why's that?"

She found his voice soft but compelling, like gentle fingers tugging the strings of a guitar. Primed as she was, she could no more not respond than a plucked guitar string can refuse to vibrate. "For one thing I was an only child."

"That right?"

His eyes were on her again, bright as searchlights. Meeting them was suddenly too intense, the light in their depths calling up memories even his touch had not. She caught a quick gulp of air, and with a toss of her head, broke the contact.

"And I never knew my mother. She died a few days after I was born."

"Aw, hell. That's tough."

She shrugged away his sympathy, finding it an irritant, like a reminder of an itch she couldn't scratch. "Not really. I never knew my mother. How can you miss someone you've never had?"

Oh, Lord, she hadn't meant to say that, at least not that way. But somehow her voice had gotten away from her, had risen too fast and too sharply, so that when she broke it off it was with a ragged sound, like something tearing.

"Oh, I don't know. I think you can." It was an easy drawl, his manner gentle but with a core of firmness that, like the hand that had held her when she stumbled, would neither let her fall nor escape.

And oh, Lord, the temptation was strong to give in to that firmness, yield to the strength she could sense in him, lean against him and share her burden. He was giving her the openings she needed; the hand was there, and all she had to do was take it.

But she had never yielded to, leaned on or shared her burdens with anyone in her life. Not since Colin. It was too late to change now.

Face it, Charly, you're alone. You always have been and always will be.

She shook herself, fighting free of the thoughts. "Anyway, I had...someone."

"Your dad?"

Her chest tightened. She gave a bark of laughter, and after a moment cleared her throat and said in a carefully neutral voice, "Housekeeper. Her name is Dobrina Ralston. I called her Aunt Dobie. She's the one who raised me." She walked a few paces, keeping step with him, conscious of the heat, of the day and of his body. Wishing, suddenly, that he would put his arm around her and hold her close to him in spite of it. Traitorous notion.

She took a breath and murmured, "I think...she loved me."

Troy couldn't answer. He was thinking of the home he'd grown up in, where the love was noisy, confident, taken for granted, a given—never, ever "I think..."

As he angled a look at the woman walking so silently beside him, he tried to think what it would be like to live in a house filled with that silence, instead of with the thud of footsteps, slamming of doors, yells and shouts and arguments and the occasional knock-down-drag-out fight, with laughter and singing, piano lessons and *Sesame Street* on television. He tried to imagine this woman in that house. He thought about taking her home with him.

That was a surprise. He told himself, Hold on, there, man, what in the hell are you thinking of? She's not some orphan stray, like that little spotted pup you dragged home when you were ten. She's a grown-up woman with issues that need settling, and whatever they are, they're for her to settle, not you.

The only problem with that was, last night he'd made the mistake of letting himself get sidetracked. And what that had done was make it hard for him to remember what his mission was supposed to be in the first place.

Yesterday he'd come to the town of Mourning Spring, Alabama, as his brother's best man with the sole purpose of rescuing one miscreant maid of honor and delivering her to his brother's house in Georgia in time for a wedding. End of story. Right?

Wrong. Today he knew it wasn't anywhere near the end of the story, or the beginning of it, either. He'd pretty much figured out that Charly's story must have begun a long time ago, right here in this town, and that maybe it was about to end where it had started. And maybe that was what it was supposed to do, all along—like completing a circle. He didn't know yet what the woman's story was, or what it was going to take for her to complete that circle, or why it was important to him that she not have to do it alone. He just knew that all of a sudden it was.

Yesterday Charly Phelps had been a name, a general description, somebody he'd heard about. Today she was a woman he'd slept with. Which, oddly enough, had nothing to do with the fact that she was also becoming somebody he cared about.

That thought was unsettling enough to demand some sort of action, so he gave Bubba's leash a tug and said, "What do you think, ol' man? Checked out all the local action?"

Bubba gave the tree he was investigating one last snuffle, lifted his leg, then ambled on over and wallowed in between Troy and Charly as proudly as if he owned them both, thumping them each a couple of times with his tail.

Troy said, "Heel, Bubba," without much hope, then turned to Charly. "How 'bout you? What's next on your agenda?"

She lifted one arm and combed her hair back from her face

with her fingers, closed her eyes and breathed, "My suitcases. Please."

They'd started back toward the car, Bubba "heeling" so well Troy tripped over him. While he was untangling himself, he looked over at Charly and said, "You sure? I'd thought you'd be wantin' your purse first thing."

She gave one of her little signature snorts, and he saw the corner of her mouth go up in that way she had that wasn't really a smile. "Oh, I do. I just think I'd like to look a little more presentable, is all."

"Whaddaya mean, presentable?" He nudged her and grinned. "Woman, are you malignin' my wardrobe? You look fine to me." He thought she looked more than fine—damn cute, in fact—in one of his V-necked T-shirts, which she was wearing tucked into her own gray slacks and without any evidence of a bra that he could see. She'd looked even cuter earlier this morning, wearing the shirt with just his boxers, but he'd had to concede that the outfit probably wasn't appropriate for running errands in a small Southern town.

He also didn't see anything wrong with her hair, which she'd washed in the shower, she'd told him, using one of those little bars of soap for shampoo. She'd been complaining about it ever since, something about it not having "body," which he'd heard women moan and groan about before and still didn't get. It looked great to him, sleek and shiny as a crow's wing, with a slippery look that made him want to touch it. And not just with his fingers. She had great hair, thick and mostly straight but cleverly cut in a way that made it bend and curve and lie just right around her face and neck. Probably cost her a pretty penny, too, if he knew anything at all about women's upkeep. But worth it. Definitely.

As for makeup, well…like most men, he wasn't real observant about things like that. He supposed, if she looked close enough, she could probably find all those flaws women worry about and like to fix, cover up or improve on. But as for him, he was more apt to notice what was *in* a woman's eyes than painted on them. And a lot more interested in what came out of her mouth, and the way it moved, the way her lips curved and quivered and pouted, than he was in what color lipstick they were wearing. But that was just him....

"I've also got to see about getting a new rental car," Charly was saying. "I'm going to have to call them and break the news about the accident, see what they're going to want me to do."

"You're insured, I hope?"

She gave him a "What kind of an idiot do you take me for?" look. "Fully. I just hope they'll be willing to deliver a car to me here. I'd hate to have to go to the nearest rental office, which is probably going to be in Huntsville or someplace like that."

"No problem if you do," said Troy with an easygoing shrug. "I'd be glad to take you wherever you need to go."

She muttered, "Thanks, that's nice of you," in a stiff, unnatural voice, as if it was a difficult thing for her, being beholden to someone. For a woman in as much difficulty as she seemed to be, she did have an overabundance of pride.

She walked a ways, watching her feet, then cleared her throat and said bluntly, "You know, once I have a car, there's no need for you to stay around." That was so close to Troy's thoughts that he gave a bark of laughter, which seemed to surprise her. She looked at him almost in alarm, and added hastily, "I appreciate everything you've done for me, I really do." She stopped there, with a look on her face that told him she was probably remembering the way they'd spent the night, realizing how that sounded in light of it, and getting more and more embarrassed by the minute. She tried again. "Um, what I mean is, I know you must have things to do, places you need to be. Once I have a car, and I get my purse back, you don't have any..."

"Obligation?" Troy said huskily, stopping her with a touch on her arm and turning her to face him. He heard a tiny break in her breathing that sounded almost like fear, and then her shoulders relaxed and her cheeks went pink, which he personally thought looked good on her. She muttered something under her breath, looking away, looking down at Bubba, looking anywhere except at him. He touched her chin, bringing her face back to him, although her eyes wanted to stay hidden under the cover of her lashes. "Hey," he said, teasing her, "why are you so anxious to get rid of me?"

She laughed—a small, painful sound—then pulled away from him and walked on. He fell into step beside her. After a moment she drew a quick, catching breath and asked, "Have you...ever done anything you were ashamed of?"

It was so out of the blue, he let go the breath he'd been holding in a gust of surprise. "Hell, yes. Hasn't everybody?" She made a small, impatient sound. Still off balance, he glanced at her and saw only a profile that looked as if it had been carved in marble. "Hey, look, this isn't still about last night, is it? Because I have to tell—"

"No!" Her eyes leaped to his face and hung on for one amazing, intoxicating moment. *Whiskey eyes.* Then she said it again on a slow exhalation and looked away, shaking her head. "No. At least...no, it's not about that. I mean in the past, like maybe...when you were young."

That was when he realized how important it was, and what it meant. That was when his heart started to beat faster, and prickles of fear mixed with excitement began to crawl along his skin. Because he suddenly knew it was her own story she meant, and that maybe she was trying to figure out a way to share it with him at last. And because he could see that opening up after a twenty-year silence might not be as easy a thing as he'd thought.

Scared to death he was going to say or do the wrong thing and make her change her mind about telling him, he gave it some thought, then said carefully, "Matter of fact most of the things I've done that I was ashamed of were when I was young. I think it goes with the territory."

She gave her head an angry shake and then for a while said nothing. Just when Troy was thinking to himself, Okay, man, that's it, that's all, you blew it—she drew an uneven breath and said, "You're talking about...like, smoking and drinking, sneaking out at night, lyin' to your mom, playin' hooky, two-timing your girlfriend—"

Troy interrupted with mock horror. "Damn, you *were* a wild child, weren't you!"

"You don't know the half of it." Her smile flickered on and off as if it had a faulty connection, and when she went on, her voice had the gruffness of embarrassment in it. "No, what I'm saying is, those kinds of things, yeah, you did them when you were young, and maybe you were ashamed then, mostly because you knew you were supposed to be. But now? Think about it. Tell me honestly—do you really regret most of the stuff you did back then? I'll bet you even brag about it."

He rubbed the back of his neck while he thought about it, then gave a soft chuckle of acceptance. "I guess I don't. No more'n I regret havin' been young."

She nodded tensely. Another moment or two went by. Then she pulled in another breath she didn't really need. "What I'm talking about is something...bigger. Something that not a day goes by you don't think about it. Something you dream about, and wake up in a cold sweat thinking about. Ever do anything like that?" Her voice had taken on a new hardness, as if, he thought, she were pushing it through clenched jaws.

He didn't say anything for a minute. He was thinking about a night lit up by burning buildings instead of stars, a night when the smells of the sea and jungle mingled with the smells of petroleum and blood. And of the friend he'd held in his arms while the life drained out of him.

He drew a careful breath of his own. "Yeah, I have."

"How do you live with it?"

He thought about it, but didn't have any answers for her. Not the ones she wanted. "I guess you just do," he said gruffly. "You move on."

She gave him a look and said no more, leaving him with a black, angry feeling that he'd failed her.

After that walk in the park, reuniting Charly with her luggage was a breeze. The officer on duty at the police station directed them to the impound yard where the Taurus's remains had been taken, where they were informed that the suitcases had been removed from the trunk of the wrecked vehicle and transferred to a locked storage facility. A short half hour's wait later, the suit-

cases had been retrieved and signed over to their rightful owner.
Even Charly had had to admit that there were some advantages
to small-town living.

Troy had figured she'd want to go back to the motel and
change, but she had him pull into the first gas station they came
to instead. He got the key for her, and she hauled a big old
garment bag and an overnight case into the hot, scuzzy little rest
room with her and shut the door.

When she came out, he almost didn't recognize her. She was
wearing a pale gray suit that fit her like a glove, with sable velvet
trim on the collar that exactly matched her hair, and a narrow
skirt that stopped just above her knees, and that, along with the
black high-heeled shoes she was wearing, made those long legs
he'd noticed this morning a sight to behold. Her hair seemed to
have all but disappeared, slicked magically away from her face
and up into some kind of twist at the back of her head, which
made her neck look a mile long—reminded him a little bit of
Audrey Hepburn. Her lips were the color of hot fudge, and looked
every bit as tasty, too. He thought he might have to rethink his
position on makeup.

He realized he was staring when Charly said, "Well?" in a
sharp, uneasy voice.

He swallowed saliva and muttered, "You look great."

"Thanks," she said dryly, and handed him her overnighter.

"Uh, don't mind my askin'," he said as he loaded the suitcases
into the Cherokee, "but is there a reason you need to get so
dressed up just to go pick up your purse? You look like you're
fixin' to go to court."

"Funny you should say that." He looked at her and saw that
she was smiling. It wasn't a pleasant look; there was something
about it that made a tingle go down his spine. Something dark,
and full of secret resolve. "As a matter of fact this happens to
be my favorite 'impress the hell out of the judge' outfit."

"I hope she ain't female," he muttered, watching her hike up
her skirt in order to lever herself into the Cherokee.

She laughed with a kind of fierce jauntiness that suited her about as well as hot pink vinyl shoes would have matched that outfit.

They drove through town in silence, except for Bubba's heavy panting and Charly saying things like "Turn left here," and "Right at the next corner." Troy felt uneasy but couldn't put his finger on why. As he drove through sun-dappled neighborhoods past white-haired ladies on riding lawn mowers, shirtless guys washing their cars and kids playing in sprinklers, for some reason he was thinking about last night again, the thunderstorm and what came after, and all the electricity and sexual tension in the air. There was tension and electricity in the air now, too, so thick he could cut it with a knife. But this time he didn't think it had anything to do with sex.

"This is it," Charly announced. "You can pull into the driveway, if you want."

Troy nodded, put on his blinkers and turned right between two brick gateposts topped with carriage lanterns. "*This* is where you left your purse?" He gazed through the windshield at the huge brick house with its white columns and graceful porches, surrounded by old trees and an aura of gentility, and let go a long, low whistle. "Okay, I think I can see why you might want to dress up a little."

She gave that snort of mirthless laughter. "Yeah, well, don't be too impressed. I grew up in that house, and trust me, it's not all it's cracked up to be." She grabbed hold of the door handle. "You can wait here in the shade. I shouldn't be too long."

"You sure you don't want me to come with you?"

She hesitated, then shook her head and muttered so softly he could barely hear it, "This is something I have to do myself." As she opened the door and stepped out, he thought she added an unsteady "But thanks."

This time Charly didn't bother to go to the front door. Instead she went straight across the lawn and through the banks of azalea bushes, following a path of stepping stones where many had gone before—the trade and service people, the milkmen and meter readers, gardeners and plumbers, delivery people of every kind and description. The pathway led to the garages and outbuildings and the parklike grounds behind the house, and eventually to the woods beyond. Once upon a time it had meandered on through those woods to the huge stone mansion on the other side, where her best friend, Colin Stewart, lived.

But first it detoured to the trumpet-vine-covered back porch, and across that to the kitchen door. Which, as Charly knew very well, was seldom locked. And it was not now. Nor was anyone in the kitchen, it being Saturday, which had always been Dobrina's shopping day. Charly closed the door carefully behind her and crossed the mellowed hardwood floor, her heart beating in cadence with her footsteps, loud in the silence. Oh, how she remembered that silence.

She knew the judge would most likely be in his study. Unless, of course, he was in his office at the courthouse. She'd thought of that possibility—that after all this, he wouldn't be here. But she remembered that on Saturdays he'd almost always waited until Dobrina had returned with the groceries before going to his office. She was betting that, like everything else in this place, the old routine wouldn't have changed that much.

And it hadn't.

The study door was closed, which meant that it was occupied. Charly hesitated, her hand on the doorknob, trying to take deep, fortifying breaths for which there was no room in her chest. Her heart was pumping wildly, taking up far too much space, and her stomach felt hollow and fluttery, the way it did when she was about to stand up before a new judge and jury for the first time. Which, in a way, was a reassuring thought; she knew from experience that none of what she was feeling would show on the outside. She knew that to all appearances she was C. E. Phelps, attorney-at-law—cool, confident and very much in control. *Let the trial begin.*

She held her breath, turned the knob and pushed the door open.

Judge Charles Phelps was seated at his desk, smoking his pipe and reading his morning newspaper. He was dressed in the Saturday-morning uniform that hadn't changed since Charly's childhood—old slacks with suspenders and a cotton dress shirt with the sleeves rolled to the elbows, unbuttoned far enough to reveal grizzled chest hair above a vest-type undershirt. He looked up casually when he heard someone come in, no doubt expecting to see Dobrina, back from her shopping.

When he saw who it was, he straightened as if he'd been poked, then peeled off his reading glasses, dropped them onto the newspaper and sat back in his chair, his fingers working the bowl of his pipe. The white tufts of his eyebrows lowered over his cold, pale eyes as he watched her close the door behind her, but he said nothing. She hadn't expected that he would. To say anything at all—a greeting, a question, even a challenge—would have given her an opening, making it easier for her. She could hope for no such concessions from him.

"Hello, Father." She said it in her best attorney's voice—dry and cool. Good morning, Your Honor.

As she stepped onto the faded Oriental rug—which had no doubt lain in that same spot since the reign of Queen Victoria— it occurred to her that she was doing so for the first time as a full-grown adult. The thought made an odd little thrill go shooting up her spine—a sense of her own worth and power that wasn't new to her exactly, but was certainly new to her *here,* in these surroundings. It was a heady feeling, a little like a straight shot of bourbon on an empty stomach. She accepted it gladly for the courage and confidence it gave her and didn't stop to remember, then, that whiskey courage is almost always false.

"I'm glad I caught you in," she continued in the same brisk, businesslike manner. "I assume Dobrina's out shopping?"

The judge nodded, making no other concession to civility.

Charly gave him a lawyer's smile, cold and dangerous. "Well. I will need to speak with her later, but right now it's you I'd like to talk to." She chose a chair, an upholstered Queen Anne wing-back, and shifted it slightly to suit her.

She'd thought about it—whether she would sit or stand. Standing would give her a height advantage, of course, but then she'd be too much like a supplicant, coming before the lord of the manor hat in hand, while a chair, on the other hand, especially a comfortable one placed at a slight angle, would put her more in the position of equal.

She sat, crossed her legs and leaned back, outwardly relaxed. "If you have a minute...?"

Her father had placed his pipe in its ashtray and was rubbing absently at a spot on his chest just below his left shoulder. "I b'lieve everything that needs to be said between us has already been said." His voice was heavier than she remembered it—thick and Southern as blackstrap molasses.

Charly determinedly brightened her smile. "Yes, well, apparently Dobrina doesn't share your belief." She paused a beat, then continued in a conversational tone, "I suppose you heard about me getting arrested last night?"

The flash of surprise in his eyes gave her a brief moment's satisfaction, before he closed them and said in quiet disgust, "Oh, my Lord."

"No?" Her face felt rigid. How much longer could she maintain the smile? "Well, I guess the local news must be runnin' a little slow this morning. Yeah, it seems that while you and I were having our little tête-à-tête yesterday, Dobrina took my purse out of my car—" she ignored his exclamation of disbelief "—and replaced it with an open bottle of Black Jack. And *then,* just to make sure that didn't get overlooked by the proper authorities, after I left she called them up and reported my rental car stolen."

The judge shook his head and muttered under his breath, something about lies, replete with distaste. "Now, why on earth would 'Brina do such a thing?"

"I don't know," Charly said lightly, "maybe you can ask her when she gets home. Personally I think she just underestimated my resources. See, I believe she thought, since I'd been away from this town for so long, that I wouldn't know anybody else, and if I were arrested with no ID and no money, I'd have no choice but to call you for help." She made an ironic clicking sound with her mouth: *C'est la guerre.*

"Failing that, well, there was always Plan B. Dobrina's a smart lady. She knew that eventually I'd have to come back here to get my purse—by the way, you haven't seen it around anywhere, have you? No? Well, I expect she'll be back soon.

"In the meantime I've had time to do a little bit of thinking, and I've decided that, misguided though her actions were, Dobrina was right about one thing.''

She paused, and felt as if she'd scored a victory when he murmured on cue, ''Which is?'' It was a small but gratifying shift in the balance of power.

She replied quietly, ''That you and I have some unfinished business to attend to.''

He made a sound somewhere between a hiss and a snort and rocked back in his chair, his hands gripping the arms almost spasmodically. His voice was harsh, his face contorted, drained of color.

Charly surged forward, pressing her advantage like a street fighter. ''Look, you can hide your head in the sand all you want, but do you really think for one minute, now that I've seen those pictures on your mantelpiece, that you can just make me go away?'' Her voice had begun to tremble and her heart was hammering painfully. Careful, Charly, careful. Whatever you do, keep it businesslike. Remember, you are your own attorney. With a valiant effort she reined in her emotions and sat back once more.

''I want to make you a proposition.''

Her father's lips curled disdainfully. ''You're in no position to be making anything of the sort.''

''No,'' said Charly quietly, ''I don't think you have that quite right. It's you who are in no position to deny me.'' She paused. Her father glared at her in frigid silence. His eyes, his face, even his skin color seemed to have frozen. She took a breath. ''I believe you know what I want. I want to see him.''

She could hear his breathing—short, shallow gasps. It suddenly occurred to her that he looked awful—even ill. She felt a quiver of doubt, uncertainty. But then his lips curved and his eyelids dropped to half-mast, and he said in that viscous drawl, ''What makes you think he'd want to see you?''

The calculated cruelty of it nipped any concerns she might have had for him in the bud. Killed them dead, like peach blossoms in a March blizzard. Once again, just as she had the last time she'd faced this man, she felt herself go cold and still. ''What have you told him?'' she whispered. ''About me?''

He jerked back, pretending insult. "I told him the *truth*."

"The truth?" And suddenly she was on her feet and leaning toward him across his desk, all resolve forgotten. "You don't know the truth!"

His eyes flew wide. "Don't I?" He coughed, then drew himself up, pressing down on the arms of his chair, his voice rising as he did. "Which truth am I in ignorance of? The fact that his mother was a spoiled, selfish girl whose wanton behavior destroyed her own reputation and one of the finest families in this town? Or the fact that she abandoned her child the day he was born and then ran away? Nevah *once* looked back?"

Charly was trembling so hard that, but for her hands braced on the desktop, she doubted she could have kept her feet. She was seething with rage, words sizzling like hot coals on her tongue. "I will...see...my...son."

"Selfish, spiteful girl." Her father all but spat the words at her. "Have you no *shame?*"

She was too angry to recoil. "Have *you?* I did *not* abandon my son, and you know it. I gave him up for adoption—on the advice of so many supposedly wise and compassionate people, not the least of which was my own father! And I did it—" she sucked in a desperate breath "—I did it so he could have the kind of warm, loving home *I* never had."

"How...dare...you—"

"How dare *you!* What did you do, *Your Honor?* Did you use your judicial power and connections to gain custody of my son? Did you adopt him yourself? In God's name, *why?* Why would you do such a thing?" He didn't answer, just stared at her from a frozen half crouch, his face like stone. Sensing victory, she straightened and gave a high bark of laughter.

"Did you actually think you'd be a better father to him than I would have been a mother? How? How could you, when you were never a father to me, your only daughter? How could you possibly think you could give him more love than I could, when you never gave *me* any? Whatever love and affection I got, Dobrina gave me. *You* were never there for me—*never*." The last word was a growl, harsh with pain. But there were no tears. There would be no more tears, not in front of him. Never again.

She turned away from him, her voice brittle now with self-control. "Did you know I used to sit in my room in the evenings, doing my homework, getting ready for bed, and I'd look out my window to see if I could see the light in your office window, just so I could feel near you? But you never had time for me. You never *listened* to me. You just judged. Hell, you aren't even listening to me now. You know that? When I walked in here, I was ready to compromise. All I wanted was to see him—not even to let him know who I am, just...introduce me as a distant cousin, or something, I don't care. Just...to *see* him. But as always, you didn't give me a chance to tell you that. You wouldn't even listen."

She had run out of words, finally. Shaking violently, gasping like a marathoner, she caught her breath and held it, fighting to regain control and somehow slow her runaway heartbeat. And in that sudden stillness, she heard a faint choking sound.

She turned, jerky and off balance, like a malfunctioning windup toy, and felt herself go numb with shock. Her father was lying across his desk in a half crouch, his arms clutched to his chest. What she could see of his face was a dreadful, slaty blue.

Charly never did remember much about what she did then. The next thing she knew, she was on her knees beside her father, who was lying flat on his back on the floor, and she was blowing into his open mouth, and pumping away at his chest with all her might and saying furiously, in time to the beats, "Don't ... you ... dare ... *die*. Don't ... you ... dare ... *die*. Dammit, I'm ... not ... finished ... *yet*."

She was still at it when Dobrina came home, she had no way of knowing how many minutes later. Then she paused just long enough to say tersely, "Thank God you're here. Call 911. My father's had a heart attack."

Chapter 8

August 4, 1977

Dear Diary,

I don't know whether to be mad at Colin, or kiss him. He did something that made me so embarrassed I could have just died, but then it all turned out okay, so I guess it was really pretty sweet. What he did was, he told me he was having this pool party at his house, and that it was just going to be Kelly Grace and Bobby and some others, nothing big, and we'd just barbecue and listen to music and hang out. So I went over, and guess who was there? *Richie.* I mean, just Richie, and nobody else. Talk about embarrassing! God, it was so awkward. There we were, just the two of us, with our bathing suits and everything, and we couldn't even look each other in the eye! But like I said, it all turned out okay. We started talking, finally—I mean, what else could we do, right?—and we both said we were sorry, and he asked me if I wanted to go with him to see

Saturday Night Fever this weekend. Of course I said yes! Even though I've seen it three times already.

Of course I didn't tell Richie about what happened between Colin and me. I'm never going to tell anyone about that, ever, ever. And I don't think I will have sex with him, either.

Thought for the Day: From now on, I am going to wait until I am truly in love. Or at least married.

Troy had taken Bubba for a ramble up the street and was just working his way back toward the car when he heard the first siren. The first thought he had was that the noise was going to set poor ol' Bubba off, and every other dog in the neighborhood along with him.

Then the fire-department paramedics came roaring past him, with an ambulance right behind them, and he stood stock-still and watched them both turn into the same driveway he'd just come out of. And God forgive him, what he thought then was, Lord help us, she's killed somebody!

Even on further reflection it didn't seem all that far-fetched a notion, considering the jagged edge the woman had been walking for as long as he'd known her. Which, come to think of it, was less than twenty-four hours. After all, what did he really know about this Charly Phelps, anyway?

Okay, for one thing, that she was the friend of somebody whose judgment and good sense he trusted. Other than that, just that she was a California lawyer who'd spent an unhappy childhood in a small Southern town, liked bourbon and french fries, pretended not to like dogs and had a soft, mushy heart she didn't want anybody to know about. Oh, yeah, and she was one hell of a lover. Passionate. Edgy. *Angry...*

He took off at a jog-trot, Bubba loping happily along beside him with his tongue hanging out. Half a block later Troy broke into a dead run.

The two meat wagons were parked in the semicircular driveway in front of the big brick house with the white columns, engines idling, lights flashing, ready to roll. No one was in sight. Troy got Bubba put up in the Cherokee and was taking the steps two at a time when the front door burst open and a paramedic came backing out onto the porch, holding an IV bottle high in one hand. After him came the stretcher, or rolling gurney, or whatever they called it, surrounded by a whole bunch of EMTs, all of them in a hurry but businesslike about it. Troy took that as a good sign, meaning whoever was on the stretcher was alive and probably stable, at least for the moment. And he couldn't see any signs of blood, which was more reassuring to him than he liked to admit.

He didn't start to breathe evenly, though, until he saw Charly come through the door, right behind the stretcher. She had one hand clamped across her mouth, and what he could see of her face above it was bone white. There was another woman with her—a tall, thin black woman with an Egyptian look about her— and the two were sort of holding on to each other, so it was hard to tell who was supporting whom. He got out of the way and let the stretcher go by, then lightly touched Charly's arm. Her eyes leaped to his in startled recognition, and he realized that until that moment she hadn't even been aware of his presence, so focused was she on the stretcher and its occupant.

"What's goin' on?" he asked in a tense undertone.

"It's my dad." She gulped air, looking like someone woken up from a bad dream. "I think he's had a heart attack."

"Oh, Lord." Troy was thinking about his own father's two heart attacks. Especially the second, the one that had killed him, when Troy was off somewhere in the service, so he never got a chance to say goodbye. He scrubbed a hand through his hair. "He gonna be okay?"

The black woman suddenly squeezed Charly's elbow, muttered, "I'm goin' with him," and pushed past her and took off down the steps.

Charly frowned distractedly, looking as if she wanted to follow. "I don't know. I have to...get to the hospital."

"Wait—hang on a minute. I'll take you."

Troy reached back and pulled the front door closed, since it

didn't seem likely anybody else was going to think to do it, and
followed the crowd down the steps, digging in his pockets for his
keys on the way. The fire-department truck was already pulling
out, and the ambulance's engine was revving. Someone gave the
black woman a hand up into the back and slammed the doors
after her, and it rolled into the street, siren wailing and lights
flashing.

Charly made it to the Cherokee before Troy did, running clip-
clop on the uneven brick paving in her high-heeled shoes. He
went straight to the driver's seat and climbed in, fired up the
engine and hauled the door shut. Then he paused with one hand
on the gearshift and looked over at her. "You know where the
hospital is, or shall I give chase?"

"I know where it is," she said tensely, poised on the edge of
the seat like a runner in starting blocks.

"That's good," Troy said in a quieter and more deliberate
voice than he usually used. "In that case what I want you to do
is, I want you to take a great big deep breath and ease on back
in that seat and relax a minute." She threw him a burning look,
riled and rebellious. He looked right back at her. "I mean it.
We're not goin' anywhere until you do."

She exhaled in an angry hiss and muttered something under
her breath—probably swearing, which he'd noticed she had a ten-
dency to fall back on in times of stress. The part he could make
out clearly was the rough equivalent of "Who the hell do you
think you are?"

He folded his arms across his chest in a way he'd seen his
mama do a time or two, and when he spoke it was in the quiet
voice he'd heard her use to quell tantrums. "Who I am is the
friend who's drivin' you to the hospital to see about your daddy,
for starters. Also the friend who doesn't want to see you wind up
in the bed right next to him." He paused to let that sink in. "Now,
the man's in good hands, and there's not gonna be anything you
can do for a while anyway. Nobody's even gonna talk to you
until they've got him all hooked up and stabilized. You understand?"

She fought it, fought him. Then she let out another breath, this one slow and weary, and sank back, closing her eyes. "You say that as if you know."

"Oh, yeah. I was in high school when my dad had his first heart attack. I don't imagine the drill's changed all that much since then."

"His first one?"

"My daddy was a stubborn man," he said softly. "I was in the service when he had the second one. By the time I got there, it was too late."

"Oh, God." She didn't open her eyes. He could see her throat move with her swallows.

"You feel like tellin' me what happened?" he asked, making it gentle but matter-of-fact, knowing how close she was to breaking at that moment and understanding how much she wanted not to.

For a few seconds she didn't say anything, and he wondered if she would. But then her lips tightened in a spasm of pain, and she whispered, "We were arguing. I was shouting at him. And he just...collapsed. I should have known something was wrong. I should have seen it coming. But I was just...so angry."

"Hey," said Troy, "this wasn't your fault."

She shook her head, a quick, violent denial. "I knew he didn't look good. His color was bad. I knew it, and I kept yelling at him anyway. I did this to him."

Troy snorted. "Woman, you do have a high opinion of your capabilities." He reached over and put the truck in gear, while she gaped at him and tried to decide whether to take offense or not. "Fact is, people don't get heart attacks from arguing—they get 'em because their arteries are plugged up with junk, due to bad genes or bad living, take your pick. If your dad hadn't had a heart attack today, he was probably gonna have it later on, most likely when you weren't even around. Look at it this way—at least you're here. No matter what happens. You understand? That's more'n I got."

She didn't reply. He drove to the square in a humming silence, wondering why he felt as if they'd just had a quarrel. Shoot, they hadn't known each other long enough to be quarreling.

But if that was so, then why was it he felt...not *angry* with her exactly, but...hurt, maybe? Certainly disappointed with her, mistreated in some indefinable way. Which was so unlike him, he kept racking his brain to come up with a reason why he felt so. What was it she'd said or done?

"Turn right at the light," Charly mumbled, and lapsed once more into brooding silence.

And that was when it came to him. That it wasn't what she'd said or done, but what she hadn't. Here he'd driven damn near two hundred miles to bail the woman out of jail, spent the whole night either making love to her or sleeping with her snuggled up in his arms, spent the entire morning helping her iron out her screwed-up affairs and now he was driving her to the hospital and trying his best to comfort her after her dad's heart attack— and he *still* didn't have a clue as to what in the hell this was all about! After all that, after all he'd been through with her and everything he'd done for her—not that he was keeping score—it really was starting to bug him that she still apparently didn't trust him enough to tell him what was going on inside her.

Dammit, it just wasn't in him to pry. Growing up in a household with close to a dozen people in it counting grandparents and the occasional extra, not to mention a career in the military and a lot of years living in barracks housing, had given him a healthy respect for privacy. He believed in offering a helping hand if it was needed and asked for, but beyond that, he believed in staying out of other people's business and minding his own.

And in a way that was the problem. Because after the events of the past eighteen hours or so, he'd begun to feel kind of like she *was* his business. Like he had a vested interest in her, or something. Put another way...

Hell's bells, man, say it plainly! You care about her.

Okay, so he did. He cared about her. Which was what made it so damn hard, not knowing what was making her hurt so bad.

Mirabella put down the phone and turned to find that the man she adored was right there, eyes steady and soft with concern, ready to fold her into his arms. She still wasn't used to the miracle of that, of having someone love her so much, read her so clearly and understand her so well, so she had to be coaxed a little bit. Which Jimmy Joe was more than up to.

"Problems?" he asked, gently massaging her neck until her muscles were ready to relax and let her head settle into its customary nest below his chin.

She tried to disguise a sniffle. "That was Charly. Her dad just had a heart attack."

"Oh, Lord. How bad is it?"

"He's alive, but at this point they don't know much more than that."

"Well," said Jimmy Joe, "that's good. That's a good sign. Once they get 'em to the hospital, they usually manage to pull 'em through."

Mirabella nodded, and then they were both quiet, thinking of Mirabella's dad, who had survived his recent heart attack, undergone multiple-bypass surgery and was currently doing fine, and of Jimmy Joe's dad, who hadn't done any of those things.

"Were Charly and her dad close?" Jimmy Joe asked after a while.

She shook her head. "I don't think so. I told you, remember? She ran away from home when she was very young."

He held her tighter. "Sometimes that makes it worse."

"Yeah, I know." Mirabella muffled another sniffle against his chest. After a moment she took a breath and said casually, "Troy's at the hospital with her."

"Oh, yeah?" She could feel his smile against her hair, and tilted her head back so she could give him a scolding glare.

"I know what you're thinking. And you can stop thinking it, because I'm telling you, I know Charly, and it doesn't mean a thing. So Troy's at the hospital. Big deal. He's your brother. If he's anything like you, where else would he be?"

"You got me there," murmured Jimmy Joe, rocking her gently with his chuckle.

Mollified, Mirabella relaxed against him once more. But her mind was anything but relaxed. It was busy, as usual, chewing over this latest development, weighing options, making plans.

Presently she drew herself up and declared, "We'll have to postpone the wedding."

"Well, now," said Jimmy Joe cautiously, "let's not get carried away. You really think that's what she'd want? With your sisters comin' all the way from California, and your mom and dad up from Pensacola and all?"

"I *know*," Mirabella wailed. "But I don't see how we can get married without the maid of honor and the best man, do you? Oh, God, now I don't know *what* to do." With that almost unprecedented admission came a sigh of vexation. Although she'd gotten considerably better about rolling with life's punches since meeting Jimmy Joe, Mirabella still didn't adjust all that well to glitches in her carefully laid plans.

Which, of course, Jimmy Joe was well aware of. So he just chuckled and wrapped her up once more in his arms and said, "Tell you what—it's early yet. Instead of goin' off half-cocked, why don't we just wait a bit and see what happens?"

Charly walked slowly down the hospital corridor, following signs and arrows that would lead her back to the CICU waiting room. She was feeling numb, maybe a little giddy, and thinking about ironies. Thinking that the corridors, signs and arrows all looked familiar to her, like some kind of *Twilight Zone* episode where no matter what she did, she kept ending up back in the same place.

Except that this wasn't a TV fantasy or a nightmare she could expect to wake up from eventually. This was real. The fact was, twenty years ago she had walked down these same corridors after giving birth to a son. She'd walked out the front door that day and stepped onto a Greyhound bus and never looked back. Now here she was twenty years later, back where she'd started from, and the man she'd tried so hard to run away from all those years was the one who'd brought her here. How was this possible? It was as if she'd spent her whole life believing she was really getting someplace, only to find that all the time she'd been wandering in a circle.

Circle of life. Birth...to death.

"You get a hold of her?" Troy was at her side, holding a foam cup full of coffee in one hand and a large soft drink cup with water in it in the other.

She nodded, and was conscious of an enormous sense of relief as she took the coffee he held out to her, as if she'd just been given a pillow to lean back on. "They'd just gotten back from lunch, and were about to head out to do some more shopping." She smiled thinly. "I was lucky to catch them—Bella's a world-class shopper."

She gestured toward the cup of water he still held in his hand. "That for Bubba?"

"Yeah, I think I'm gonna go see if I can find a better place to park. I tied him to the door handle so he can lie underneath the truck for shade, but I think I saw a place just down the hill where I can pull in close to some trees. Besides—" his grin flashed briefly "—it's farther away from here in case he decides to cut loose and start howlin'." He touched her arm and lowered his voice. "You gonna be okay here?" His eyes were dark and solicitous.

He has such incredible eyes.

The impropriety of the thought startled her. She nodded, her throat tightening with guilt, and said, "Sure."

"Okay, then. Be right back."

He turned, almost bumping into Dobrina, who was coming from the nurses' station. "Any news?" Charly asked without much hope as she and Troy moved from the doorway of the waiting room to let her pass.

Dobrina shook her head while giving Troy a measuring look. Then she drew herself up to her full height, which was considerable, and thrust out her hand. "I'm Dobrina," she announced before Charly had a chance to make the introductions. "And you'd be...?"

Charly couldn't help but be amused by the way Troy practically snapped to attention. Dobrina had that effect on people. "Troy Starr, ma'am. Charly's friend."

"The one she called on to get her out of jail."

Thus relegated to the position of mannerless child, Charly

rolled her eyes and threw up her hands, while Troy said humbly, "Yes, ma'am."

Dobrina was giving him what Charly had always called her supermom look—the one she'd swear could see straight through a person, or at least down to what was deep inside. Apparently in Troy's case she approved of what she saw, although *he* probably wouldn't have guessed that from her expression, which reminded Charly of an old-fashioned schoolteacher about to smack somebody with her ruler. But Charly had always been able to tell when Aunt Dobie was melting—something about the way her eyes turned a soft gold, with fine little wrinkles underneath.

A warm wave of memory soaked through the numbness inside her to settle around her heart, and she had to look away.

"Humph," said Dobrina, still looking at Troy down the length of her nose as if he were a truant schoolboy and the apple he was offering her had a worm in it. "Where you from?"

"I'm from Georgia, ma'am. U.S. Navy, recently retired."

"Georgia." She gave a dubious sniff. "Retired, you say? Look pretty young to be retired, to me. What you plannin' to do with the rest of your life?"

Troy rubbed the back of his neck. "Well, ma'am, I haven't quite figured that out yet."

"Well, you best get to figuring." Dobrina leaned forward and tapped him on the chest. "You got to do something worthwhile with your life."

Troy gave Charly a look of appeal. She knew how he felt, but could only offer him a shrug of sympathy. When it came to Aunt Dobie, it was every man, woman or child for him- or herself.

A moment later, though, inspiration came to his rescue. Holding up the cup full of water, he said, "Yes, ma'am. Uh, would you excuse me? Gotta go tend to my dog. Nice meetin' you." And he fled, visibly perspiring.

"Seems like a nice young man," said Dobrina with a judicious sniff, looking after him.

"A regular Boy Scout," Charly murmured, frowning as she watched Troy's classically masculine, broad-shouldered, narrow-hipped form turn a corner far down the corridor and disappear from view, her thoughts so far removed from anything remotely Boy Scout-ish she considered it a wonder Dobrina's God didn't smite her on the spot.

She was experiencing two very different but equally perplexing emotions. First there was the old flip-flop feeling in her chest, the unmistakable symptom of sexual attraction, and the stomach-churning guilt that went along with that. Her father had just had a heart attack, for God's sake—this was no time to be falling wildly, head over heels in lust!

But it was the second feeling she found most worrisome, even frightening. Certainly the most difficult to understand. For twenty years she'd existed, rising and falling, succeeding and failing, pretty much on her own resources, dependent on no one. So why was it only now she should feel this sense of weakness, disorientation and fear, as if she were blind and her trusted guide dog had just walked off and left her in the middle of a catwalk with no handrails?

Realizing that Dobrina was giving her one of her looks, she shrugged and added, "I haven't known him very long." And she thought, My God, what an understatement. I only met him yesterday. How can that be?

"Well, we may just as well sit," Dobrina said abruptly, giving Charly's elbow a squeeze as she marched past her into the waiting room.

Charly managed a nod but stayed where she was for the moment. She was feeling too shaky and jangled to sit. She sipped bitter, lukewarm coffee and listened to the distant beeping of monitors, the muted murmur of voices, the ringing of telephones, and tried to make sense of the chaos into which her life had so unexpectedly descended.

It seemed impossible. When she'd woken up in the dark of yesterday morning she'd been a successful Los Angeles attorney, about to fly to Georgia to participate in her best friend's wedding. How could things have gone so wrong so quickly?

"I can't believe this is happening," she said softly. "I never meant for this to happen." Then she looked over at Dobrina, and saw that the woman's eyes were closed and her hands were clasped together on top of the big black handbag that was resting on her knees. She was rocking herself slightly and her lips were moving. It was with a small jolt of shame that Charly realized she must be praying.

But after only a moment Dobrina's eyes opened and she said gently, "Of course you didn't, child."

Charly moved slowly toward her, arms crisscrossing her waist, still clutching the cup of cold coffee as if it were a talisman protecting her against harm. "I went back for my purse." Her teeth were chattering. She clamped them together and gave a painful laugh. "After all that, you know what? I forgot it again."

Dobrina was sitting ramrod straight, staring straight ahead at nothing. Her head dipped twice and she said in a soft, faraway voice, as if she were talking to herself, "I know...I know. I'm sorry for doing that. This is my fault...my fault. I should never have interfered."

Charly waged a silent war with her own anger and lost. She went to sit in the chair next to Dobrina, reached over and put her hand over the other woman's clasped hands and gave them a squeeze.

"You know what?" she said tightly. "It's not either one of our faults. It's *his* fault." She jerked her head toward the waiting-room door.

Dobrina came to herself with a little gasp, pulled a hand free and gave Charly's a slap. "Don't you go sayin' that, now. I won't have you to talk that way. I won't."

"Oh, God." Charly put her head back and closed her eyes. After a moment she said tiredly, "You always do that—make excuses for him. Take his side...protect him. Why is that? You, of all people. You know what he's like."

"Oh, I expect I know him better than anybody does." Charly heard the sigh of an exhalation, then unexpectedly a chuckle. "I know he's a stubborn old fool."

"And yet you've stayed with him all these years."

For a moment there was silence. Then in a soft, musing tone that made her sound like someone else, someone much younger, Dobrina said, "I almost left him once."

"Really?" Charly sat up and opened her eyes. "When was that?"

"Oh, yes—yes, I did." Dobrina was nodding, still looking straight ahead, looking into the past now. "Oh, that was when you left, child. But then he brought the boy home. He needed me then. So what could I do? I stayed."

He brought the boy home. Charly felt as if she'd been struck in the chest. "The boy—" she had to stop for air "—you mean, my son. He brought...him *home?* You mean...you raised my son? *You* did?"

"I did." Dobrina dipped her head, then drew herself up proudly. "I raised him, just like I raised you." She reached for Charly's ice-cold hand and gripped it hard. "He's a good boy— a *good* boy."

Charly's face felt like a mask. She fought desperately to keep the mask intact—she had to. Behind it there was complete devastation. "Tell me about him," she whispered. "Please. Tell me, where is he? What is he doing?"

"Why, he's just finishin' up his sophomore year at Ol' Miss," said Dobrina, beaming, as eager to share her child's accomplishments as any proud parent. "Premed—oh, he's so bright, that boy. He's aimin' to be a doctor, you know."

Charly's laugh was high and musical, one note away from a sob. "His father always wanted to be a doctor."

"He should be home now," Dobrina went on, as if she hadn't spoken. "They just finished with finals last week. But he wanted to go off with some friends of his, you know, went down to New Orleans to celebrate." Suddenly she was rocking herself again, her eyes looking lost and her voice gone rusty. "I called and left word for him to come right home."

Charly couldn't breathe. She pressed a hand against the ache in her heart and whispered, "He's coming here?"

Dobrina didn't seem to hear her. She was mumbling, "Oh, sweet Jesus, I don't know what he's gonna do when he hears. I just don't know...."

"He and my father—" The words came out much sharper than

Charly intended. She swallowed hard and finished in a mumble, "Are they...close?"

Dobrina's face lit up. "Oh my, yes. He's the apple of your daddy's eye, that boy. Oh, yes, they're close. Real close. Just like a father and son."

Father and son. But what about me? I was his daughter! She clutched at another breath, pulling it into herself like a security blanket, and asked with desperate brightness, "What's his name?" She'd named him Colin Stewart, after his father. "Did you...did he keep...?"

Dobrina was nodding. "It's Colin on his birth certificate, but he's called Cutter. Cutter Phelps." Of course, Dobrina pronounced it the Alabama way: *Cuddah.*

"Cutter..." Charly repeated it in a daze. She was once more, in spite of all her efforts, on the verge of tears. "I just wanted to see him," she whispered, "That's all—not even to let him know it was me, you know? Just...see him. I told him—my father—I was going to no matter what he said. That's what upset him so badly. Was it so much to ask? Does he hate me that much?"

"Oh, child," Dobrina said, her own voice cracking. "He doesn't hate you."

"Yes, he does!" Charly knew she sounded like a hurt little girl and was powerless to stop herself. "He's never forgiven me for what happened. I don't think he ever will."

Dobrina slowly rose to her feet, clutching her pocketbook. Charly could see now that she was trembling.

"Look," she said in a rush, her own voice shaking, "I know it was all my fault—getting pregnant, and...what happened to Colin. I know I shamed him. But what happened to Colin...he was *my* friend, dammit! I know he was a Stewart, but I lost someone I *loved.* But he's never forgiven me, even after all these years. I thought—"

Dobrina whirled on her then, suddenly and magnificently angry. "Oh, you stubborn, stubborn child. You're just as bad as he is! Can't see the truth, even when it's right in front of your face." Charly's mouth opened, ready with her defense, but the older woman threw out a hand and silenced her with a gesture. "It's not your havin' a baby or that poor boy's death your father can't forgive you for—it nevah was. Don't you know that? It's your *leavin'* he can't get over. The fact that you left, and you nevah came back. Like to killed him when you did that. I thought it would. If it hadn't a' been for the boy..."

Charly rose slowly, shaken to her core. "Why did he do it, Aunt Dobie?" she asked in a breaking child's voice. "Why did he bring him back? He was so adamant about my giving up my baby. And then, after it's too late, he goes and does...what he did? I don't understand."

Dobrina gazed at her for a long moment, her eyes darkening slowly to the blackness of inexpressible sorrow. "Don't you see, child? He was hopin' and prayin' it *wasn't* too late. All he evah wanted was what was best for you. You were his little girl, his only child, and all he could see was how havin' that baby was goin' to ruin your future. He thought he was doin' the best thing. Then, after the boy was born, and you were gone, he saw what he'd done was wrong. He went and got the boy and brought him home, and then he waited...."

Charly could barely bring herself to whisper it. "Waited?"

Tears glistened on Dobrina's proud, tragic face. "For you, child. He waited, all those years, for you to come home."

Chapter 9

September 3, 1977

Dear Diary,

School starts tomorrow—oh, joy. I can't believe summer vacation is over already. So much has happened—which of course *you* know about. I still can't believe I'm writing to a book like it was a real person. Although I guess I'm sort of getting used to it.

Anyway, I'm not really sorry to be going back to school. It's going to be such a bitchin' year—can you believe I'm a junior? Kelly Grace and I are both sorry now that we didn't try out for cheerleaders last spring when we had the chance—I know we would have made it, you should see some of those cheerleaders!—since we are both dating football players. We've become quite the foursome, K.G. and Bobby, Richie and I. Colin says we could probably still make the flag twirlers. No offense, Colin, but being a member of the marching-band auxiliary isn't quite the same as being a cheerleader, if you know what I mean! Oh, well. I know we are going to have a lot of fun this year anyway.

   Thought for the Day: I just hope I'm not coming down with the flu or something. I've been feeling kind of sick lately. Wouldn't that be the pits!

Thunderheads were starting to build in earnest over the mountains by the time Troy got Bubba settled in a nice shady spot with his water dish and a rawhide bone to gnaw on. A breeze had sprung up, which he thought might mean the unsettled weather was about to move on through. He hoped it would cool things off; it was hard enough, having a dog to take care of, without worrying about the heat. He was beginning to regret the impulse that had made him invite Bubba along for company, although it had seemed like a good idea at the time, when he'd thought all he was doing was making a short foray to the mountains of Alabama to bail somebody out of jail. Little had he known.

He left Bubba looking forlorn but resigned and started back up the slope to the hospital. He was feeling a mite put-upon, if the truth were told. And to make matters worse, feeling guilty for that. He hadn't been raised to keep score when it came to helping people out, but on the other hand, he didn't much care for being treated like a handy crutch, either, something without either thoughts or feelings that could be easily ignored when it wasn't needed.

But as soon as he spotted Charly pacing up and down on the walkway in front of the emergency entrance, he felt a familiar hitch in his breathing and a knot of desire forming in his belly. And he thought that actually, having to haul a dog around with him for a few days wasn't *that* big an inconvenience.

She'd taken off the suit jacket. The silky black thing she'd been wearing under it—which, if you asked him, looked too much like a slip to be called a blouse—left most of her chest and shoulders and every inch of her arms bare. Except for the dusky place where the seat belt had bruised her, her skin looked flawless. And unfashionably pale, especially in contrast with her hair, which was coming loose from the slicked-back hairdo to slash across her neck and cheekbones like black-ink commas. It surprised him some that he found that so attractive, considering he'd been raised in a sun-belt culture where anybody without a tan was considered to be either too poor to afford one, or sickly. He thought maybe it was Mirabella who'd started him thinking otherwise, with her redhead's coloring and skin you could almost see through. Funny, he thought, how a person's tastes and opinions could change almost overnight.

She'd managed to find herself another cigarette. She glared at him as he approached, daring him to say something about the fact that she was smoking. She looked wired and tense, like a caged cat, he thought, with her ears laid back and her tail twitching, just waiting for someone to lash out at.

Not wanting to disappoint her, he folded his arms across his chest and *tsk-tsk*ed in mild reproach. "How in the world did you manage to find one of those things here? This is a hospital."

She tipped back her head and blew smoke with an audible hiss, then quipped sardonically, "Ah have had to depend on the kindness of strangers." And immediately she took another drag, her narrowed eyes a warning.

So he just shook his head and moved up beside her, resisting a strong desire to put a comforting arm around her shoulders. He wanted to touch that silky skin so badly he knew he'd better not. Instead he asked casually, "Had any news?"

She threw down what was left of the cigarette and stepped on it. "Still nothing."

He suddenly realized that she was trembling. He could feel it, even though they weren't touching, could almost hear it, like the humming of high-voltage power lines. His jaws clenched. He let out a breath and said softly, "Waiting's tough." But the same vibration had begun deep down inside him, as if it were a contagion he'd caught from her.

He wondered how much more of this he was going to be able to take. He was a patient man, but right now he wanted to grab her and shake her, slap her, scream at her, anything to bust loose whatever it was she was insisting on keeping bottled up inside. He'd never seen anybody wound so tight.

He was trying his best to be reasonable. All right, so her father had just had a heart attack. So they obviously had some unresolved issues, which he could see might make it that much harder. So she had plenty of reasons to be upset, and maybe he was being selfish to expect her to share her personal problems with him, a stranger. But last night she hadn't treated him like a stranger. And she'd had reasons enough then to be upset, surely—lady gets off a plane from L.A., drives to Alabama, loses her purse, crashes her car, gets arrested and thrown in jail—who wouldn't be at the end of her rope? And she'd turned to him for comfort the only way she'd known how, instinct driving her to seek the nearest warm body. Even now, in the cold light of day, it was something he understood.

But he'd had the feeling then that there was more to it than the obvious stuff, the accident and getting arrested and all. That there were things going on with her she wasn't letting him in on. He felt that more than ever now. This wasn't about her father having a heart attack. This was about whatever it was that had happened all those years ago to drive a young girl out of this town and away from her home and family, something she was ashamed of to this day. Something it still gave her nightmares and chills to think about.

Dammit, why couldn't she see that he was there to help? And he didn't mean just driving her around and picking up her meal tab. He understood things like nightmares and cold sweats all too well. Why wouldn't she trust him?

And why did it bother him so much that she didn't?

"Hey," he said, disappointment filling his throat like gravel, "how 'bout gettin' something to eat?"

"I'm not hungry," she muttered, shaking her head, behaving, in his opinion, like an obstinate child.

"You sure?" he asked, cajoling her like one. "It's been a long time since breakfast."

She aimed a frown past him, edgy and restless. "No. You go ahead."

The need to touch her was a greater hunger than the one gnawing at his belly. To contain it, he tucked his hands against his ribs and clamped down hard on them with his biceps. "Hey," he said, forcing a lightness he was a long way from feeling, "you need to eat. Trust me—I know."

Her eyes flicked at him, full of controlled fury. "What are you, my mother?"

Patience, he thought. And he found that, in spite of all his efforts, his hand had found its way to her elbow. Her skin felt like cream on his fingers. "Come on, I'm buyin'."

"Damn right you are," she snapped, "since in case you hadn't noticed, I still haven't got a purse."

"Don't worry, I'm runnin' a tab. Hospital's got a cafeteria, I noticed. That okay with you?"

She looked at him as if he'd lost his mind. "God, no. Look, if you're going to make me eat, it's going to have to be worth it. A burger and fries, or no deal."

He shook his head and muttered about her father lying in ICU with a coronary and her stuffing herself with french fries, but the truth was, the idea sounded damn good to him, too. "Okay," he said, "it's a deal. Do you need to tell anybody where you're going? What was her name, your dad's housekeeper—?"

"Dobrina." She gave her head a quick, hard shake that was almost like a shudder. "No. Let's just go."

He dug in his pocket for his keys, and they started down the hill, Troy automatically shortening his stride to accommodate those high-heeled shoes she was wearing. Though she seemed to get around in the infernal things pretty well, he had to admit. Which probably had to do with her being a big-city lawyer, he reminded himself, and on her feet in shoes like that all day. For some reason it was hard to think of her that way, even dressed for it like she was now. His mind kept wanting to put her back in his boxers, or better yet, in nothing but those spangly drops of water, fresh from the shower....

Bubba was bouncing around at the end of his leash like a paddle ball, tickled to death to see them back so soon.

"How come he's not howling?" Charly asked, giving the dog a wide berth and a wary look.

"I don't know," said Troy, "I think maybe he's gettin' used to it."

He had to leave poor old Bubba squirming and whining, though, scared he was going to get left again, while he went to start up the car and get the air-conditioning going. And the next thing he knew, there was Charly untying the dog's leash herself, and bringing him around to the back of the Cherokee. And cussing up a storm while she was doing it, too, trying her best, in her elegant suit and high-heeled shoes, to keep from being trampled on by a great big clumsy and overly enthusiastic pup. It was a sight guaranteed to melt the heart of any red-blooded Southern man.

The look on her face was a clear warning to him not to give voice to what he was feeling just then, so he hid his grin and limited himself to a brisk "Where to?" as he climbed in behind the wheel. "Your friend Kelly's okay?"

She gave another one of those funny little shudders. "God, no, anyplace but there."

He threw her a look of curiosity. "Why not? She doesn't serve hamburgers?"

"Oh, I'm sure she does." She put her head back against the headrest and closed her eyes, laughing softly. And the warm feeling inside him congealed. Once again he felt shut out, excluded, barred.

After a moment she sat up and began pulling pins out of her hair, combing through it with her fingers. She gave it a final shake that seemed to magically put all the pieces back in their original places and dropped the pins into the console cup holder.

"It's just that I'd rather not run into anybody I know right now," she said tightly, "if you don't mind." She let out a breath and looked away, out the window. "Hell, when this news gets out—about the judge's heart attack—I imagine the people in this town are gonna be lookin' to lynch me."

"Oh, come on."

"You think I'm kidding." She gave him a brief, hard look,

then turned away again. "They *will* blame me. Trust me, I know."

"Come on, how could they? You just got here."

She gave her patented snort of laughter. "Oh, please. Judge's wayward, runaway daughter shows up in town, judge has a coronary—who are they gonna blame? Besides—" she snatched a breath and finished sardonically "—it wouldn't be the first time I killed off one of this town's leading citizens."

He waited a minute to be sure he'd heard her right. Then he whooshed out air in a startled laugh. "Whoa, I think you're gonna have to explain that one."

She waved a dismissive hand. "It's a long story."

Like his brother Jimmy Joe, Troy had a long fuse, but even he had his limits. He clamped down hard on his temper, but he could feel his heartbeat accelerating and the heat starting to pump through his veins. He drawled with deceptive softness, "Like I said before, I'm not goin' anywhere. Why don't you just try givin' me the short version?"

"The short version?" Her voice was brittle with her own suppressed anger, which Troy had enough sense to know he wasn't the true cause of. "You want the short version. Okay, how's this? Rebellious young girl living in small Southern town gets pregnant out of wedlock, refuses to do the decent thing and go off to an aunt's house out of town for the duration to save the families embarrassment and shame, et cetera. Baby's sensitive teenage father commits suicide, girl gives birth to a son, girl puts baby up for adoption, girl hops the next bus out of town. End of story." She stopped it there on a choking sound.

Troy didn't say anything. He drove in narrow-eyed silence while his brain processed all that and his heart pounded like a demon against the wall of his chest. He kept thinking, Wow. And, Okay, you asked for it. And Wow again.

Finally, though, he was hearing those words *End of story*. And then he realized, *Not by a long shot*.

This morning he'd thought about circles and coming back to the beginning in order to find the end. And he still thought there was something in that notion. But if Charly was telling him a story, then the part he'd just heard was maybe the first few chapters. All that had happened a long time ago. That was in the past. It was pretty plain to him that there'd been some new chapters added since then. Yesterday that rebellious girl, now all grown up, had come back to that small Southern town to make peace with her past, and instead something had happened, something that had hit her like a Scud missile.

And today? Today he figured she was walking wounded, just trying to figure out a way to live with the pain from one minute to the next.

What troubled him was, he couldn't for the life of him think of anything he could do to help her. He was a United States Navy SEAL, doggone it, and feeling helpless didn't sit well with him.

He cleared his throat, knowing he had to say something. "Is that the thing you're so ashamed of?"

She looked confused for a moment, then remembered and shrugged. "Some of it." Her voice turned bright and harsh as neon. "Hey, I bet you're sorry you ever answered that phone, huh?"

Troy gave a little "Huh!" of surprise. Because the truth was, he didn't know how he felt about that. There was no use denying there'd been a time or two in the past twenty hours or so when he'd had second thoughts about what he'd gotten himself mixed up in.

He looked over at Charly, and for a change she was looking back at him. She had her head tilted at a cheeky angle and a wry smile on her lips, but her eyes were clinging to his, searching and unsure. Maybe he imagined it—it was just for a moment, before he had to pull his gaze and attention back to the business of driving—but he couldn't shake the notion that he'd seen something in the deep-woods shadows of those eyes. Something looking out at him...like a little **girl in** her secret hiding place, hoping against hope he was about **to find** her but expecting him to turn away before he did.

It gave him a strange and, **for** a strong man and former navy SEAL, a damn unsettling feeling. It made him feel like crying.

"So, what do you do, now that you aren't in the navy anymore?" Charly asked between bites of her Double-Whammy Super Deluxe Cheeseburger, chasing stray globs of special sauce with a fingertip. "When you're not bailing delinquent bridesmaids out of jail, that is."

Since his own mouth was full, Troy couldn't answer right away. He chewed and thought about it while his gaze rested idly on Bubba, who'd already polished off his three burgers and was sitting at attention with his jaws dripping and his eyes locked onto Troy's dinner like heat-seeking missiles. He knew what Charly was doing, and he was inclined to let her get away with it. Hell, he'd known guys pinned down and taking heavy fire to pull their kids' pictures out of their pockets and start exchanging stories about birthday parties.

He swallowed, wiped his mouth with his napkin and cleared his throat. "Not too much, actually. Marybell's had me doing—"

"Marybell?"

"Yeah, you know, Mirabella." Charly was looking so stunned, he had to smile. "She didn't tell you, huh? That's what Jimmy Joe calls her. Guess it's startin' to rub off on the rest of the family."

She put a hand over her eyes and murmured, "Oh, my Lord."

"Anyway," Troy went on, "I've been doing some things for her—handyman stuff, you know—gettin' things ready for the wedding, remodelin' the house to make a nursery for Amy. Which isn't as easy as it sounds, let me tell you. Hell, I remember boot-camp instructors who weren't as hard to please. You know how she is—got to have everything just so."

Charly smiled wryly. "Sounds like Bella." She shook her head as if she'd just had her bell rung. "Jeez...*Marybell.*"

After a moment she gave a sort of cough and aimed a frown in Bubba's general direction. "So, how is she?"

"Mirabella? She's fine, I guess. Seems real happy." Troy thought his smile must be a carbon copy of the lopsided one Charly had just been wearing; it was the way Mirabella affected people. "Sometimes it's kind of hard to tell. She can be pretty intense."

Charly chuckled in agreement, and there was a moment's silence that seemed almost companionable.

The hospital with its cool corridors and beeping monitors and high drama seemed a long way off. They were the only occupants of the fast-food restaurant's outside tables, since it hadn't seemed fair to leave poor Bubba tethered to the Cherokee in the heat while they dined in air-conditioned comfort. The breeze Troy had had such hopes for earlier hadn't lived up to its promise, and the day had the lazy feel of a long late afternoon not quite ready to turn itself over to evening. The insect hum and heat shimmer combined with a stomach full of cholesterol and too little sleep the night before was making Troy feel drowsy and relaxed. He wondered if they were affecting Charly the same way.

He was thinking about asking her if she wanted to go back to the motel and change her clothes, and thinking about the various possibilities of where that might lead, when she suddenly coughed and said, "Well, I hope she is."

He said, "Pardon?" having completely lost the thread of the conversation.

She had picked up a french fry and was studying it minutely. "Bella. I hope she's happy. She sure deserves to be." She sounded gruff, almost angry.

"Doesn't everybody?" Troy said cautiously.

She hitched a shoulder and popped the french fry into her mouth. "So they say."

"I sure can't think why she wouldn't be happy," he said after a moment, leaning forward on his elbows to steal one of her fries. "Seems to me she's got it all—beautiful little baby girl, a good man who happens to think she's the most wonderful woman ever born..."

"Oh, please." She made a sound that was more cynicism than laughter and looked away. "Like all it takes to make a woman happy is to keep her barefoot and pregnant? That is just so...Southern."

"Well, now," Troy drawled, "last time I looked, women had the vote down here, too. We got women doctors, lawyers...hell, we even got women politicians."

"Oh, Lord, don't get insulted." She laughed and shook back her hair, and he could see it was the physical part of an effort she was making to banish the darkness of her thoughts. "I'm just havin' trouble picturing Bella living in the South, is all."

"Lots of people do," said Troy, with a little shrug to show he wasn't arguing with her, or trying to convince her of anything. Which he wasn't. "More an' more all the time."

"Well, anyway," she said lightly, "she sure does think your brother walks on water. You ask me, the man sounds almost too good to be true."

Troy had to look down to dilute his smile. "Well, I'm afraid he's the genuine article. Yeah, she got herself a good man there— definitely the pick of the litter."

"The pick of the *litter*?" Charly laughed, one of the first sounds of real amusement he'd heard her make, then angled a look at him from under her lashes he could have sworn was flirting. "What about you? You and your brother anything alike?"

"What? Aw, hell no." He squirmed in the hot plastic seat, all of a sudden feeling something he'd never felt before: self-consciousness, the back of his mind clicking away like an adding machine, totaling up the pluses and minuses of his character and looking for the first time in his life as if it might come up with a deficit. Nothing like a woman, he thought ruefully, to test a man's confidence.

"Naw," he said, brazening it out, "Jimmy Joe's a whole lot smarter'n I am. Sweeter, too." He grinned at her, showing all his teeth. "But I'm cuter."

She laughed again, but this time he couldn't hold her eyes. She looked away, reaching abruptly for her drink.

He watched her lips close around the straw, watched her throat move with her swallow, thinking of all the things he could have said then, all the things he wanted to say...wondering what was in her mind, and if it was anything like what was in his. Because he was thinking again of making love with her, not the way he already had, but the ways he'd like to.

And it occurred to him that in a way, having sex with somebody made it even harder to get to know them. Kind of like two different radio signals trying to come in on the same frequency. Sometimes it was tough to make sense out of either one.

"So," said Charly, taking a breath, "you don't know what you want to do? Now that you're out of the navy, I mean. I thought the service was supposed to train you for something."

"Oh," Troy said dryly, struggling to get his thoughts back under control, "they trained me for a lot of things. Most of which aren't much use in civilian life. It's not like I was a mechanic, or a chef, or a computer engineer or a pilot or something. SEALs..." He let it trail off.

"You never did anything else?"

"Oh yeah, sure—for the last few years I've been training other SEALs. And for a while I was Master-at-Arms." She raised her eyebrows. "Law enforcement," he explained, and waved it off with a gesture. "Look, it's not that there's nothing I can do. It's more a matter of finding something I *want* to do."

"And...?" She was giving him her undivided attention, her eyes sharp as sherry wine.

"Don't know that yet." He shrugged and shifted around in his chair; he was finding it unnerving, having all that passion and intensity focused on him for a change. "The navy—being a SEAL—that's a tough act to follow. I don't know how to explain it, except that there's an edge...kind of a high you get, being in dangerous situations. You can get used to it, you know? Makes normal life seem pretty tame by comparison. Flat." He was quiet for a moment, turning his paper iced-tea cup around and around, watching it make wet rings on the plastic tabletop. "I just don't want to wind up like these guys you see—you know the ones I'm talkin' about—they hit the high point of their life back in high school, making the winning touchdown in the big game, and nothing ever gets quite that good again."

"Like Kelly Grace," Charly said softly. "High school was undoubtedly the high point of her life. And Bobby Hanratty and Richie..."

Richie. It suddenly occurred to Troy to wonder if the handsome, strapping football player in the photograph he'd seen was the one who'd gotten Charly pregnant, all those years ago. Somehow, though, the kid hadn't struck him as the sensitive type, definitely not the type to commit suicide. And there was something missing in Charly's voice when she spoke of him....

He died.

He remembered now. There'd been the other one, the slender, sweet-looking boy wearing the band uniform. Colin, that was his name.

A little chill of intuition shivered down his spine.

"Anyway," he said harshly, "I don't want that to be me." He got up, gathering trash. "You want to go back to the motel and change, or anything? Or you want to go straight back to the hospital?"

Charly got up, too. "I think I should get back to the hospital," she said. "If you don't mind."

"No problem."

Their gazes intersected as she came around the table, held for a moment and then parted almost like old friends. Troy wondered if he was imagining it, or if there was something new between them...something warmer, maybe. A little less edgy.

When they pulled into the hospital parking lot the sun was setting behind a black pile of thunderheads. The breeze had sprung back up, too, warm and brassy with the smell of distant rain.

Charly took hold of the door handle and turned to him, her face pale and tense in the twilight. "You can just let me out here, if you want to. No need for you to wait around."

Okay, maybe he had imagined that things had changed a little bit between them, that she was finally starting to consider him a friend instead of just a kind stranger. He was surprised by how much it pained him, having her keep shutting him out again and again. What kind of person did she think he was, for God's sake, that he'd just drop her off on the hospital steps, when for all either of them knew the worst possible news might be waiting for her inside?

Then he remembered her eyes, and the hopeful, lost little girl he'd seen locked away inside them. For a moment his throat seized up on him. "Oh," he said, forcing words through so they sounded scratchy as burlap, "I b'lieve I'll come on in with you for a while, if you don't mind. Just let me get my dog squared away."

She nodded, and he noticed she didn't seem inclined to argue with him anymore about facing whatever was waiting for her in that hospital all alone.

Since he didn't have the sun and the heat to worry about, he was able to park a little closer to the hospital. He left Bubba tied to the Cherokee's door handle and walked Charly in through the emergency entrance and down the long hallway to the CICU, one hand casually on her waist, as if it belonged there.

They found Dobrina alone in the waiting room.

"Asleep," Charly whispered, pausing in the doorway. Troy could feel her body relax.

"That seems like a good sign," he offered.

She nodded. "I can't believe she's still here." Troy gave her a quick look but didn't say anything. She let a breath out softly, shaking her head in wonderment. "She's been with him since I was born, you know that? Thirty-six years. I don't know how she's stuck by him all these years."

"She got any family?" Troy asked.

"She had a husband once. I think he was killed in Vietnam, or something." She paused, her head tilted to one side, thinking about it. "You know, I really don't think I ever asked. I was a kid, you know? And as far as I was concerned, she was *my* family. And then..." She gave herself one of those little shakes that was more like a shudder and turned away, but not before he saw the sadness in her eyes. Such terrible sadness, it made his whole face hurt just to look at her. "I sure never thought she'd still be with him," she said in a light, brittle voice. "I guess that's loyalty."

To Troy it seemed pretty obvious that it would take more than loyalty to keep that proud, elegant woman at a man's side for thirty-six years, but it didn't seem like the time to point that out. He'd noticed that it didn't seem to matter how old people got; when it came to their parents' love lives they were blind as bats.

At the ICU nursing station, they were told that Judge Phelps was in stable condition and resting comfortably.

"Can I see him?" Charly asked, her voice tight.

"He's asleep right now," the duty nurse told her, "but you can go in for a few minutes." She gave Troy a warning look. "Family only, one at a time."

"It's okay," said Troy, "I'm just with her." To Charly he said softly, "I'm gonna go make a phone call. You be okay?" She nodded, her eyes unfocused. "Be back soon," he said, and then he did something that surprised them both. He leaned over and kissed her.

He left her there and went off, jangling like an old jalopy, to find himself a phone and some badly needed privacy.

Charly had been in ICUs before, in her professional capacity, but never when the person hooked to all the tubes and wires was someone to whom she had an emotional connection. She had expected it to be an upsetting experience; she'd prepared herself for fear, helplessness, even pity. What she hadn't expected, as she stood just outside the glass partition gazing at the man lying so inert and pale and stripped of every shred of dignity, was to feel angry. Especially since she had no idea who it was she was angry with—him, herself or God.

She went toward him slowly, the beeping of the monitors timing her own pulse, the anger like a weight around her heart.

How could you do this to me? Is this it, then, the ultimate punishment? To leave me with your death on my head, and everything between us so wrong? Will I have to find a way to live with this now, too?

She was struck by how small he seemed, this man who had loomed like such a giant in her life. This man whose love she'd craved, whose approval she'd yearned for, this man she'd rebelled against and finally tried to run away from, only to find that his specter would dog her every day of her life. This man she'd tried so hard to prove herself to that she'd actually made a success of her life against all the odds.

How many times, when the struggle had seemed beyond her capabilities, had she flogged herself onward with the thought that she could *not* go back, would not go back until she'd succeeded, until she'd made something of herself beyond even her father's expectations? And that someday...*someday*...she'd come back here and show him?

He waited, all those years, for you to come home....

"Oh, God, how ironic," she whispered.

How terribly ironic that when she finally did come back to show her father the successful woman and respected attorney she'd made of herself, it was to discover that all that time, her greatest failure had been in staying away.

"I didn't know...I didn't know," she said in the voice of a heartbroken child. "How could I know you'd do such a thing? You never even told me you loved me...."

And suddenly she knew that *that* was the reason for the anger. And that it always had been.

"Don't you *dare* die," she whispered fiercely, just as a tear surprised her by sliding off the end of her nose and dropping with a tiny *plip* onto her father's blue-veined hand. It seemed to her a betrayal of the vow she'd made never to cry in front of him again, even though he was sound asleep and would never know. She jerked around, swiping at her eyes with a furious hand.

She froze. Her mind, her emotions, her body process-es...everything stopped. Someone was there, outside the glass partition, a tall young man, watching her with familiar eyes, red rimmed now with fatigue, and fear, and fury. She knew him instantly, from the photographs on her father's mantlepiece. He was the toddler with the floppy-eared dog, the boy with the baseball glove, the proud graduate in his cap and gown.

He was her son.

Chapter 10

October 18, 1977

Dear Diary,

Well, it was a big night for Mourning Spring High School. It was Homecoming, and we played Parksville and won. Bobby made two touchdowns and Richie even made one, which is pretty good considering he plays mostly defense. The way it happened was, he intercepted a pass and ran it all the way back for a touchdown. It was really bitchin'. Kelly Grace got junior princess—I knew she would. So she and Bobby get to be in the Queen's Court at the dance tomorrow night. I'm going with Richie, natch.

I should be really happy, right? Well, I'm not. I've never been so miserable in my life. I'm so scared, I don't know what to do. I can't talk to anybody about this. I haven't even told Kelly Grace. I know I have to, eventually, but...you know what? Sometimes I think I'd rather die.

I have to tell Colin. (Oh, by the way, the marching band did really well tonight, too. They did a whole medley from

Grease, since this year's theme is the fifties. It was bitchin'.) I haven't seen much of him since school started. We don't ever talk anymore like we used to. Guess I'm going to have to pretty soon, though, huh?

Thought for the Day: I guess there's nothing like sex to screw up a good friendship.

She'd imagined it a thousand times. Dreamed about it. Made up romantic scenarios in her head. Especially in the early years, when she was still young and naive enough to believe in happy endings. Then had come the working years, when the struggle to get through college, then law school, bar exams and her first, dreadful job with the public defender's office had kept her too busy and physically and emotionally exhausted to dwell on personal heartaches.

But in the past few years, when adoption stories were so often in the headlines and searches for both adopted children and birth parents seemed to have become the latest yuppie fad, she'd begun to think about it again. She'd even gone so far as to consult one of the senior partners, who had given her the names of a couple of lawyers he knew of who handled such matters, and also the names of some reputable private investigators. She'd carried the numbers around in her briefcase for weeks, waking up in cold sweats after nightmares filled with anguish, rejection and shame. She discovered that somehow in growing up she had lost the ability to tell herself those fantasy stories wherein she composed both sides of the dialogue, and could always count on things to come out the way she wanted them to. In the end she'd thrown the numbers away.

Maybe someday, she'd told herself. But first she had to go back to Mourning Spring. After that…she'd see.

But oh, God, in her wildest dreams and worst nightmares she had never imagined this.

My son. Mine and Colin's.

Colin Stewart Phelps.

Cutter. He's called Cutter.

The ICU nurse was talking to him now, touching his arm, guiding him away from the glass partition. Charly could hear his voice, muffled but tense with anger. She could see the tension in his strong, young body, the flush of anger on his smooth cheeks, the shadows of exhaustion and fear around his eyes—*Colin's eyes*—as he twisted around to stare back at her.

Flinging her father a last, desperate look, Charly started after her son. But she seemed scarcely to be moving. Oh, God, she'd had this nightmare so many times—her body weighted and weak, her heart trying to leap out of her chest as she strained to run, to reach out, to pursue! Her throat aching with the pressure of her own voice screaming his name...and making no sound at all.

But she must have made some sound, because just as he reached the waiting-room doorway he turned his head and saw her. For a moment he seemed to freeze. Then he pivoted and came back a few steps, holding up a hand like a traffic cop to stop her in her tracks.

It worked. She halted, and a few feet away from her, so did he. Even with that distance between them, she could feel his body shaking. Her heart melted, aching for him.

Dear God, she thought, I've already hurt him so much. What am I doing here?

"What the hell are you doing here?" he demanded in a cracking voice. Such a young voice. "This is *family*."

"Cutter," Charly said in a sticking voice, trying out the name for the first time. "I'm—"

"I know who you are," her son cut in. He had his grandfather's voice, Charly thought. And his manner, too, as he bulldozed right over her feeble attempt to respond. "What the hell are you doing here? Haven't you done him enough hurt? You want to kill him, is that it?"

"*Cutter!*" Dobrina stood just inside in the waiting-room doorway, her face the color of old ashes, her eyes shooting fire from the shadows of their sockets, a high priestess about to call down the wrath of the gods upon all their heads. "Cutter Phelps, you mind your language *and* your manners, you hear me, boy?"

Cutter stood his ground, his eyebrows lowering in a way that reminded Charly so much of the judge it almost made her smile. "She's got no right," he muttered, riled and furious. "*He* wouldn't want her here."

"How do you know?" Dobrina demanded. "He tell you that?"

"Look," Charly began in an airless croak, "I don't—"

Her son rounded on her then, jerking away from Dobrina's restraining hand. "Well, *I* don't want you here, okay? So you can just go back to wherever you came from. You are not needed here, understand? You are not welcome here. So you can just...go. Right now. Go on, get out of here. Leave us alone!"

I don't want you here. The words were like a wind in her ears, drowning out even the sound of her own pain. She could see Dobrina's lips moving, knew her own throat must be forming words in reply, but she heard nothing.

Go...now. Cold as she was, numb as she was, somehow she found a way to make her body obey. Just as she had twenty years before, Charly left her son, walked away from him down a hospital corridor and did not look back.

"So that's about the size of it," Troy said into the phone. He gave a half-embarrassed chuckle and lowered his voice even though there wasn't anybody around him to hear it. "I'm tellin' you, little brother, I'm startin' to feel like maybe I've bit off more'n I can chew."

"Well, now, that's a new one," said Jimmy Joe.

"I mean it. I used to think I could handle myself in just about any situation, you know? But this...ah, hell, I think I'm outta my league here, man." He let his breath out in a hiss of frustration and ran a hand over his hair. "I don't know what the hell's goin' on."

"Goin' on? With what? Who? You mean—"

"I mean with *her*—Charly."

"Ah."

"She's got...stuff goin' on here. She's havin' a pretty hard time with it—I don't just mean her dad havin' this heart attack, either. I'm pretty sure it's more complicated than that. Anyway, I'd like to help her, you know? Only she won't tell me much about what's goin' on, and I...well, hell, *you* know how it is. I don't want to be stickin' my nose in where it doesn't belong, but..."

"Uh-huh," said Jimmy Joe. And then for a few minutes there was silence, while all sorts of things flew back and forth along the wires unspoken, the way they do sometimes between guys who are close to one another but unaccustomed to expressing their deepest feelings in words.

Then there was a little throat-clearing sound, and Jimmy Joe said, "I ever tell you how I came to meet Mirabella?"

"I heard the story," said Troy cautiously. "Picked her up in your truck, right? Somewhere out in the Texas Panhandle in a blizzard? Delivered her baby on Christmas Day and made the national news."

His brother chuckled. "Well, there was a little bit more to it than that." He paused. "See, I'd run into her before all that happened, over in New Mexico. I noticed her right away—hard not to, you know, pregnant as she was, and lookin' like she does. Anyway, I kept wonderin' about her—what she was doin' out there like that, pregnant and all alone, so close to Christmas. The more I thought about it, the more it didn't make sense to me. And the more it bothered me. But I was like you—I didn't think it was any of my business, didn't think it was my place to ask."

"Uh-huh," said Troy, listening intently now.

"Well, then, of course, the more I got involved with her, the more I wanted to know about her. And I kept tellin' myself it still wasn't any of my business. And then somewhere along the way I came to a point where..."

He paused, and Troy prompted, "Yeah?"

"I knew it *was* my business," said Jimmy Joe.

"Ah." And there was another of those silences, vibrant with unvoiced truths and revelations. Presently Troy let out a breath and said gruffly, "So, how do you know?" He coughed. "When you've reached that point, I mean."

His brother's chuckle was one he'd never heard before—gentle, contented and wise. "You'll know."

After that there wasn't much Troy could do but say his goodbyes and sign off, feeling not a whole lot less frustrated than when he'd dialed. He was just hanging up the phone when he saw Charly coming down the hallway. He shoved his calling card back in his billfold and started toward her, still jabbing with it at his hip pocket. Took a couple of steps, got close enough to get a good look at her face and stopped, while his insides turned to ice water.

"Bad news?" he asked softly.

"What?" Her eyes lost their glaze and focused on him. "Oh, no, no, it's okay, he's asleep. No point in staying. Let's go, okay?" Her voice sounded breathy but with a little catch in it, as if, he thought, she'd been running with the hounds of hell on her tail.

As tuned to her as he was, it took him a beat longer than it should have to notice the two people down at the end of the corridor by the ICU, the place Charly had just come from. But he still had a lot of his SEAL reflexes, and when a distant movement flicked at his peripheral vision, he glanced that way first, then focused in a little harder. He could see it was the housekeeper—Dobrina, was it?—standing in the entrance to the waiting area. But who was the guy with her? A young guy, real young. Hardly more than a kid.

"Who's that?" he asked, keeping it as casual as he could.

Charly didn't even look, just hunched her shoulders and muttered, "Nobody. Let's just go, okay?" She sounded as if her jaws had been wired together.

Which was about the way Troy felt, too. There was a red-hot poker of tension shooting up through his neck muscles, right between his jaws and into his temples. He kept having to remind himself to unclench his teeth.

"Where would you like to go?" he asked politely when they were outside in the soft purple dusk, with the breeze lifting their hair and offering up in return the summer smells of honeysuckle and rain, and the music of frogs and bugs and night birds.

Halfway across the concrete apron where the ambulances parked to unload their passengers, she suddenly halted, swaying up on her toes with the abruptness of it.

"I don't know," she breathed on a long exhalation, lifting her face to the sky so that her hair brushed the upper part of her back. He didn't want to notice the way it slithered across the bare skin above that little black top she was wearing, but he did. And it made his stomach curl, "I don't care. I just want to get away from this place. I *hate* hospitals." He noticed then that her eyes were closed.

He didn't think about what he did then—maybe it was just a kind of self-preservation thing, because it had become too damn hard to look at her, seeing all the little telltale signs that told him how bad she must be hurting. The way her mouth didn't move quite right, twisting when she wanted it to smile; the way she kept grabbing those quick, shallow breaths, like a child trying not to cry; the way she hid her eyes from him, as if even in the purple twilight they might give away more than she wanted them to. Then again it could have been from motives as pure as the instinct to comfort another human in need, or as impure as his own need to answer that curling in his belly with some kind of action. What did it matter?

In the end probably not at all.

He stepped up behind her and brushed the powdery soft skin of her upper arms with his palms. When she shivered, he slipped his arms around her and pulled her against him with a sigh, not realizing until he'd done it how much he'd been longing to.

"Don't know anybody who doesn't," he murmured, slurring his words against her hair, "hate hospitals..."

She didn't answer with words, but moved against him in a subtle way and tilted her head to one side in unspoken invitation. He didn't need to be asked twice, though he did pause for a moment before taking her up on it to enjoy the view from where he stood, letting his eyes feast on snowy slopes and sweetly rounded hills...disappearing into black silk not *quite* soon enough to hide their rosy seashell crests. And with his hands where they were, it was so easy to turn his palms up and cradle them both and thus encourage them even more fully into his sight. And then to explore with his thumbs those hard little peaks, through the covering of silk that shielded them from all other eyes but his.

He did those things, and when he heard her gasp, *then* he finally lowered his mouth to take what she'd offered him—the most vital and vulnerable part of herself...the side of her neck. Closing his mouth over the taut cords, he pressed his tongue against her pulse, timing its frantic cadence to his own. And then began to suck gently.

Heat and pressure weighted his body; his head seemed to fill with a soughing sound, like the rush of wind through trees. Still, he felt her trembling, heard her voice saying, very faintly, "Oh...God."

And then another sound. A long, eerie wail.

Bubba.

Troy held himself still while the breath drained from his lungs and his head slowly cleared.

"What is that animal?" Charly growled. "A damn *wolf?*"

"He knows we're here," mumbled Troy. "Musta heard us, I guess." He eased his arms from around Charly's body, half of him thinking he'd like to kick the damn dog into next week, and the other half telling him it was just as well he'd interrupted when he had. He didn't know what it was about that woman, but in close enough quarters she was downright dangerous. Touching her did have a way of making him forget where he was.

He kept his hand on her back, though, as they made their way through the Emergency parking lot to where he'd left the Cherokee.

"What do you want to do now?" he asked, fishing for his keys. "You hungry?"

"Lord, no," she said in a voice thick with revulsion, clip-clopping along in her high heels. She threw him a look. "Are you?"

"Nope." Not for food, anyway. "Just askin'."

He unlocked the doors for her, and she climbed in while he was giving Bubba a halfhearted scolding and getting him settled down in the back with the suitcases.

"Why don't you put him in the middle seat?" Charly asked, sounding impatient. "There's more room."

"You want him slobberin' all over you?"

She made an angry, snorting sound. "I'm washable. Those suit-cases aren't."

"Well, okay," said Troy, "but remember, you asked for it."

Naturally Bubba was thrilled to be allowed back into the seat he considered to be rightfully his. And the first thing he did was wallow on over to personally thank the woman responsible for his good fortune, which meant burying his nose in her hair and licking and snuffling on the very same part of her Troy'd had his own mouth on a few minutes ago.

Charly stood about a minute of it, then muttered, "Okay, dog, that's enough. *Sit.*"

To Troy's amazement Bubba instantly went and flopped down on the seat and stayed there, grinning from ear to ear.

Shaking his head and muttering "I'll be damned," Troy climbed behind the wheel and started up the truck.

Charly angled a look across her shoulder to him. "Let's go back to the motel. I'd really like to get out of these clothes."

Well, now. He thought there were probably half a dozen ways she could have said that, and most of them wouldn't have meant anything other than what the actual words said. But the way she chose wasn't one of those ways. Her voice seemed to come from way deep in her throat, with a certain burr to it that affected him about like long painted fingernails drawing lazy patterns on his naked back.

He paused with his hands on the wheel and turned his head toward her. He couldn't see her eyes, since they were in shadow. But in the lights shining in from the parking lot he could see sweat glistening on her throat and across the top of her collarbone, giving her skin a translucence that reminded him of the insides of seashells—what was it called? Mother-of-pearl.

"Okeydokey," he said. And noticed, as he put the Cherokee in gear, that the same burr that had been in her voice seemed to have taken over his now, too.

Young as the night was, B.B.'s Barn was already jumping when they pulled into the Mourning Springs Motel and parked in front of number 10. A good ol' rockabilly beat was thumping, and faint whoopin' and hollerin' sounds could be heard even from across the street. A couple of MSPD patrol cars were parked out front.

"Well, it's Saturday night," said Charly when Troy remarked on the activity, eyeing the patrol cars. "What did you expect?"

"You want to go over for a while? Have a beer? Bite to eat? Dance?"

She shook her head, then swiveled it back to him. For a long moment they looked at each other, just looked...and listened to the sounds of distant revelry and intimate tensions, of drums and pulses and breathing sounds all mixed together. Without his being aware of movement, the space between them seemed to shrink...the beat of the drums got louder, became deafening. No—not drums. It was his own heartbeat he heard.

Her mouth was there, his for the taking, and there was probably nothing short of a missile barrage that could have kept him from it. He pushed his hand under her hair, cradling first her sweat-damp nape, then moving on up to the back of her head, weaving his fingers through her hair like a shuttle through a skein of silk. And slowly, slowly, he brought his mouth to hers. It was a journey of inches that seemed to take a lifetime, while inside him the heat and hunger mushroomed and the suspense became an exhilarating high, like the rush of adrenaline just before a jump.

Their open mouths met, melded. Became one indistinguishable whole. Her breathing quickened; her pulse throbbed beneath his fingers. Their body rhythms merged and accelerated, rising to the same inevitable crescendo.

She felt lush and ripe in his arms. The sweat on her skin gave it a slippery, giving feel, as if he could melt right into her and lose himself there. It wasn't the first time he'd kissed her, God knew, but it felt like it. And at the same time, it felt like coming home.

He wasn't sure what it was that stopped him; his brain wasn't exactly capable of analytical thought just then. But suddenly there he was, pulling back, easing himself away from her, turning slowly in his seat until he was facing front again, and his whole body pulsing and pounding like an overheated steam engine. He sat there staring through the windshield, trying to focus his eyes and get his mind functioning again—and all he could hear was that damn hillbilly band across the street.

That must be it, he thought, feeling dazed and jangled, like a man who'd just come within an eyelash of walking over a cliff. There was something about a honky-tonk bar and a cheap motel that sure could make a man lose sight of the paths of righteousness.

He didn't know when he'd ever felt so lousy. He could feel Charly shivering in the seat next to him and knew that in another second she was going to say something—ask him what was wrong, or maybe suggest they go inside. If she did, he didn't know what he was going to tell her. He didn't know what was wrong, and he sure as hell didn't want to go inside.

Which was hard to figure, considering he'd never wanted a woman as much as he wanted her, not in his whole life. If it was possible for a man to die from an overdose of desire, then he was surely a goner. But—and this was what didn't make a whole lot of sense to him—he didn't want her like *this*. Not a repeat of last night, mind-blowing as it had been. That had been *then*. This was now. The closest he could come to explaining it was that there'd been a lot of water under the bridge since, and for him, at least, it had brought them to an entirely different place. Much as it surprised him to realize it, mindless sex just wasn't going to do it for him. Not tonight. Maybe never again.

It was then, as he sat there with the cold shakes of adrenaline withdrawal crawling through his insides, that he heard it: his brother Jimmy Joe's voice.

You'll know.

And he felt something inside himself shift, as if his own personal compass had just spun around and the needle was pointing steady and true at due north, and for the first time in a long time he knew exactly where he was and where he was going.

Still staring straight ahead, he cleared his throat and said tensely, "You want to tell me what's goin' on?"

Her laugh was dry, sardonic. And not entirely steady. "I thought that was pretty obvious."

"Don't try to snow me," he snapped, "because it ain't gonna work." He wasn't angry, but he didn't care if she thought he was.

What he wanted was to break through that brittle shell of self-control she'd wrapped herself in, and if getting her angry back at him was what it took, that was fine with him.

"I don't know what you mean," she said in a voice just a little too breathy for the icy disdain it was trying to portray.

"You're wound so tight I can hear you squeak. Look, I don't know what's goin' on with you—"

"Jeez, my father just had a heart attack!"

"Don't give me that—this isn't about your father. Not all of it, anyway. Maybe you and your dad have some issues—"

"Issues?" She said it on a note of mocking laughter, as if it was a word she hadn't expected to hear out of a Georgia redneck like him.

"Hey," he said, "you've been in this shape ever since I met you. You think I can't see it? Lord, woman, what kind of fool do you think I am?"

For a change she didn't lash back at him but sat instead in hunched and sullen silence. He touched her shoulder and felt her flinch.

He took a breath and said more gently, "Look, we both know what happened last night was...I don't know, some kind of escape thing. You as much as told me so, remember? You said you'd had a hell of a bad day, and all that. And I can understand that. And today hasn't been so great, either. I understand that. But let me tell you, if you think you can...if you think I..." He stopped there, his hand clamped across his mouth, realizing finally that no matter how he said it, it was going to come out wrong. That any way he did it, it was still going to be a rejection.

"I didn't hear you objecting." Her voice was soft and dangerous.

He gave a huff of painful laughter. "No," he said through his fingers, "I didn't have any objections. Then. And just so we understand each other...the only thing I'm objecting to now is your motives."

She muttered something both sarcastic and profane under her breath and lunged for the door handle. He caught at her arm, but not in time. She twisted out of his grasp and wrenched the door open.

"Where do you think you're gonna go?" he asked quietly. "Room keys are in my pocket."

For a long, tense moment she stayed poised there, like a bird about to launch herself skyward. Then she slammed the door shut and jerked herself around, tense and shaking. Bubba, finally roused by the noise and the hope of freedom, came to snuffle inquiringly at her hair. She twitched it angrily away from him and said, "Stop it!" in a choked whisper, then gave up and sat with her eyes closed in silent misery while the dog expressed his sympathy and concern for her in the way that dogs generally do.

Troy watched while strange sensations—aches and tuggings, softenings and tightenings—followed one another through his chest. Finally, taking pity on her, he barked, "Quit it, Bubba." And then, gently stroking her wet cheek with the backs of his fingers, he said, "Look, why don't you just tell me what's going on? All I want to do is help."

Oh, God, Charly thought, please don't do this to me. She could take just about anything except his gentleness...that damn... kindness. First the dog and now *him*.

Please God, don't let me break down. Don't let me start to cry. If I do, I'm afraid I won't be able to stop.

"Who was that in the hospital?" His voice was soft, inexorable. "The kid I saw talking to Dobrina? Somebody you know?"

The pressure in her chest was terrible. In desperate need of air, she caught at a breath—but there was no place to put it, and she had to let go of it unsatisfied.

"No," she whispered, "I don't know him."

"Seemed like he knew you," Troy persisted, staring ahead through the windshield. "Whoever he is, looked to me like he hates your guts."

Pain stabbed her like a knife. She gave a high squeak of laughter. "Well, he probably does."

His head jerked toward her. "But you don't know him."

"Nope." She met his gaze defiantly, eyebrows arched, ironic

little smile firmly in place. But she couldn't hold it. The instant before it crumpled, she turned her face away.

"I only saw him once before," she said, in a voice that ripped through her throat like claws. "That was on the day he was born. The day I gave him away." She listened to stunned silence for a moment, then produced a laugh that tinkled in her ears like things breaking. "He's changed a lot in twenty years."

"You mean to tell me—" he had to stop to huff out air "—that was your *son?*"

"Yep, that's what I'm telling you. That was—*is*—my son. Colin...Stewart...Phelps." She drew the name out, then added, "They call him Cutter," pronouncing it the Southern way: *Cuddah.*

"Good Lord," Troy whispered. He shook his head like a dazed fighter. "But, hold on a minute, didn't you tell me you gave him up for—?"

"Adoption. Yep," said Charly, "I surely did. Signed the papers right there in that very same hospital, as a matter of fact. Then I...hopped on a Greyhound and skipped town."

"Charly, why—?"

"Why? Well, see, there wasn't really much use in my stayin' around here, was there? Not after I drove my child's father—who also happened to be the only son of the town's oldest and most beloved family, not to mention my best friend—to commit suicide. Was there? My father sure didn't think there was, and most of the townfolk agreed with him, Kelly Grace bein' just about the only exception. Oh—and Dobrina, of course. Like I said, I think she loved—"

"Come on, Charly." His voice was harsh as a slap. "Why are you doing this?"

She swiveled her head toward him. It seemed to take all her strength, as if the moving parts had rusted. "Doing what?"

"Talkin' like this. Tryin' to pretend like it doesn't—"

"What do you *think* I'm doing?" The sound of her own voice shocked her. It sounded like the cry of an animal in pain. "Lord, what I'm *tryin'* to do is *survive!*"

Bubba was on his feet again, whimpering. Charly threw up both arms to protect her face from another tongue-washing while Troy stuck out his arm to hold the dog back, and somehow or other, the next thing she knew they were tangled up with each other, his arms were around her instead, and she was fighting him, using her upraised fists to push him away, pummeling mindlessly at his rock-hard chest.

Chapter 11

November 3, 1977

Dear Diary,

Well, I did it. Today after school I broke up with Richie. News sure does travel fast, because a little while later Kelly Grace called and wanted to know what happened and why I did it, and all. She's mad at me that I didn't tell her first, and because now she and Bobby can't double date with us anymore. I didn't tell her the real reason why I did it. I just said Richie and I weren't getting along, which is true. He kept on saying if I loved him I'd let him go all the way, and I guess he's probably right about that. Anyway, I'm pretty sure I don't love Richie. I don't want to marry him, that's for sure! If I did that, I'd have to stay in this town forever, and I have bigger plans than that. First I'm going to California, and then I'm going to college, and after that...who knows?

Then a little while ago Colin came over. He'd heard about Richie and me already and wanted to know what was wrong. He told me he's been worried about me for a long time because I haven't been myself. We went for a long walk in the woods. It was a really nice day, sort of cold, but sort of warm, too, the way it is sometimes. And all the leaves are down, and the squirrels were running around all over the place, chasing each other up and down the trees and being real cute. So anyway, I finally told Colin. We both cried, and then we sat and talked for a long time, until it got too cold to stay out and almost dark besides. Neither one of us knows what to do. Colin says I have to tell the judge, though, that's the first thing. I know I have to, but I don't even want to think about it. I think maybe I should tell Aunt Dobie first. Maybe she'll know what to do.

Thought for the Day: Isn't it funny how one little tiny thing can change your whole life forever?

Even Charly knew it was no contest. How could it be? He was an ex-SEAL, for God's sake!

She put up more than just a token struggle, though, fighting him partly out of panic and partly because she simply didn't know—had never known—how to give in gracefully. She called Troy a son of a bitch, with every embellishment she could think of, as well as some she was shocked she even knew.

To her surprise he seemed to approve of that. He kept encouraging her, crooning things like, "Yeah...that's right...go ahead, get it all out, now," which only made her madder. She'd been going it alone for more than twenty years, her entire adult life. As far as she was concerned, crying was weakness, to be avoided if at all possible, and if not, then to be indulged in, like other weaknesses, in limited amounts and in strictest privacy. She couldn't remember the last time she'd cried in someone's arms.

Oh, yes, she could. And it was that memory—of two frightened teenagers walking in the woods on a lovely November day while the leaves and their worlds fell down around them—that was finally her undoing. Once again, as on that cold November day, she felt as though her world were coming apart, turning upside down. No longer was she Charly the independent and strong-minded career woman, Ms. Phelps the cynical and disciplined attorney. Instead she was back in those Alabama woods again, and she was Charlene Elizabeth, sixteen and in trouble, sobbing out her fear and desperation in her best friend's arms.

"I...left him," she sobbed. "He was...so little. He was...my baby."

"I know," Troy crooned. "I know...shh...it's all right."

"They let me hold him...just for a minute. He had such tiny little fingers...oh, God, he was so beautiful. And then he—he started to fuss, so I gave him my finger to suck on. And I got this feeling...all through me...like shivers, only warmer. Sharp, like pain, only...it wasn't. It was wonderful...the most wonderful thing in the world. And then they—they took him away. They took him right out of my arms. And it hurt so much...oh, *God....*"

"I know," Troy whispered, "shh...I know." His arms tightened even more securely around her, his hand cradled the back of her head and his cheek rested on its top as he bowed his body, making of it a sanctuary, just for her. And she burrowed into his encompassing warmth like a wounded animal into its den.

"It hurt so much...I didn't know what to do. I just wanted to get away from there. I had to go. I had to. I didn't know...oh, *God*—I didn't know...."

"Shh, it's okay. What didn't you know?"

"He...the judge...my father. He took my baby home. I don't know—I think maybe he adopted him—but...he was there all the time. He was right there, and I didn't know. I thought...all this time I thought he was *gone.* I thought my baby was lost to me forever, and all the time he was *here.* And I didn't know...I didn't know...."

"Of course you didn't know. How could you?"

"They thought...they thought I'd come back," Charly whispered brokenly. "But I didn't. I never came back. Oh, God..." The pain overwhelmed her. This was worse than anything she'd ever known before, worse than Colin's death, worse even than having her baby taken from her. Because this was her own doing...her own fault. Her own failure. And it could never be undone. How could she ever live with this?

Troy was stroking her hair. His hands were warm and steady, but his voice sounded strange, as if he had a bad cold. "What do you mean, you never came back? You're here now, aren't you?"

She shook her head rapidly, brushing her face against his front. "It's too late...too late. He hates me."

"Ah, now, it's never too late."

"Yes, it is." She sat up, pulling reluctantly against the gentle restraint of his arms. God, she felt awful. Her sinuses ached, her head felt like a balloon that had been blown up too tight and her nose was running a stream.

She was looking fruitlessly around her for something to stem the tide when Troy matter-of-factly reached into the console between them and pulled out a small, travel-sized box of tissues.

"There y'go," he muttered as he passed her a good-sized wad.

She took them without a word, blew and reached for more. Troy plucked a bunch and handed them over. She mopped her eyes, pressed them to her nose and muttered, "Boy Scout," glaring at him over the balled-up tissues.

Troy gave a chuckle that was partly a sigh and eased himself back in his own seat, moving as if his body hurt. "Naw," he said gruffly, "I guess you'd have to blame that on ol' Bubba. You travel around with a pup, you better have a load a' clean-ups handy." As if on cue, they both craned around to look at the dog, who was sitting erect in the middle of the seat, gazing at them in complete and utter perplexity. They both said, at exactly the same moment, "Hey, ol' Bubba," then looked at each other and laughed softly. Together. A gentle and comradely silence washed over them like a healing balm.

Troy cleared his throat. "About your son—it's not too late."

Charly blew her nose, then shook her head and said in a stuffy but firm voice, "Yeah, it is. He hates me. And I don't blame him."

"He doesn't hate you. Hell, he's just young, is all. This was bound to be a shock to him, too, you know—you showin' up out of the blue. He's probably as upset and confused as you are. You need to give him some time. He's gonna come around.''

"Oh, God.'' Charly suddenly groaned and leaned her head back against the seat, closing her eyes. Just for a moment. Then she opened them again and stared avidly at the ceiling, wishing she could find the answers she needed written up there. If she only looked hard enough... "I wish...I knew what to say to him,'' she whispered. "How will I ever get through to him? I don't...know how.''

"Hell,'' said Troy roughly, "just talk to him. Look, I know it won't be easy. It's not somethin' that comes naturally to you, talking about your feelings—''

"You're damn right,'' Charly cried, as she felt the pain well up in her all over again. "It hurts too damn much!''

"—but you gotta do it anyway. You need to tell him what you just told me, about what happened, how you felt. Give him some time to think about it, and he's gonna come around. Believe me.''

She swiveled her head toward him, compelled by something in his voice, something she'd been too caught up in her own pain to notice until that moment. The cracking, breaking sounds of a strong man's emotion. As she stared at him, at his recruiting-poster face, his beautiful, compassionate eyes, a new and formless panic began to creep over her, jangled and raw as she already was. Who in the world is this man? she wondered. How was it she was sitting here telling him things she'd told no one else in twenty years? How could she feel so safe with him, when he was everything she'd been running away from her entire adult life? What was happening to her?

And another, even more frightening thought—could it be, that this was what Mirabella had felt like, that long dark night with Jimmy Joe in his truck?

No! something in her protested desperately. No, no, no.

"How the hell do you know?'' she demanded in self-defensive anger. "You don't know anything about it!''

He scrubbed a hand across his face, making a faint scritching sound, then turned his head slowly toward her. And she noticed with another pang of panic, and an indefinable sorrow, that his normally clean-cut face was all shadows—shadows of whiskers on his cheeks and jaws, shadows of fatigue around his eyes. He'd had as little sleep as she had, she realized. And it wasn't even his trouble.

The ever lurking tears welled up again in the back of her throat. To contain them, she drew a breath and held it the way a stubborn child does, containing at the same time a powerful urge to reach out and touch his face, to smooth away the shadows with her fingertips.

"Maybe I don't," he said softly. "But I do know this—I know what's important. And I know how to fight. And I know that if something's important enough to you, you fight for it even if it hurts."

She couldn't answer him. He held her eyes for a long moment, then turned abruptly and reached for the ignition key, started up the Cherokee's engine and threw it in reverse.

"Where are we going?" Charly demanded with a gasp, letting go of the breath she'd been holding. Her voice thickened with suppressed sobs. "Aren't we going in?"

"Uh-uh," Troy muttered as they bumped out onto the highway, "I'm gonna feed you first. And don't tell me you're not hungry, either," he added as she was opening her mouth to do just that. "It's been a long time since that b-u-r-g-e-r this afternoon. You're gonna feel a whole lot better once you get somethin' in your stomach."

Somewhat to her surprise, the mention of hamburgers made the ache in her throat ease a little. Her mouth even started to water as she conceded grudgingly, "Well, okay, I guess we can go to the drive-through."

"Uh-uh. No way. No drive-throughs. For a change you're gonna eat some real food."

"I'm not going in any place! Not looking like this!"

"Fine. You can wait in the car."

She sulked in silence for a minute or two, then turned to glare at the implacable profile of the man who had somehow taken charge of her life. Why, she wondered, didn't it anger her, worry her, frighten her more than it did?

And again the thought crept around the edges of her consciousness like an unwelcome pest—like a mouse in the kitchen: Mirabella, was it like this for you? Is this how it happens?

"What are you," she said in a surly tone, "the food police? What do you care what I put in my stomach?"

He lifted one shoulder in an easygoing shrug that made her want to yell like a shrew and punch him. "Hey—you are what you eat. Hell, it's no wonder you're havin' a hard time coping with everything. When was the last time you put a vegetable in your mouth?"

"This afternoon," she said promptly.

He snorted. "French fries don't count."

"I was referring," she replied in a haughty tone, "to the ketchup."

There was soft laughter from him then, and a subtle easing, like the wafting of fresh breezes through the air between them. Charly felt her face muscles relaxing as she leaned back against the headrest, perhaps even wanting to smile. She felt battered, drained, exhausted, but—and when she tried to come up with a word for it, the best she could do was...*safe*. She thought it must be something like spending a long, terrifying night in a storm-tossed sea, all alone in a leaky rowboat, bailing like mad for her very life, and the Coast Guard had just shown up and hauled her on board. The storm might still be raging, but she knew she was safe now, and in good hands.

And even though she had always taken pride in her aloneness, coming so close to foundering, she realized, had been somewhat of a chastening experience for her. She was far too relieved to have been rescued to mind that she wasn't alone anymore.

Troy managed to find his way to the supermarket he'd noticed yesterday on his way into town without asking Charly for directions. He was glad of that, since she finally seemed to be relaxing a little, and he hadn't wanted to rile her if he could avoid it. She sat up when he pulled off into the parking lot, though, roused and suspicious.

"What's this?" she demanded to know, in her edgy, camouflage tone.

"Like I said—real food." He rolled the windows down and pocketed the keys. "Sit tight—keep Bubba company. Be right back."

"I swear, if you bring back yogurt," she said darkly, glaring at him through the window, "you'd better be prepared to wear it. *Or* anything green!"

"Yes, ma'am." He gave her a mock salute and went off smiling to himself.

It took him longer in the store than he expected. When he came out, when he first walked up to the Cherokee, his heart did a hard flip-flop, because he couldn't see either Charly or Bubba inside. But when he got closer, he could see that what she'd done was recline her seat all the way down, and it looked like she and Bubba were pretty much sharing it. She had her arm around the pup's neck, and he had his big ol' head tucked in underneath her chin and both of 'em were snoring away like babies.

Troy stood there for a minute just looking at the two of them, the woman he'd only known for a day, and his very own dog. His heart was still doing flip-flops, and there was a wicked little pulse going like a hammer in his belly.

Oh, Lord, he thought. Oh, dear Lord. What am I gonna do about this?

Charly and Bubba both woke up when he opened the door, jumping apart like a couple of kids caught kissing in the closet. The dog, who had the better sense of smell, started whining and drooling, while Charly righted her seat and raked her fingers through her hair and generally tried to look as if she hadn't really been napping, just resting her eyes for a minute.

Troy plunked the sackful of groceries on her lap and climbed in behind the wheel while she was poking through it, looking for something she could object to.

"What's this?" she asked, holding up the first thing she came to, which was a foil sack, warm to the touch and fragrant enough to drive poor ol' Bubba half-crazy.

Troy gave her a smile. "Rotisserie chicken. Lemon pepper."

She sniffed. "Barbecue's better." And a moment later,

"Whole-grain bread? Didn't they have any sourdough?" And finally, "*Milk?* You must be kidding."

"That's right," said Troy placidly. "Low fat."

She did some of that swearing under her breath he hadn't heard for quite a while, then said in a suspicious tone, "Okay, where are the vegetables?"

"They're in there."

"Where? What kind? I don't see any—hey," she exclaimed as he made a left at the main road instead of turning right, "where are we going? The motel's back that way."

"Yeah," he said, "I know." And then he took a breath and let it out slowly while he thought about how he was going to explain to this beautiful, sexy, incredibly desirable woman why he didn't care to be alone with her in a motel room.

As galling as it was to have to admit it, the truth was, he just couldn't trust himself with the woman in a situation that afforded him both the means and the opportunity to take her to bed. He'd always considered himself a man of fairly good character where women were concerned, and with strong enough willpower to keep himself within the boundaries he'd set for himself. But for some reason, with this woman, all bets were off. God help him, every time he got close to her, he found himself doing things he had no business doing, and wanting to do things he had no business even *thinking* about. Not with somebody he'd known for less than twenty-four hours. Not with somebody in the state she was in, and based on what had happened last time they'd been alone together, maybe not exactly capable of making her own best decisions, either.

But he didn't want to explain all that to Charly, partly because he wasn't comfortable letting her know just how vulnerable to her he was, and partly because he was pretty sure she wouldn't see anything particularly wrong with it. Not that he thought it was usual for her to go jumping into the sack with a guy within hours of making his acquaintance, or that she'd somehow been overwhelmed by his own personal charms. Hell, no. He didn't have any illusions about that. She'd been emotionally vulnerable and he'd been available, that was all. End of story. And as far as he could see, those circumstances hadn't changed a whole lot.

Well, okay, except in a couple of ways. For one, they'd already made love one night. And a memorable, most enjoyable time it had been. Which would make it a whole lot harder to avoid doing again.

And for two...well, to put it bluntly, now he cared about her. Which made it a whole different story.

"It's a nice evening," he finally managed to say through the truckload of gravel in his throat, keeping his eyes focused steadfastly through the windshield as he tried to tiptoe his way around a lie. "Nice and warm...doesn't look like it's gonna rain. Thought we'd have us a picnic. You know of any place around here we can go and park?"

There was an odd little silence before she said, "Yeah, actually. I do." He could tell by the sound of her voice that she was looking straight at him, and knew that he was taking a risk, meeting her eyes, even for a moment. He chanced it anyway, but she'd already turned her head away. "It's not too far from here," she said softly. "Bear right at the fork."

Beyond the place where the main highway out of town branched off, the road got curvier and began to climb. A little farther on she told him to turn right where a sign said, Mourning Spring Park—No Camping—Closed at Dusk.

"Ignore that," she said. "Everyone does."

"Ah," said Troy dryly, "let me guess—the local lovers' lane?" Lord, he hoped not.

She didn't reply. The narrow paved road wound down and down. Troy was conscious of trees he couldn't see, and lush vegetation closing in around them, shutting out the stars. At Charly's direction, he pulled into a wide graveled clearing, parked and turned off the engine. In the Cherokee's headlights he could see picnic tables and trash cans and the trunks of large trees. A car parked down at the far end of the clearing started up its engine and pulled slowly past them, lights off.

"Sorry, kids," Troy muttered. He rolled his window down and he sat for a moment, listening to the music of the night...the ticking of the cooling engine, the rhythmic singing of frogs, the screech of cicadas in far-off trees, the rush and tinkle of running water, the rustling of leaves. And closer by, the breathing sounds of the dog in the back seat, and of the woman next to him. The air felt cool and moist on his skin and smelled of ferns and moss and rotting leaves and rich, dark earth. Eden must have smelled like this, he thought.

He left the car's headlights on while Charly carried the sack of groceries to one of the picnic tables and he got Bubba's leash on him and secured it to a nearby trash can. Then he hauled out the blankets he'd started keeping in back to protect his new upholstery when he'd first got the pup, and gave them a good shaking. He got the battery-powered emergency lantern out from under the front seat, set it on the picnic table and spread the blankets out on the ground. When he came back from turning the car lights off, Charly was already carrying the grocery bag over to the blankets.

"You don't know what's been on those tables," she said with a shudder. "And you don't even want to."

They settled themselves on the blankets, out of reach of Bubba, whose leash allowed him as far as a corner and no farther. One by one, not looking at each other, they laid out the things Troy had bought, placing them on the blanket between them—save one, wrapped and cushioned in plastic, which he set carefully aside. From a tree nearby an owl hooted his hopeful question, and Troy thought again of Eden. He was beginning to have doubts about whether this picnic had been such a good idea after all.

He got out his pocket knife and began whittling at the loaf of bread, cutting off huge slabs while Charly laughed at him and muttered, "Boy Scout."

"Nope," he said placidly, slathering the slabs with spicy-sweet honey mustard, "SEALs."

He then turned his attention to the chicken. The first piece, covered with greasy, well-seasoned skin, he meant to offer to Bubba, since the poor guy was whimpering and slobbering all over himself and just about to pee himself in his excitement and anticipation. But when Charly saw what he was doing, she snaked out her arm and snatched the chicken out of his hand just in the nick of time, exclaiming indignantly, "What are you doing? That's the best part!" And poor ol' Bubba gave a woof of disappointment as he watched her pop his morsel into her own mouth.

Troy just shook his head in resignation and went back to slicing, while Charly defiantly cooed and licked her fingers with exaggerated smacking sounds. In the lantern light he could see the sheen of grease on her lips and fingers, along with a wicked gleam in the look she slanted his way. He knew she was teasing him, taunting him, tryin' her best to get his goat. He just couldn't quite be sure whether it was the food she was giving him a hard time about, or something else entirely.

"Here you go, guy," Charly was crooning to the dog, "you can have this instead."

Well, that got Troy's attention off of Charly's lips and the busy pink tongue she was cleaning them with barely in time for him to rescue a drumstick from Bubba's slavering jaws. Which was just about more than the poor dog could handle; he gave a brokenhearted yip and sat back on his haunches, quivering all over, until Troy got the meat pulled off the bone for him. Then it disappeared in one gulp, before Charly'd even had a chance to utter a squawk of indignation.

"Never give a dog a chicken bone," Troy explained to her. "They splinter—might get caught in their throats."

She made a vaguely acquiescent sound deep in hers and slowly licked her lips. Then, keeping her eyes fastened on Troy's mouth, she tore off a piece of the chicken and held it out to him, dripping skin and juices. "This is so-o good," she murmured. "You've got to taste it."

Before he could even recall why he shouldn't, much less tell himself not to, he'd opened his mouth and let her place the fat, juicy scrap of meat on his tongue. "Mmm," she crooned. "See?"

It probably was delicious, but you couldn't have proved it by him. All of a sudden his mouth had gone bone-dry, and his tongue wanted to stick to the roof of his mouth. He swallowed with an audible gulp as she wiped her thumb across his lower lip.

She pulled off another piece and put it in her own mouth, then licked her fingers, sticking them in her mouth one by one and slowly drawing them out again.

Troy wanted to grab her and shake her and demand to know what the hell she was trying to do to him, but he was afraid if he moved, if he so much as opened his mouth, he'd find himself kissing her instead. He felt light-headed and bottom heavy, as if all his blood had suddenly surged into his lower body. Which it probably had. Lord, but the woman was dangerous.

Bubba was whining again, figuring his turn was way overdue. Charly told him sweetly to mind his manners, then fed him the part of the back with the tail on it. The poor dog was so grateful it was almost pitiful to watch him. Troy knew just how he felt.

"You ever have a dog?" he asked her, his voice an unrecognizable croak.

She shook her head. "I always wanted one when I was a kid. Most of my friends had them." She cocked her head to one side, and her voice took on a dreamy tone. "I wanted a great big woolly bear of a dog, you know? Something lazy, like a St. Bernard, so I could cuddle up with it on the rug and read a book, or something. Stupid, huh?" She broke off another piece of chicken and studied it for a moment before absentmindedly letting Bubba steal it.

"So why didn't you get one?"

She shrugged and went for the chicken again. "When I was…oh, about eight, I guess, my father got me this little mouse thing—a gerbil. Maybe a hamster. Anyway, it died—I don't remember why, I must have done something wrong—and my father said I couldn't have any more pets because I wasn't responsible enough to take care of them properly."

Troy cautiously cleared his throat, finding it necessary once again to tiptoe around his own emotions. "Don't know very many eight-year-olds that are," he muttered.

Then he figured he'd better rescue the chicken before she fed the whole thing to the dog, so he took it from her, pulled off a nice big piece of skinless breast meat and held it out to her. She leaned over and took it into her mouth, and he felt a tingle go through his fingertips and all the way up his arm and into his scalp. He thought it was a damn good thing he had his hands full.

"What about later on?" he asked her in an airless mumble. "When you were grown-up and on your own?"

She answered him with her mouth full. "Mmm—I live in an apartment, work long hours—wouldn't be fair. It's better this way, actually. No responsibilities, nothing tying me down. I can do what I want to—come and go as I please."

"Uh-huh," said Troy. He wanted to ask her if she ever missed having somebody around, somebody to be there and happy to see her when she came home at night, somebody to curl up on the rug with and read a book, somebody to massage her feet for her when she'd been in court wearing those high-heeled shoes all day. Not that a dog could do that for her. He tore off another piece of chicken and held it just out of her reach and said, "Doesn't that get kinda lonely?"

Her eyes met his above the morsel of chicken, dark as the woods around them, each one holding a tiny glowing lantern in its center. "I've been alone since I was sixteen," she said softly. "Except for a few good friends, like Bella. That's the way I like it." Without taking her eyes from his, she leaned over and took the meat from his fingers, making sure her lips caressed his fingers before curving in a smile of seduction and challenge.

Bravado, he reminded himself. Pure bravado.

"How'd you do it?" he asked her in a casual way, focusing on the conversation with all his willpower as he doled out Bubba's next portion. "Just out of curiosity. I mean, jeez—sixteen years old and just off the bus in California? Lots of kids do it, and I don't think very many of 'em manage to grow up to be lawyers."

"I had some money—my college fund. It was mine, so I took it. And I had a fake ID—everybody did, didn't you? So we could buy booze and things like that? Anyway, that helped. I was able to get a job, and the police didn't hassle me."

She told him about it between bites, about how she'd found herself a room at the Y and a job in a fast-food restaurant, not enough to live on, but it made her college money last longer, long enough for her to find a job working as a live-in maid for the family of a Beverly Hills attorney who hadn't been fussy about her documentation. And how, with the security of a safe place to live and enough food to eat she'd been able to go to school at night and earn her GED, then community college, all the while saving every penny she could toward the day when she would finally enroll in UCLA. And after that, law school, and with the recommendation of her former boss, a part-time job with a law firm.

She gave it all to him, the bare bones, anyway, while they reduced the chicken to the same condition—with the eager assistance of a big old Lab puppy. Troy had meant to make them some nice hefty sandwiches with the whole-grain bread and the mustard he'd brought, but somehow he just never got around to it. Instead they took turns feeding each other—and Bubba—little bits and pieces of that chicken, and talking, and licking the juices and the grease off of each other's fingers, and they never even noticed that they were getting closer...and closer...and closer to each other, until there was hardly any room between them at all, and licking fingers got to seem like kind of a superfluous thing when there was something better right there handy.

He never did know who started it, or just whose slick and lemon-peppery lips first became too great a temptation for a questing tongue to ignore. Spicy breaths flowed together and became a warming sweetness, like sun-ripe fruit. Lips and tongues slid over and around and slipped between, tangling together with a joyful abandon that was like otters playing in sun-dappled water. Her skin felt warm on his fingers, as if it had just been kissed by the sun. When he spread his fingers across her cheek and pushed them into her hair, the sunlight came inside him, filling him up with heat and nourishment and light.

He brought her to him slowly, pressing her into him with the utmost gentleness, and as he sank into her mouth he felt himself rising, growing larger, becoming stronger, and her with him, as if some benevolent and approving god were lifting them up toward the light. Lifting them into the sun.

And that was when he knew. Exactly how and where and when

it had happened, he didn't know, but somehow, somewhere along the way, she had become *his* sun.

The realization shook him so that he tore himself away from her, reeling and disoriented, Icarus tumbling to earth.

He opened his eyes and was surprised to find that it was still night. "Time for veggies!" he said in an adolescent croak as he groped behind him for the package he'd set aside.

"I was hoping you'd forgotten," Charly mumbled. The words sounded bumpy to him, as if she were shivering.

"I'll just bet you were. Close your eyes," he ordered.

"Why?"

"No questions. Just...trust me, now, okay?"

He heard a breathless and miserable "Okay." Then and only then did he trust himself to look at her. She sat with her legs under her, hands clenched in her lap, shoulders hunched. Her head was high, though, and with her eyes closed her face wore the sad, noble expression of martyred saints. In the lantern light her skin had a cold, bluish look to it, so that what she reminded him of more than anything was a lovely sculpture made of ice. The images of sunshine seemed like a fading memory with no sensory reality to it, like looking at summer-vacation snapshots in the dead of winter.

"Okay," he said softly, "open up, now—your mouth, not your eyes."

A moment later she gave a little hiccup of surprise and pleasure. "Strawberries! But that's not—"

He silenced her with a berry. "Sure they are. Chock-full of vitamins and fiber."

"What? Well, okay, but how come there's no hot fudge to dip them in? Or champagne?" But she was laughing when she said it.

"Shut up," said Troy, laughing too. "Here—have another one—they're good for you."

"I will if you'll share it with me." Her eyes were shining with laughter and challenge.

What could he do? The laughter was so good to see, and he couldn't bear for her to lose it. So he leaned across the space he'd put between them and took what she offered...first the fruit, then her mouth. Strawberry wine...

"Not a very original idea, I'm afraid," she whispered after a while.

"Hard to beat a good cliché," he replied, half-drunk on the taste of her.

But this time, like the older and wiser Daedalus, he knew better than to fly too near the sun; given a second chance, he managed to stay emotionally far enough away from her to keep them both from falling.

"I'd like to go back to the motel now," said Charly. "Please." The strawberries were all gone, and the laughter with them.

Troy was doing his best to gather up their trash while Bubba snored on his feet. His body ached all over from the strain of unconsummated passion. Charly was trembling, he imagined, for the same reason. And he almost—almost—gave in. God knows he wanted to. But in the end he took a deep breath and said gruffly, "Naw...thought we'd stay here a while longer."

"Someone might come." She blurted it out breathlessly, then cut herself off as if she regretted the impulse that had made her say it. After a moment she started again in an entirely different tone, lifeless and wooden, trying hard to sound as if she didn't really care all that much. "That's why, isn't it? Why you wanted to do this. You don't want—"

"Oh, I want, all right," he said harshly, breaking in because he couldn't bear the sadness in her voice another second. "I want you so bad I don't know if I'm gonna be able to stand it."

"Well, you certainly have me." Her whisper was slow and tentative. When he didn't reply right away, she made an impatient sound and looked away. "I don't know how I could possibly make that more obvious."

For a minute or two Troy went on fiddling with the blanket, smoothing it out, making it neat, while his thoughts and feelings chased and tumbled around inside his head like squirrels playing in the woods, his heart going a mile a minute and a sweat coming on. How in the hell am I going to explain this? he thought.

He knew a lot of guys who were good talkers—sounded like TV soap operas, some of 'em—when it came to telling a woman the kinds of things they liked to hear. Troy hadn't ever tried to be one of them. He'd always believed if he couldn't tell a woman what she wanted to hear and have it be the truth, it was better to keep his mouth shut, and there'd been a few times he knew he'd caused a woman some disappointment and heartache because of that philosophy. In the long run he'd figured it probably saved both the woman and him a whole lot more grief than it caused. This was the first time in his recollection where the truth was both too complicated for words and too important for silence.

"Hey," he said gruffly, "come on over here." Not knowing what else to do, he reached for her, put his arms around her and pulled her against him. She came stiffly at first, until he growled, "Pretend I'm a big ol' St. Bernard dog." Then she gave a moist, uncertain laugh but snuggled close, and he eased them both down on the blanket so that her head was pillowed on his chest in the nest just below his shoulder. When her hand began to rove across his chest, heading south, he corraled it gently and held it cradled right over his rapidly beating heart.

"Look up there," he said thickly. "It's clearing off—look at the stars."

"Lord," she said in a wondering tone, "you really are a Boy Scout."

"No, ma'am," he growled, "not hardly."

He kept staring up at the stars, trying to think of a way to explain it to her. For some reason all he could think of was a cartoon movie he'd seen while he was growing up—*Peter Pan*, it was—and there'd been this crocodile that had bitten off Captain Hook's hand, along with a clock that for some reason never seemed to run down, and then followed him around the rest of his life trying to get at the rest of him.

"What's funny?" Charly mumbled.

"Nothin'." How in the hell was he supposed to tell her that he reminded himself of a crocodile, and she of Captain Hook?

But it was the truth. He knew he didn't have Charly, no matter what she'd just said. All he had was just a little bitty piece of her. And dammit, he wanted the rest—the whole Charly, every last bit of her. Because the taste of her he'd already had was part of him now, like that ticking clock in the ol' croc's belly. She was inside him, part of him, and he wasn't going to ever be able to get her out of his system or his consciousness again.

"Problem is," he said after a long, long time, heaving a sigh, "I'm in love with you."

Save for some soft breathing, there was no reply. Her head felt heavy on his chest. Troy raised his head in order to look, then lay back again, while his heart pounded in his throat. She was sound asleep.

Chapter 12

December 5, 1977

Dear Diary,

Well, I finally did it. I told the judge. Aunt Dobie made me. Well, I could have told her it was a big mistake. What I should have done is just left town while I had the chance. Funny thing, it seemed like he was madder at Aunt Dobie than he was at me. I heard them yelling at each other for a long time after he sent me to my room (isn't that funny? Here I am Pregnant, and he sends me to my room, like I'm a child!)

Anyway, of course the first thing he asked me was who's the father. Naturally he thinks it's Richie. You should have seen his face when I told him it wasn't! Now he really thinks I'm a slut—big deal, on top of everything else, right?

By the way, Richie called me a slut the other day. I didn't know he had such a mean mouth. I'm glad I found out his true nature, though. I don't know how he found out—not from me, that's for sure! Besides Colin, I only told Kelly

Grace, and she promised me she wouldn't tell a soul. I should have known better. She probably told Bobby, and he told Richie, and so I'm sure the whole town is in on my big secret by now.

Thought for the Day: I'm sure glad I didn't sleep with Richie.

PS *I think I just felt the baby move!!*

He woke up in Eden. Or maybe a Walt Disney movie—he'd been thinking of both, he remembered, just before falling asleep with Charly wrapped in his arms and her head cradled trustingly on his chest.

His arms were empty, now. So was the place across his legs where Bubba like to sprawl whenever he got the chance. The nearby sounds of rustlings and cracklings eased any concerns he might have had about that, so he saw no reason to deny himself the luxury of a slow and peaceful awakening.

Though it was already getting too warm where he lay, dappled by sunlight slanted through the branches of ancient trees. The air smelled of the life cycle of growing things—of new shoots pushing through sun-warmed soil, of flowers and ripening fruit, and of dead leaves slowly returning to the earth from which they'd come. He thought again, fleetingly, of circles.

A pair of cardinals flitted across his line of vision, chasing each other. Somewhere in the distance a mourning dove was calling. And all around him, permeating all his senses...water. He could hear it tinkling, trickling, whispering, feel it on his skin, see it swirling like gold dust in the shafts of sunlight, smell it, even taste it, cool and brassy on his tongue.

He sat up, and the breath left his body on whispered words of awe, *"Oh, man..."*

Straight ahead and on his right, cliffs of black limestone rose into the pale blue sky, their faces glistening with moisture that looked eerily, from this distance, like a woman's tears. Water seemed to spring from the rock itself, seeping from nooks and crannies where sword ferns and wild primroses flourished, cascading down over ledges and outcroppings festooned with vine tendrils and carpeted with the lush emerald green of moss. At the base of the cliffs the water splashed and trickled into a dark green pool, from the banks of which rhododendrons reached up...and up toward the cliff heights with flower-laden branches thick as arms, like virgin priestesses offering bouquets to their gods.

Troy was a Georgia boy born and raised, and he was used to red clay soil and woods filled with deer and possum and wild turkeys. But this...well, he'd seen places like it in South America and Africa, but he'd sure never expected to run into such a sight in northern Alabama.

"Good morning," Charly called to him softly, "welcome to Mourning Spring."

He saw her, now, standing barefooted in the shallow stream where the spring water emptied out of the pool and ran away to disappear into a culvert they'd driven across in darkness the night before. It sure did look to Troy like she was wearing his boxers again, although how she could have managed to sneak a pair out of the motel room without him noticing was beyond him, and was doing kind of a delicate little do-si-do with Bubba, who was wallowing around and trying his best to use her for a maypole. Of course, being a Lab, any form of water the pup could manage to get himself into, he thought he'd died and gone to heaven, so he was being even more enthusiastic than usual.

Troy got up and went over to her, telling himself it was to see if she needed any help with the dog, but mainly because he had a sudden and profound hunger for the warmth and the smell and the feel of her. He stopped on the edge of the bank, close enough to see that it wasn't his boxers she was wearing after all, since not even in the wildest days of his youth had he ever owned a pair with pictures of Tweety Bird on them. Nor, in his best recollection, a T-shirt bearing the portrait of a bad-dispositioned Puddy Tat. He had to admit, though, that on her they looked pretty damn cute.

"Mornin'," he said. And when she remained stubbornly out

of his reach, in a voice husky with ripening desire, "This place sure is somethin'."

"I guess it is." She said it with the indifference of a hometowner as she switched the leash from one hand to the other, while Bubba wallowed around behind her, plowing through the stream with his nose in the water. "Anyway, it's how the town got its name. If you look at it just right, it sort of looks like a woman crying."

"Yeah," said Troy, "I saw that." He just wished to goodness she'd get out of that water, because otherwise in about a minute he was going to have to take his shoes and socks off and go in after her.

"Anyway," she went on, sounding like a tour guide at a national park, "it's supposed to have been an Indian campsite at one time. Supposedly there wasn't a spring here, then, but there was water down below, in the creek. According to legend, one day there was a huge massacre on this spot, and the village was pretty much wiped out. And when that happened, the ground shook and tears began to pour from the rocks. So they say. Thus the name—Mourning Spring."

"Makes sense," said Troy. "Earthquake probably opened up seams leading to some underground river. There's limestone caves all up through these mountains, in Tennessee...Kentucky. Missouri." *Come on...get outta there.* He had to grind his teeth together to keep from saying it out loud. What was the matter with her, anyway? She was acting like she didn't want him within ten feet of her.

"We used to come up here a lot when I was growing up," she said, as Bubba gave himself a shake, spangling her long, slim legs with rainbow drops. "Picnics...birthday parties. And later on, when we got driver's licenses...naturally it was everybody's favorite party spot."

"Naturally," said Troy as inspiration struck. He snapped his fingers and said, "Hey, Bubba, come on outta there now. You heard me, come on." Bubba raised his head and stared at him for a minute, then ambled on over to see what he had to offer, towing Charly behind him. Which, of course, had been Troy's intention.

"Of course," she said as she followed the dog onto dry land, "that was before this was officially a park, so they didn't have that rule about closing at dusk back then."

"That right?" Troy took Bubba's leash from her, noticing as he did so that the skin around her eyes and across the tops of her cheeks had a stretched, transparent look. Something about that slowed him down, and at the same time made his breathing catch and his heartbeat quicken. "Who'd they make it a memorial to, do you know?"

A movement of her head directed his gaze toward something he'd seen before but hadn't really noticed—a big block of granite sitting near the edge of the pool. Fastened to the face of it was a brass plaque, on which he could clearly see the words In Loving Memory. And now, for the first time, he noticed the name: Colin Patrick Stewart. And the date: March 17, 1978.

It was hard for him to haul his eyes back to Charly's face. The breath he'd just taken felt like an anvil in his chest. "Colin," he said softly. "He was your friend, wasn't he? The one in the band uniform. The one who died."

She nodded, her face suddenly vulnerable and unshielded as a child's. "They found his body right there." Again she used only her head to show him the place. "On the rocks, halfway in the water. He didn't drown, though. They said it was the fall that killed him."

"My God," Troy exploded. He realized that he was trembling with reaction—anger, shock, horror. "Why didn't you tell me? Why'd you let me bring you here? Jeez, Charly—"

"No, it's okay—I wanted to come." There was something peaceful about the way her eyes were resting on the granite block, their color deep and dark as the pool beside it. But they had a certain shininess, too, that reminded him of things so fragile that even a whisper could shatter them—things like bubbles, or the mirrorlike surface of a pond. "I haven't been here since...it happened," she whispered. "I guess...I needed to see."

He drew a deep breath, calming himself, and put out his hand and gently brushed her cheek with the backs of his fingers. It felt moist and cool to the touch. "He was the one, wasn't he? Your baby's father. The one who committed suicide."

"Yeah." She caught her breath with a sound much like a hiccup. "He was."

"Jeez, Charly..." But as shaken as he was, there was no hesitation in him; all the frustration and doubts of yesterday were gone. Last night his heart's compass had shown him the way, and the needle was still holding fast and true this morning. He stroked her cheek once more, and then, with utmost care and tenderness, reached across to her opposite shoulder and turned her toward him, then folded her into his arms.

A sigh went through her, and she softened against him, but there was no trembling, and no sobs. For a time he held her like that, while Bubba, perhaps miraculously, perhaps sensing her need, or maybe just plain tired out, sat at attention beside them, patiently standing watch.

"You want to tell me about it?" Troy asked presently, his heart swelling when she nodded. And so she began, even while he walked her slowly back to their blanket, got Bubba tethered once more to the trash can, found them seats on the nearest picnic table, where they sat side by side with their feet on the bench, holding hands.

"He was my best friend," she said. "The best friend I ever had."

Until now. Charly gazed down at her hand, lost in Troy's bigger one, the words like a song inside her, a song she'd never really listened to until now. But it's true, she thought. *This man is my friend.* It seemed like a miracle to her. Dazed by it, she had to wait a moment before she could go on.

"We'd been together, played together, since we were babies. And even when we got older, it seemed like we just had this...connection, you know? We told each other things we never told anyone else. And...well, he was just always there for me. Sometimes it was almost like we were the same person." She laughed in that tender, careful way you do when tears threaten. "I used to imagine we were really twins, and that our parents had conspired at our birth to separate us. That was, until I got old enough to realize they expected us to marry some day. That would have been a little much, even for Southern Gothic, don't you think?''

"So, your parents were in favor of you guys getting married?" Troy's eyebrows came together as he thought about that, and Charly knew what he must be wondering.

"Oh, yeah—I think they just assumed we would, since we'd always been so close, and all."

"So why—?"

"Why didn't we?" Pain blocked her voice, cramped the small muscles in her face so that it was impossible to say anything for a while. I can't tell you that. Anything but that. I'm sorry...I'm sorry. I promised.

"I'm not sure I can explain," she whispered. Still, she had to try. "I...loved Colin. He was the sweetest, dearest person I've ever known. Sensitive...kind. He was going to be a doctor, you know. He'd have been a great one, except that it would have been hard on him if he ever lost a patient. He had a heart like mush." She dashed away tears, and when she lowered her hand it seemed a natural thing to add it to the one already in Troy's keeping. "I adored him. But it was never anything to do with sex...boyfriends and girlfriends, you know? I used to tell him all about my little crushes and flings, and he'd give me advice. We were *friends,* that's all."

"So how—?" Troy stopped to clear his throat.

"How did we make a baby?" Charly finished for him, her lips making a lopsided smile. She took a breath and looked away, laughing softly. "Well, in a word—I'm not proud of this, you understand—I guess you could say we were...*drunk.*" At his startled exclamation, her eyes flicked back to him. "Oh, not that it was that simple."

Restless suddenly, fragile with shame even now, she pulled her hands from his and used them both to comb her hair back from her face. "See, I had a crush on this boy named Richie—"

"The football player."

"That's the one. Anyway, it was Fourth of July, and Richie had finally asked me out—we were going to go to the big picnic and fireworks show the town always put on, double-dating with Kelly Grace and her boyfriend, Bobby. Well, when my father found out, he threw a fit—said we were going with the Stewarts, Colin's family, like we always did, and that was that. With the judge, there were no arguments. So...we cooked it up, Colin and I. We'd go together like they wanted, but in the midst of the festivities we snuck off and I joined up with Richie and Kelly and Bobby. Well, Richie and Bobby had somehow managed to get a hold of a bottle of Black Jack.''

"Uh-oh," said Troy. "How old did you say you guys were?"

She turned to smile at him ruefully. "Sixteen."

"So is this one of those things you were talking about that you're ashamed of?"

"No," she retorted, "it's one of those things I was talking about that you're *supposed* to be ashamed of, but aren't." But her heart was pounding, and she couldn't sit still. She slid off the picnic table, and took a step away from him, holding her hair back with both hands. "Listen, it was not an uncommon form of recreation for high-school kids back then. I imagine it's still not."

"I imagine you're right," he said carefully. And after a pause, "Look you don't have to talk about this if you don't—"

"No, I want to." She threw him a look across one shoulder. He was sitting hunched forward with his hands clasped between his knees, his beautiful eyes focused on her, reaching out, it seemed to her, like a strong and steady hand. The hand of a friend. She turned back to face him, shaking her hair free, letting her breath out slowly. "It's just...you have to understand, I've never told this stuff to anybody before. Give me a minute, okay?"

"Take all the time you need," he murmured. "I'm not goin' anywhere."

She came back and sat on the splintery bench beside his feet, rocking herself slightly. After a moment she cleared her throat and went on, "So there we were, out in the woods, drinking Black Jack and Coke and watching fireworks and making out like mad. Just when things were starting to get out of hand, I don't know what happened, I just sort of...froze up. Chickened out. Got scared, I guess. But at the same time, I was…pretty wired, you know? Confused as hell.''

"I can imagine.''

"Yeah, well, you can probably imagine how Richie was taking it, too. To say the least, he was furious with me. Anyway, I took off for home, walking. And naturally, since I was upset, I went straight to Colin's house, looking for him. He'd gone home after he left me with Richie, so our folks wouldn't know we weren't together. We were the only ones there—everyone else was still at the fireworks show. We got a bottle out of his folks' liquor cabinet—I don't even know what it was—and took it up to Colin's room and started drinking it right out of the bottle, passing it back and forth. We were sitting on Colin's bed. I was upset, crying. And I imagine my hormones were working overtime— his, too. He…put his arms around me—just to comfort me, you know? That's the way he was. But then…somehow…I don't re- member…all of a sudden we were kissing. And…it just *hap- pened*.''

Then, for a little while there was silence, save for insects' hum, the whisper and trickle of water and Bubba's snores, while Charly sat quietly waiting for her breathing to return to normal. Troy waited with her, saying nothing, his hand in her hair, gently strok- ing.

"I don't remember much,'' she whispered, "about afterward. Except that I felt awful…so ashamed. I don't even know how I got home that night. The next day, Colin came over, and we sat on *my* bed this time, and he held me and we talked—I cried— and he told me I shouldn't be ashamed, that we'd both had too much to drink, and we should just forget it ever happened.'' She gave a sharp, hurting laugh. "Which I would have been only too glad to do.''

"Except,'' said Troy, clearing his throat, "somebody had other plans.''

"Yeah.'' Charly sat up straight and waggled her shoulders, as if it were possible to ease the weight of memory. "I actually had a terrific summer,'' she said, struggling for a lighter tone. "Richie and I patched things up, and he apologized for his behavior that night, and we spent the whole summer double-dating with Kelly and Bobby. Had a great time. School started—our junior year—and it looked like it was going to be so much fun. Bobby and Richie were football heroes, and Kelly and I were doing our bit as adoring groupies, hanging on to our guys' big strong arms. Except for the fact that I'd sworn off sex, which annoyed Richie no end, and was sick to my stomach every other day, everything was fine.'' She drew in a breath. ''Just…fine.''

There was a thinking silence, and then Troy said slowly, in a voice raspy with disbelief, ''So…you're telling me that Colin…your best friend, and the father of your child, this sweet, kind, sensitive boy…committed suicide—*killed* himself—rather than *marry* you?''

She swiveled her head toward him, meeting his frown with a clear, steady gaze. ''So it seems,'' she said evenly. *I'm sorry, I'm sorry….*

''That doesn't make sense.''

Charly shrugged and looked away again. ''Nevertheless, it happened.'' But her voice had begun to tremble, and she wondered what she would do if he persisted. How long would she be able to keep the truth locked inside her heart, now that *he* held the keys?

She waited, heart pounding and shoulders tensed, while Troy's mouth opened and the questions poised there on the tip of his tongue. But at that moment, Bubba came out of his doze with a warning woof. And then they both heard it—a car, whining down the grade.

''We'd better be getting back,'' Charly mumbled, trembly with relief and danger narrowly avoided. ''There might be word from the hospital.''

Troy nodded, and without another word, went to untie Bubba's leash. Sick with uncertainty, Charly glanced at him, but his face was so grim and thoughtful she couldn't bring herself to look at him again. She gathered up the blankets in silence and helped him stow everything in the Cherokee, finishing just as a minivan pulled into the clearing, disgorging several laughing, shouting children in assorted sizes.

As they pulled away, Charly turned to fasten her seat belt, taking advantage of the opportunity, as she did so, to look back unobtrusively at the granite memorial, poignantly spotlighted now by a shimmering ray of sunlight. Tears stung her eyes. *I did it, Colin. I did it. I kept my promise. And your secret...*

She only hoped and prayed that honoring her vow to one friend hadn't just cost her another.

They drove straight back to the motel without stopping for breakfast, since Troy figured he still had enough groceries left from last night to tide them over until they could get something hot—starting with coffee. He unloaded the car while Charly made for the shower, and then, since the rooms at the Mourning Springs Motel weren't equipped with phones, he went down to the office to see if there'd been any messages.

The desk clerk was real glad to see him, since Troy hadn't officially asked to extend their occupancy or paid for their two rooms, as was the local custom, in advance. Troy thought about telling him to cancel one of the rooms, but he didn't, even though it gave him an unfamiliar, hollow feeling in his belly when he thought about sleeping in a bed alone, and Charly a mile away in the room next door. A cold, lonely feeling.

In the end he paid up both rooms for the next couple of days, and then asked if there'd been any messages for either him or Ms. Phelps. The desk clerk hmmed and muttered and poked around and finally came up with a piece of folded paper with the name "Charlene Phelps" written on it. Troy took it back to the room with him and laid it on the dresser. Then he took Bubba outside and fed him.

When he came back in, Charly was standing there with her hair dripping on her shoulders, wearing tan slacks and a white bra, holding the piece of paper in her hand. Her eyes reached for him and held on tight, and this time he could see her in there plain as day, that little lost girl, waving at him from their woodsy depths, crying out to him for help.

"It's from Dobrina," she said in a flat, scared-sounding voice. "She says my father wants to see me."

* * *

"You gonna be okay?" Troy asked her as they approached the ICU nursing station.

Charly nodded, although her jaws felt so tense she wondered why her teeth didn't crack.

"Well, okay, then. I'll be right here waitin'." He touched her elbow and abruptly left her.

Even though she'd prepared herself for it, his absence left her off balance, as if the room were rocking. She put a hand on the station counter to steady it.

"You can go on in," the duty nurse said. "He's been askin' for you."

Asking for me. It was the unreality of those words that carried her the last few steps around the glass partition and into her father's tiny room.

It seemed quieter than the last time she'd been there—less busy. Gone was the aura of urgency that hovers like gunsmoke over the battlefields where struggles for life and death are fought. In that quietness she felt some of her tension ease, and a little— just a little—of the fear seep away.

The upper half of her father's bed had been cranked high so that he lay in a semireclining position. He was apparently dozing; his mouth was hanging half-open and his eyes were closed. The skin on his face looked slack and pleated, Charly thought, as though the person inside it had shrunk.

She moved toward him cautiously, wondering if she ought to wake him. She was still a few steps from the bedside when his eyes opened and he said in a hoarse and groggy voice, "Thought you'd have left by now."

She cleared her throat, but couldn't think of anything to say. How *did* a person respond to a statement like that? State the obvious? Argue? The last argument she'd had with this man, she'd almost killed him.

Her father's eyes traveled slowly over her, but avoided her face, while his eyebrows drew together and lowered in the intimidating way she remembered. Then he coughed and said gruffly, "They, ah, tell me you saved my life. I wanted to thank you."

Charly gave a high, stressed laugh. She wasn't sure what she'd expected, but it sure wasn't this. "*Thank* me?" Since I'm probably the one that caused this... She looked away, her arms folding themselves across her body in a purely reflexive defense posture. "Listen, I'm sorry," she said in a hurried mumble, desperate to get the words out before she ran completely out of courage. "I didn't mean to upset you. I shouldn't have barged in on you like that. I didn't know you were sick. I'm sorry."

The judge's hand brushed the sheet in a gesture of dismissal. "Well, I didn't know, either." He gave a soft grunt of a laugh. "Took ever'body by surprise. 'Brina's been tellin' me for years I needed to shed a few pounds—guess I shoulda paid more attention to her. Well, she'll get t' say she told me so for the rest of my natural life. That ought t' make her happy."

"How are you?" Charly asked, taking a cautious step closer. Her heart wouldn't stop pounding, and her throat felt scratchy and dry. She wished she had a drink of water. "Have the doctors said? How bad was it? Are you—?"

"Am I goin' t' die any time soon, you mean?" He glared at her from under his eyebrows, then relaxed back against the pillows with a deep exhalation. "Oh, they've got to run all sorts of tests, yet. They'll wait till I'm out of the woods for that, but I expect I'm lookin' at some surgery—only question is how many arteries need bypassin'." His voice faded into a weak-sounding cough.

Charly looked around in sudden panic. "You're tired," she muttered. "I should probably go."

Her father raised his head and shifted around, gruff and restless, like a bear rousing from his winter's nap. "Sure, go on. Maybe you should." And then, as Charly was turning uncertainly, beginning to move away, "Guess you saw the boy...got what you came for...."

She turned back with a sharp exhalation, feeling as if someone had just grabbed her around the chest and squeezed hard. "Yes. Yes, I saw him. But that wasn't what I came for. How could it be? I didn't know he was here." Easy...easy.

What was she doing? The man was sick, he'd almost died and

here she was, yelling at him again. She shouldn't be here, shouldn't be saying this!

She clenched her jaws and reined herself in, but the words came out anyway, in a constricted growl. "I came...to see *you*."

Her father flinched back against his pillows, glaring at her with the poignant fierceness of a battered eagle. "Why?"

She jerked away from him, turning her back on the bed and the beeping machines, one hand clamped to the top of her head, the other clenched against her stomach, fighting for control. I can't do this, she thought. Not here, not now.

How many years had she thought of this moment, how many times had she rehearsed what she would say to him, to her father, the man lying in that bed...the man whose approval she'd longed for so desperately all of her life? How many times had she asked herself, Now? Do I deserve it now? And answered herself, No— not yet. Go a little farther...climb a little higher...achieve a little more...and then maybe. And now finally, feeling worthy at last and come to demand what she'd worked so hard to earn, to find that she'd been chasing a fantasy all along.

Why? he'd asked her. Why did you come?

Why, indeed. It was time she faced the truth. The one thing she wanted from him, he couldn't give her. Her father didn't want her. Didn't love her. Never had, and never would.

"I'm sorry," she whispered. "I shouldn't have. This was a mistake. I'm sorry—"

"No!" It was a faint echo of her father's familiar stentorian bellow, but it still had the power to stop her in her tracks. She turned and saw that his mouth was working in an odd way. Incredibly he looked like a child trying not to cry. "No...don't go. I'm the one...I'm the one who should be saying that...I'm sorry." His voice was one she'd never heard before, frail and quavering. Frightened, she wrapped her arms across herself, but couldn't stop herself from trembling.

He paused, then, and made an impatient gesture. She could almost see him gathering his strength, and when he spoke again it was in a reassuringly sonorous tone, weak but steady.

"I b'lieve it's true, you know, what they say about a close

brush with the hereafter changing your perspective.'' He coughed, shifted and went on gruffly, ''You were right. I never was a father to you. After—after your mother passed away, well, you were just so small, then...plain scared me to death, if you want to know the truth. So I left you to Dobrina. It was easier, you know. Not to feel. And I...well, I b'lieve it got to be a habit, one I didn't know how to break. Maybe never occurred to me I should. When you left...'' He moved a hand just slightly, but it was enough. Charly clamped a hand across her mouth, stifling a sob of protest in her throat.

I can't do this, she thought. I promised myself I wouldn't cry.

''When you left,'' her father went on in a quiet, trembling voice, ''I thought I'd been given the judgment I richly deserved. But I brought the boy home regardless, and appealed to the Lord in His mercy for a second chance. For a long while I thought He hadn't seen fit to grant it to me. Then it came to me that maybe He'd just given it to me in a different way—that the boy was my second chance. Now I see—'' he coughed again, and lifted his head to glare at her through eyes rimmed in red ''—I see that the Lord has been more merciful to me than I ever could have imagined. And now that I have been given that chance, I ask you—''

Oh, God, Charly prayed, *please* don't do this. Please don't let me cry.

But it seemed the Lord was busy right then, answering someone else's prayers.

''I ask you...to forgive me.''

''*Forgive you?*'' Charly squeaked, still managing to hold back sobs even as, in spite of all her efforts, the tears began to overflow. ''But *I'm* the one that left. I ran away and never let you know...how I was or where. I *meant* to hurt you. I did—I know that now. But at the same time I just wanted you to love me.''

''I always loved you,'' her father said stiffly, jerking as if she'd struck him. ''Always.''

''I only wanted you to be...proud of me,'' Charly whispered, dashing away tears. ''That's why I didn't come back—I wanted to make myself...someone you could be *proud* of. I didn't know...what a terrible thing I was doing—to you...to my son....''

"What you did to me, I deserved," her father said, then slowly shook his head and was very much the judge again, for a moment. "The boy did not. You will have to find a way...find the courage...to do what I have done. Beg his—"

"I think it's too late for that," Charly interrupted in a low voice, desperately needing a tissue. "He won't—"

"He will." Her father put his head back on the pillows and closed his eyes. "Give him some time—he's a good boy, but he can be stubborn at times." He paused, and his lips curved themselves into a wry smile, one Charly was used to seeing in her own mirror from time to time. "Has a lot of his mother in him."

She touched her nose with the back of her hand, astonishing herself with a laugh that was more than half a sob.

"Talk to the boy."

"I will," she whispered. "I'll try." Then she looked down at her father's gray, exhausted face, and fear clutched at her once more, turning her body cold. Fear for him, and for the son she'd hurt so badly. And for herself. It's not too late, she prayed. Please, don't let it be too late...for any of us.

"Charlene..." His eyes were open again, searching her face like a man lost. He lifted his hand slowly, reaching toward her.

Inside her chest Charly felt a strange, *giving* feeling, as though something hard and constricting—a band, or a chain, perhaps—had broken. Where for years there had been only pain, something warm and healing began to flow.

"Daddy." She reached out blindly and grasped her father's hand, and finally whispered the words they both needed so badly to hear. *"I forgive you."*

Chapter 13

January 5, 1978

Dear Diary,

Well, it is official. Yesterday the school principal called and told the judge that I will not be allowed to come back to school tomorrow when it starts up after Christmas vacation. So I guess I am now officially the Town Slut. Nobody is speaking to me—and I do mean *nobody*. Not even Kelly Grace. She acts all nervous around me, like maybe she thinks what I have is catching or something. Well, I could tell her it is, and if she doesn't watch herself she might catch it too, but not from me!

Colin's parents won't let him come over anymore. He's not even supposed to call me, which I think is totally unfair. We write each other notes, though, and hide them in this place we know of in the woods. Colin thinks he should tell that he's the father, but I don't want him to. If he does, our parents will probably try to make us get married, and I for sure don't want to, not to Colin or anybody else, either. I don't know about you, but I think sixteen is way too young to get married, pregnant or not!

The judge wants me to go to stay with his sister, Aunt Irene, in Birmingham until after the baby is born. What a horrible thought! I can't stand Aunt Irene, and Uncle Wesley is worse. Besides, this is my home. My friends—if I have any left—are here. The judge is really mad at me because I told him if he tried to make me go I would run away and never come back. Also because I won't tell him who the father is. He says I'm the stubbornest and most selfish and immature person he ever saw. Maybe he's right, I don't know. I get to feeling so scared, sometimes. Like, I get this sick, hurty feeling inside when I think about...things. About Colin, and getting married, and going away, and having a baby. So I just try not to think about it at all, which is getting harder all the time, now that the baby is moving around inside me. It's kind of neat, but...weird, too. Spooky.

One thing I didn't tell you. I don't know why, I guess I was in a State of Shock at the time. Anyway, back when I first told Aunt Dobie about the baby, she asked me if I wanted to get an abortion. I didn't know what to say—I didn't even know you could do that—legally, I mean—but I guess they passed a law or something so now you can get one anytime you need one. So I didn't say anything, and Aunt Dobie never said any more about it, either. I'm glad she didn't. I don't know what I would have done. I was pretty mixed up, and besides, it kind of wasn't real to me then. It's getting real now, though—boy, is it ever! I saw the pictures in these books the doctor gave me, so I even know what he looks like. Oh by the way—did I tell you? I think it's a boy.

(Almost forgot) Thought for the Day: I guess that was it. Isn't that enough to think about?

Troy was pacing the floor in the ICU waiting area, taking breaks now and then to glare at his watch or to minutely examine the carpet mosaics with a Blue Ridge Mountain theme that adorned the walls. Those mosaics served two purposes, it looked like to him, being both decorative and a convenient cushion for fidgety family members driven to beating their heads against stationary objects.

It was a compulsion he could well understand and sympathize with, at the moment. He might have been considering those extreme measures as a way of releasing his own tensions, if it hadn't been for the fact that the young man sharing the waiting room with him looked as if he might be needing to blow off some steam himself, and Troy thought he ought to do his best to set the boy a good example of manly patience and fortitude.

But *damn* if he didn't feel just like an expectant father. Or anyway, like he thought an expectant father might feel, which was, first of all, worried about the well-being of someone he cared about, knowing she was in a lot of pain right about now. And most of all, helpless and frustrated because there didn't seem to be anything he could do to help her.

He thought about calling his brother again to see if he had any more good advice to offer, since Jimmy Joe had actually been in this situation a time or two, the last time pretty recently, as a matter of fact. Then he remembered how, on that occasion, while Mirabella was giving birth to little Amy Jo in his truck, his little brother hadn't had a whole lot of time to spend on pacing and hand-wringing, since his role in the delivery had been a good bit more active than that.

Which, Troy thought, was *his* whole problem in a nutshell. He was used to being in an active role himself. He'd been in tense situations a good many times before, sometimes when lives—a lot of lives—had hung in the balance. But he'd been prepared for those situations, well armed and well trained to handle anything that might arise. He'd known what he was supposed to do, and how to do it, no ifs, ands, or buts.

Right now he didn't have a clue.

The boy, for example. Cutter. Lord, it was hard for *Troy* to believe that tall, good-lookin' young man could be Charly's son—he couldn't even imagine how it must be for her, seeing him like this, and for the first time since the day she'd given birth to him. He thought it must be hard for a parent to see their kids all grown-up, even when they'd gone through all the stages with 'em—from cute, drooling babies like Amy Jo, to bony ten-year-olds with chipped front teeth and bandages on their knees like Jimmy Joe's boy, J.J., and all the ones between. But this scowling, hostile twenty-year-old who already thought he knew all the answers? How would you even know where to begin?

It's not too late, he'd told Charly, with all the confidence of somebody who doesn't know what the hell he's talking about. Now, looking at the kid, he wasn't so sure of himself. He kept thinking he ought to do something to help things along, say something to the boy, maybe strike up a conversation, find out what made him tick. But he didn't, partly because Troy remembered what *he'd* been like at that age, bullheaded and sure he knew everything there was to know about the world and everybody in it, including himself. And partly because he was...well, galling as it was for a former U.S. Navy SEAL to have to admit, the fact was, the kid had him just about scared to death.

Lord help Charly, he thought grimly.

Then inspiration struck. "Hey," he said, digging in his pockets for change, "I'm goin' down to the Coke machine. Can I bring you somethin' back?"

The kid flicked him a glance, then went back to studying the piece of carpeting between his feet. "No...thanks."

At least, Troy thought, somebody'd taught him manners. "You sure? How 'bout a soda, or somethin'? I'm buyin'." Ah, hell—that's tryin' too hard.

"Naw," the boy muttered, "I'm fine."

"Well, okay," said Troy.

So then, of course, since he'd said he was going to, he had to take a walk on down to the damn vending machines and get himself a can of iced tea he didn't really want. While he was there, he got a Coke for Cutter, just in case the kid could be persuaded to change his mind about accepting it. He was on his way back to the sitting area with a cold can sweating in each hand when he saw Charly coming from the direction of the ICU, wiping her eyes with a wad of tissues. His heart started to pound.

They came together just outside the waiting-room doorway. "Hey," he managed to say in an undertone, fear thickening in his throat, "how'd it go? Everything okay?" Damn, but he wished he could put his arms around her, touch her, at least, but he couldn't because his hands were full of cans.

"Yeah," she said, dabbing at her nose with the tissue, "it went fine." But she wasn't meeting his eyes.

She took the Coke he'd brought for Cutter, absently mumbling "Thanks" as she popped it open, then drank from it deeply, like someone parched. As she lowered the can with a long exhalation and a soft, unabashed burp, her gaze slid past him, aimed like a searchlight's beam through the doorway and into the waiting room. She had kind of a shiny wet newborn look about her that for some reason brought a lump to Troy's throat.

"You sure you're okay?" he whispered, touching her arm now that he had a hand free.

She finally jerked her eyes to him, and to Troy it was like having the sunlight hit him full in the face after a long time in darkness. "I'm fine," she said softly. "Really. It went...very well. I'll tell you about it later. Right now I have to talk..." She gave a slight nod, looking once more toward the sitting area, where Cutter had risen to his feet and was waiting for her, primed and tense as a fighter waiting for the bell to ring.

So then what could he do, when every instinct in him wanted to be ridin' to her rescue, swords drawn and guns blazin', and the damn dragons were nowhere in sight? *Nothing.* That was the only answer he could come up with, and the only one he'd been coming up with, and it was about to drive him crazy. Charly was on her own. And all the help he could give her was to nod his head, swallow nails, step aside and let her go and get her heart broken.

Because he knew damn well that was what was going to happen; he could see it in the kid's face. Twenty years of hurt and anger were written there, plain as day. No way that boy was going to let it go, not yet and not without a fight. Maybe not ever.

Lord...help Charly...please.

As she walked toward her son with the Coke can clutched against her stomach like a bride's bouquet, Troy wondered if it was to keep her hands from shaking.

Cutter watched her come, standing his ground with his arms folded across his chest, stiff necked and bristling, until she got to within hand-shaking distance. Then he shifted abruptly, turned a shoulder to her and said stiffly, "Okay, you did what you came to do. You saw him, you talked to him—now you can leave."

"Cutter," Charly said in a voice so low Troy had to strain to hear, "I'd really like to talk to you. Do you think we could—"

"I've got nothin' to say to you." The boy flung the words like knives, and Troy felt each and every one of 'em right in his own heart.

Charly didn't flinch, though. "That wasn't what I asked," she said in a stronger voice. "I said I'd like to talk to *you*. Maybe you could just listen to what I have to say?"

While she was saying that, Cutter's chin pushed up and then jutted out, and Troy, watching, felt a shiver of recognition that almost—*almost*—made him laugh. It reminded him so much of Charly, the first time he'd ever laid eyes on her, coming down the hallway that night he'd bailed her out of jail. Lord, he thought, if the kid had very much of his mother in him, then Charly was in for the fight of her life.

"There's nothin' you have to say that I want to hear."

"Maybe you should hear me out before you decide that," Charly countered. She cleared her throat. "Look, my father and I just talked. We both said some things that needed to be said. And...it was a good thing. Maybe a new start. Don't you think you could...give us the same chance?"

She hadn't touched him, but he shook himself away from her as if she had, taking a step backward and holding up his hands. "Look," he said, "I'm glad you and Pop talked—I really am. That's between you and him, all right? And if that's what makes him happy, then...fine. But you and me? That's somethin' else again." He turned from her, enough so Troy could see his face plainly, and the struggle that was going on inside him—the struggle between the little boy he'd been and the man he wanted to be.

"I'm not tryin' to be mean," he said in a man's voice...a boy's mumble. "All right? I just want to make sure you understand, I don't want you in my life. I don't need you, okay?"

"Cutter—"

The hand came up again, demanding silence as he fought his inner battle for control. Finally he pulled in a sustaining breath. "There was a time I did. I used to say my prayers every night—'God bless my mama and keep her safe and bring her back.'" In spite of all his efforts, his voice cracked. He drew another breath. "But that was when I was little, okay? I'm not a kid anymore. I don't need a mother, and if I did, it wouldn't be you. Dobie and Pop, they're my mama and daddy. You had your chance, and you blew it when you walked out on us. You've got no place here. So you can just...finish up your business and go, okay? Go back to...where you came from—I don't care. Just...leave us alone."

Troy watched as the smooth young face seemed to crack like old china, finally letting loose the tears the kid had been trying so hard to contain. And he thought, That's one more thing he's gonna have a hard time forgiving her for.

As for himself, Troy was discovering that there was nothing in this world quite like the pain of watching somebody you care about—somebody you love—get hurt. He'd had things happen to him before—like his dad dying, buddies getting killed—but at those times, it seemed like there'd been a kind of a buffer, a sense of unreality, of shock, that he guessed must be nature's way of protecting people from things that might otherwise be more than they could handle. Here, there was nothing between him and the pain, nothing at all. He could see it like a crushing burden pressing down on Charly's head and shoulders, and feel the weight of it in his own chest. And added to it, the sharp, cutting agony of helplessness, of wanting so badly to help her, and knowing there wasn't a damn thing he could do.

He was barely aware of it when Cutter brushed past him, heading for the exit. His eyes were on Charly, and he was moving toward her like a man wading through a swamp.

"Hey," he'd just managed to say through the muck in his throat, and was reaching for her, had just touched her shoulder when they both heard a sound.

They turned at the same moment to see Dobrina standing in the doorway. She hesitated a moment when she saw Troy, then gave him a polite nod and came on in. She had a big handbag over one arm and another, smaller one, clutched to her chest.

"You been in t' see your father?" the housekeeper asked, ze-roing in on Charly with her fierce, deep-socketed glare. "He's been askin' for you."

Charly whispered, "Yes, ma'am," and brushed at her cheeks as if she had no right to tears. Then she cleared her throat and said in a stronger voice, "Yes, I did, Aunt Dobie. We had a good talk. Um, Cutter just—"

"I saw him leavin'." The woman's voice had the hard-edged, angry sound of too much emotion. "Best to leave 'im be, for a while. Just leave 'im be. He's young, you know—he don't un-derstand...." She paused, her head moving from side to side, as if she'd lost her way. Then she looked down at the pocketbook she was holding and thrust it at Charly. "Here, honey, I brought you your purse." She lifted her head up. To Troy it looked as if she was bracing herself.

Charly reached for the purse, murmuring thanks and sniffling a little, but instead of handing it over, Dobrina shook her head and clutched her arm with one strong, brown hand. "The Good Lord forgive me for takin' it—and for puttin' that bottle a' whis-key in your car, too. I know I shouldn't have done what I did." Then she drew herself up, proud and fierce once more. "Maybe it wasn't my place to interfere, but I wasn't about to let you leave again. No, sir—not after the way you and your father were talkin' to each other, just yellin' and hurtin' each other, and nobody speakin' the truth. There's been enough a' that in this family. And enough, I say, is *enough*."

With that, she let go of Charly's arm and reached into the big handbag she had slung over hers and pulled something out. It was a book—Troy could see that much—about the size of a prayer book, green leather, embossed in gold, letters he couldn't quite make out. But he heard Charly give a little gasp of recognition as Dobrina placed the book in her hands.

"I found this," the housekeeper said in a cracking voice, "after you went away. Maybe I shouldn't have read it—I expect that's somethin' else the Lord's gonna have to forgive me for, and you, too—but I thought...well, I thought maybe there'd be somethin' in there to tell us where you'd gone." She laughed soundlessly through the tears that had begun to stream down her smooth, nut brown cheeks. "Well, there was, I guess. Yes, there was somethin', all right. But honey, California's a mighty big place.

"I never told your father, nor Cutter, either. It wasn't my place. That's yours, Charlene, honey—yours to keep or to share. That's up to you. But that boy a' yours—he needs to know the truth. Time he knew the *whole* truth, child—about his daddy—" Charly gave a small, involuntary gasp "—and how it was with you all. You give that book to Cutter to read, honey. You give it to him, now. It's *time.*"

She patted Charly on the arm and turned away, nodding, while Charly stared at her, her face bone white and glistening, like a marble statue in the rain.

"Miz Phelps?" The young ICU duty nurse was standing in the doorway, looking like a little girl in her lavender cotton scrubs. "Ma'am, the cardiologist would like to talk to you. Long as you're here..."

Both women started forward at the same time. The nurse flicked a glance at Charly as she beckoned the housekeeper past her. "I meant *Mrs.* Phelps—sorry about that." And to Dobrina, she said, "Ma'am, if you want to, you can just go right on in." She gave Charly an apologetic smile and went back to her station.

She left behind her a stunned and vibrating silence. And then the air exploded from Charly's lungs.

"Aunt Dobie? *When? How* long have you—?"

"Nineteen years last April," Dobrina said with quiet dignity, standing straight as a pillar with her hands clasped loosely at her waist. She lacked only one of those tall, pointed crowns, Troy thought, and she could have been a golden statue guarding the entrance to an Egyptian pharaoh's tomb. "One year to the day after you left home." Her chin rose a fraction of an inch higher. "It was *his* idea. I nevah asked for it."

He heard a peculiar creaking sound and realized it must be Charly, trying to swallow, trying to speak. And then she was moving toward the other woman, slowly and wobbling a bit, like someone just getting on her feet after being sick for a while. "I'm...glad...Aunt Dobie. I really am. I'm just...surprised. I never—I didn't know my father..."

"No, you didn't," said Dobrina softly. "Nor your son, either. It's time you did, child. Time you did." She patted Charly's hand once more, hesitated for just a moment, then continued on to the ICU and the husband that needed her.

"Oh, boy. Wow. I can't believe it. Married. Oh...boy." Charly kept it up, a breathless, whispered monologue as she and Troy hurried through the hospital corridors. "My father and Aunt Dobie. Wow."

"Why is that so hard to believe?" Troy asked when they were outside on the concrete apron, blinking in the unexpected light of a brilliant Sunday afternoon.

She threw him a look, letting go of a little gust of laughter. "You don't seem very surprised."

He shrugged. "Figured she had to have a better reason for stayin' with the man all those years than just bein' his housekeeper. She loves him. It was right there in her face, plain to see—guess you've just been too preoccupied with everything else that's been goin' on to notice."

"Wow," she said in a wondering tone, staring at her feet. After a moment she shook her head, and they started across the heat-shimmery parking lot, Charly still agitated and wanting to move a lot faster than Southerners generally like to in the summertime, those with any sense. Troy took hold of her elbow to slow her down a little, and she looked up at him with confusion darkening her eyes. There was some anger there, too, sparking and flashing like bomb bursts in a night sky.

"You don't understand," she finally burst out. "You'd have to know my father. All he cared about was appearances—what people thought, fitting in, being accepted. That's why he was so upset when I got pregnant. That's why he wanted so much for me to marry Colin.''

"I don't follow you."

She heaved an impatient little sigh and rolled her eyes. "Colin was a *Stewart*. In this town that was like royalty—poor as church mice, but old blood. You're a Southerner, you should know how it is—was…can be *still*, some places. The Stewarts go back two hundred years, at least. They were the original founders of this town, owned most of it until the war. My father's people, on the other hand, were carpetbaggers—founded a fortune on the misfortunes of people like the Stewarts.''

"Lord," said Troy, "that was over a hundred years ago."

"Yeah, but that's the old Southern question, isn't it? How many generations does it take before you belong?" She gave a soft, ironic laugh. "My father is a fourth-generation Alabamian, and still felt like an outsider all his life. My marrying Colin would have given the acceptance *he* always longed for to the next generation, at least." She paused. "I didn't have all this insight back then, you realize. I was just a kid, and mad at my father because it seemed to me all he cared about was how we looked to other people. I can't imagine that he'd ever have married—''

"A black woman?"

"Well, yeah, no matter how much he may have loved her."

"Things change," said Troy softly. "Times change. People change."

She gave a suspiciously moist laugh. Looking down, he discovered that there were tears dripping off the end of her nose. Something inside him did a slow and painful flip-flop, and he finally did what he'd been wanting to do, unable to do for so long. He stopped and turned her toward him and folded her into his arms. "Be happy for them," he said huskily into her hair.

"I am. I am…I was just thinking, you know…about Cutter. I wonder if he calls her Mom."

"You heard him—he calls her Dobie." His voice was rusty as old nails. "That boy knows who his mama is."

Suddenly becoming aware of something wedged between his

body and hers, he raised his head and held her a little ways from him. "That book," he said, tipping his head toward the leather-bound volume she still held, cradled with her purse against her breasts. "Dobrina said she wanted you to give it to Cutter. What is it, a Bible? Some kind of family thing?"

She looked down with a faint air of surprise, as if she'd forgotten the book was there. He heard a sharp catch in her breathing.

"It's my diary," she said softly.

Charly said, "I can't imagine I was ever this young."

She was sitting cross-legged in the middle of the bed, in a motel room that reeked of fried chicken and biscuits and mashed potatoes with gravy, Troy having decided it wasn't the best time to be nagging somebody about their eating habits.

"Listen to this.

'Dear Diary.

I'm not going to write very much tonight, because *Welcome Back, Kotter* is on, and I have to finish my homework. I just think John Travolta is so-o bitchin', don't you? I wonder if he's married, and if he's not, if he'd ever consider being interested in a skinny girl from Mourning Spring Alabama with no boobs and a great personality.'

'Thought for the Day—'

"I was supposed to think up something profound, you understand—

'I'm thinking of getting a padded bra.'

"Can you believe it?"

"Hard to," said Troy, eyeing what he could see of her breasts underneath the portrait of Sylvester the cat that adorned the T-shirt she was wearing. He'd just come out of the bathroom, where he'd indulged himself in a longer than usual shower, complete with shampoo and shave, and all the other miscellaneous activities men do in private, seldom admit to, and would never, ever call primping. He'd done all that mainly to give Charly some time alone to look over that old diary of hers, in case she needed the privacy. But as a result he was feeling fresh, clean and sexy as hell, and maybe it was just the frame of mind he was in, but as far as he was concerned, neither her breasts nor any other part of her looked like it was in any need of improvement whatsoever.

"Here's another one.

"Today I wore my new platform shoes to school. So did Kelly Grace. I had to sneak mine past the judge and Aunt Dobie in my backpack, but it was worth it. I think they look bitchin', especially with my new jeans. Brooke Shields, eat your heart out!"'

She rocked back and looked up at him. "God—remember that? Platform shoes. Bell bottoms...designer jeans."

"Sideburns," muttered Troy, rubbing his clean-shaved jaw.

"Leisure suits," Charly sang, laughing.

"With bell bottoms..."

"...in bulletproof polyester!"

"Afros!"

"Pooka beads! Mood rings!"

"Saturday Night Fever!"

Charly put her hand over her heart in a mock swoon. "I must have seen that movie six times, at least. John Travolta was *bitchin'!* Did you guys say that, too—bitchin'? The equivalent of 'Way cool, man...totally awesome,' you know? Like... outasight?"

"Not within earshot of my mama, I didn't," said Troy dryly, going to sit on the edge of the bed, close enough to touch her, but not doing so. He felt off balance and unsure of himself, like a dinner guest finding himself witness to a family crisis. How close should he come? How close would she allow him? How much right did he have to share such intimate revelations?

She chuckled and went back to the diary, reading aloud under her breath now and then, slowly turning pages, smiling at first. But gradually her face changed, losing all traces of laughter and finally acquiring that tight, fragile look that he knew the wrong word, the slightest touch could shatter.

"Here." Her voice sounded breathless and unsteady. "July 4—this is where it starts. No, wait—" she flipped pages "—a little before that. Here we are—July 1. 'Dear Diary, Guess what! I think Richie Wilcox likes me.'" Her head came up and her eyes sought his, bright with fear and hope, like a kid about to take her first jump off a diving board and wondering if there was gonna be anyone there to catch her when she did.

"Go ahead," he said, but something had tightened around his chest so that his voice was as airless as hers. He scooted his hand across the bedspread toward hers.

She took it and clasped it tightly, twining her fingers with his as trustingly as a child. And he felt something burst inside him, spreading liquid warmth all through him...warmth, and strength and certainty. When once again she bowed her head over the diary in her lap and began to read aloud the words, thoughts and feelings she'd transferred there from her heart so long ago, any doubts he'd had about his right to share them with her had gone. Right then and there he knew his place was *here,* right here beside her, holding her, comforting her, protecting her, in any way he could, as far as he was able, for as long as he had breath left in his body.

So he held her hand while she retraced the rocky and painful pathway of her seventeenth year. When her voice trembled and broke, he moved unhesitatingly closer, sat beside her and wrapped her in his arms and held her. And when her tears finally came, he soaked them up in the front of his shirt.

The last entry he read for her: "'Today I am leaving this God Forsaken place forever....'"

Troy finished in a cracking voice, then closed the diary and put it aside on the nightstand while he and Charly held on to each other, laughing and trembling. Part of that, he hoped, he wanted to believe, was a kind of giddy joy in each other, in comradeship discovered, in the newness of having someone to cling to in a time of trouble. And part, he knew, was sheer relief—on her part, that the past had been faced at last, and on his, that she'd finally allowed him to share it all with her.

All, at least, except for one small part. There was still the promise she'd never broken, the one secret she hadn't dared to share with another soul, nor even commit to the pages of her diary. Troy was pretty sure he knew what the secret was, and he had an idea Dobrina must have guessed it, too. He wondered if Charly even realized how clear the answers were, to anyone who knew the whole story—to anyone who'd read her diary.

And whether, even now, she'd be willing to risk letting her son in on the secret she'd promised his father she would keep for him forever.

A silence had fallen over them, filled with the trip-hammering of heartbeats and little slowing-down sighs. To Charly it seemed almost like the aftermath of lovemaking, except that she felt in no way satiated, or even drowsily content. The sultry intimacy of Troy's body heat energized her like a cold shower, frosting her body with goose bumps; the fresh-soap smell of his sweat filled her head with a low-level buzz, like the first drink of champagne.

She stirred and turned toward him, her hand finding a nest in the hard-muscled hollow of his belly, just below the V of his ribs. She let it ride there for a moment, rising and falling like a leaf on a wake, wondering if she dared let it drift toward more-interesting places, wondering whether he'd deny her again, and how she would cope if he did.

She was a long way from understanding what it was that made Troy Starr tick—though to be honest, until now she'd been too preoccupied with her own pain to even try. Certainly she'd never met anyone in her life quite like him, had never even imagined they still made guys like him—and they probably didn't, at least not in L.A. He was...definitely one of a kind. Well, okay, maybe one of a pair, the other being his brother Jimmy Joe, and she could definitely understand a little better now what it was that had made a bright, sophisticated lady like Mirabella fall in love with the redneck truck driver from Georgia.

Mirabella, Charly remembered, had once told her she'd thought of Jimmy Joe as a knight. Her very own knight, come thundering to her rescue that Christmas Eve in his big blue Kenworth charger. Crazy, Charly had thought at the time. Romantic lunacy. Her best friend had simply lost her mind.

And even if it were true, and even if Charly did happen to need rescuing—which she most certainly did not—there were no more knights. Surely Jimmy Joe had to be the last one left in the world. They just didn't make them anymore. Or did they?

Boy Scouts, now...that was another story. And as far as she was concerned, there was one too many of them in *this* room.

"Ma'am, you mind tellin' me what you're up to?" Troy's voice was groggy, the words slurred.

Charly's hand had left the soft-firm flesh of his belly to skim across the front of his boxers like a kingfisher over the surface of a pond, sending shivers rippling through his body. Her laugh was soft and dangerous. "I warned you about that 'ma'am' stuff."

"Let me rephrase the question, Your Honor." His breath caught; her hand settled...became an excruciating warmth. "*Woman*, what in the hell are you doing?"

"That's better," she purred with the deceptive laziness of a lioness watching a herd of gazelles. "I'm trying to seduce you, of course."

He laughed weakly. "Now, *there's* a challenge."

Her hand moved on, riding downward along the hard ridge of his thigh, then slowly up again on the softer inside. He felt his bones melt. Heaven...no, torture. Her thigh came between his; her body weight shifted and slid lower, caressing his side. Her warm breath poured over his stomach...her tongue made darting forays into his navel.

A groan, composed of equal parts pleasure and agony, rose from deep in his belly. "Didn't you ever hear of *overkill?*"

She chuckled, modestly pleased. "I wasn't sure what it would take. I've never seduced a Boy Scout before."

She was unprepared when his body suddenly hardened to iron beneath her and his legs came around her like steel coils. The next thing she knew, she was on her back with her arms imprisoned above her head, pressed deep into the pillows, with her heart pounding, heat thundering through her body and Troy's body hard and hot on top of her.

"Where do you get this 'Boy Scout' stuff?" he growled as his mouth came swooping down, taking quick, possessive nips from her throat, from her lips, startled and open. Her lips grew swollen and tingled like fire; her breaths came sharp and hurting. "You have a damn short memory." His grip on her arms became a caress, sliding upward toward her wrists; his fingers wove themselves through hers. His mouth sank into hers, and his tongue trapped her whimper of need deep in her own throat.

His kisses took possession of her; sensation became a deluge, a monsoon, wiping out thought. Her body arched mindlessly, seeking him, while her legs shifted, making a place for him between. Her breath came in soft, tiny cries.

"After last night," she gasped, when his mouth finally released hers to explore the pulsing cords along the side of her neck, her lips moist and throbbing, slurring the words, "I thought—"

"I know what you thought." He pulled back suddenly, bringing her with him, and kneeling between her legs, with one swift motion tore her T-shirt up and over her head and threw it impatiently aside.

His fingers dipped beneath the elastic waistband of her Tweety Bird boxers, yanked them down over her hips. She drew her legs up one at a time, watching him, wide-eyed and trembling, as he pulled them off and hurled them away and then lifted and settled her, naked, astride his thighs.

"Lady, for somebody as smart as you are—" his voice was thick and guttural, his hands gentle on her arms, a feather's touch with the power of a lightning strike "—you don't know very much about what makes a man tick. Not a damn thing, as a matter of fact..."

His hands left her arms to travel down her sides, over her hips and back up again, where they found her breasts aching for his touch. And gently nested them. And then, not at all gently, squeezed and rolled and tugged the hardened, nerve-rich nipples, an exquisite agony she felt in the deepest parts of her, felt in the soles of her feet, in the nape of her neck...so sweet an agony she cried out and arched her back, pushing her breasts deeper into his hands, pressing her soft, vulnerable body against the unyielding hardness of his.

Bewilderment filled her, mixed with a need so sharp and bright it felt like despair. Together they made a pressure inside her that was not unlike tears.

"I don't understand," she whispered, her head thrown back, eyes tightly shut, frightened without knowing why. "What...is it you want from me?"

His chuckle was a liquid, tickling warmth at the base of her throat. "More than you can give me right now, darlin'...I know that."

"I want you," she cried, dizzy, cold with wanting. Trembling...trembling. "Isn't that enough?"

"Not even close." His hands were a moving, liquid warmth, flowing over her body, her sides, her belly, her thighs. She felt his fingers come between her thighs...an intimate intrusion that made her gasp...and yearn.

"Okay..." Her throat, her whole body tightened. She lifted her hands to his shoulders, then curled them around his neck and hung on with a kind of desperation as, trembling, she choked out the words she'd never said to a living soul before. "I...*need* you."

"Getting warmer," Troy murmured, intimately cradling her. Helplessly she began to rock against his hand. "What I want," he whispered as his fingers stroked her, and her breathing became whimpers, "I want you to look at me." His fingers slipped into her body...slowly, gently...a lightning bolt, tearing her apart.

"Open your eyes...*look at me.*"

Somehow she did, and found his eyes like beacons in the darkness. Beautiful eyes... She clung to them desperately, while his fingers pushed deeper, probed for her body's center, searched, it seemed to her, for her very soul. Clung to them while her world, her reality, her heart was shattering into a million pieces, and her body dissolving into shuddering, throbbing chaos in his hands.

"Now...say my name. *Say my name.*"

"Troy! *Troy...*"

Chapter 14

February 4, 1978

Dear Diary,

Well, it's out now. Colin confessed. He says he didn't mean to, but I guess yesterday he got in a big fight with his parents—about me, of course—and he didn't like what they were saying about me, and the baby, and all, and anyway, he just blurted it out that it's his baby, too.

I'm not as sorry as I thought I would be. It was getting pretty lonely there for a while. It's pretty neat, actually, having somebody to share things with. Like, today Colin came over and I let him put his hand on my stomach so he could feel the baby move. I told him I think it's a boy. He says he thinks so, too.

I've been thinking that maybe it won't be so bad after all, marrying Colin. He is my best friend. At least he understands me, and I know him better than anybody else. And we can still go to college, at least Colin can. The judge says he will help us until he finishes school—I don't know if that includes medical school or not, though. It seems like that takes an awfully long time. Our baby will be ten years old by then. And I will be twenty-seven—almost thirty.

Thought for the Day: I guess I am probably not going to make it to California after all.

On Monday morning Troy left Charly making local calls on the phone in the motel office while he and Bubba went across the highway to use the pay phone at B.B.'s Barn. Half an hour or so later they met back in number 10 to compare notes.

"My father is better," Charly said, getting the most important question out of the way first. "I talked to him for a few minutes. He sounded pretty groggy, but he says they might start running tests tomorrow, and that they should know about the surgery by the end of the week. Then I called Aunt—oh, boy, it seems funny calling her that now, you know it? Aunt Dobie? I mean, she's my stepmother! Wow." She gave a low, bemused laugh and shook her head. "That's gonna take some getting used to. Anyway, I talked to her—she's at the house. First thing she asked me was if I'd showed the diary to Cutter. You know how she is— tact isn't her strong suit."

She took a breath and turned away from him, pushing her hair back with both hands, leaving her face unguarded for a moment, and vulnerable as a child's.

"You going to?" Troy asked softly. All morning he'd been watching, wary and uncertain, for some sign, some indication of where she meant to go with this thing, whether she meant to fight for her son or give up the battle. Knowing it wasn't just her life, her future on the line now, but his, too.

Charly let the breath out in an audible hiss and, instead of answering him, said, "She wants us to stay at the house." She made a small sound that might have been a laugh. "I asked her how Cutter felt about that."

"What did she say?"

One corner of her mouth lifted in a sardonic little half smile.

"You know Dobrina. She just went, 'Humph! It's not up to Cutter, it's up to *me*.' Anyway, I told her there wasn't much point, since we were probably going to be leaving town soon."

Troy raised his eyebrows. "That so? Thought you had a court date."

Her gaze shifted past him to a far upper corner of the room, and she let out another of those testy-sounding breaths. "Yeah, well...that's another thing Dobrina had to tell me. Apparently the charges have been dropped—surprise, surprise. Oh, except for the reckless driving." She shrugged, her lips tilted wryly again. "They're issuing me a traffic citation. There go my insurance rates."

"You get a hold of the car-rental outfit?"

"I did—called their 800 number. The good news is, they're going to bring me another car. The bad news is, the soonest they can get one here is late this evening or first thing tomorrow morning."

"That doesn't sound too bad," said Troy. "You in so much of a hurry to leave? Thought you had some unfinished business to take care of."

He said it in that overly careful and even tone people use when they know they're walking a fine line with somebody and don't want to push too hard. Because Troy thought he knew where Charly was right now—on the edge, and scared to death she was gonna slip and fall.

Last night she'd come close to taking that flying leap she'd been avoiding all her life, the one into the black abyss—the terrifying uncertainty of "I love you." He'd thought he had her, brought her right to the edge, held out his hand and asked her to trust him enough to take the leap with him, but at the last second she'd stepped back onto firmer ground, the safer and more familiar ground of "I want...I need."

Troy knew what it was like to jump into blackness without any idea what might be waiting for him below. He knew what it was like to freeze up in the doorway, too. He knew that pushing somebody under those circumstances was the worst thing you could do, and that for most people the paralysis was temporary, and sooner or later they'd work their courage up in their own way.

The thing that scared him was, he'd also known some people who never did get up the nerve to make that first jump.

"What about you?" she asked him, once again avoiding the question. "Did you talk to your brother? Are he and Bella—?"

Troy was nodding. "I guess there's good news and bad news there, too. The good news is, they're home safe and sound from Atlanta, which is by no means a given, in case you've never driven in Atlanta traffic. The bad news is, Mirabella's all in a tizzy."

"Which is not an unusual state for Bella to be in," said Charly dryly. "What is it this time? Aside from prewedding nerves."

"Well...seems her sister Summer pulled in late last night."

"Summer...yeah, I know her. She's the younger one—the one with the kids. But she was expected, wasn't she? I mean, she was coming for the wedding—"

"That was the good news," said Troy, kind of scratching his head. "Bad news is, she came in drivin' a U-Haul truck."

"A U-Haul—"

"Seems she's up and divorced her husband."

"Oh, my God."

"Yep. Packed up everything and moved here, lock, stock and barrel."

"Bella didn't need this." Charly bit out the words, beginning to pace angrily. "What rotten timing. What a lousy thing to do to your sister!"

"Well," Troy said in a placating tone, "from what Jimmy Joe tells me, she didn't have a lotta choice. I guess her husband has a problem with gambling, or something? Anyway, he took every-thing—even mortgaged the house without telling his wife. Forged her signature, cleaned everything out, then split. The bank fore-closed on her, so she packed up everything she had left, including the kids, in the old U-Haul, and here she is."

Charly clapped a hand to her forehead and closed her eyes. "Oh, my Lord," she breathed. "Poor Bella."

"Bottom line," said Troy quietly, "she's really needin' me to finish that nursery for her, so her sister and the kids can have the spare room.''

"Well, of course—you should go back." Charly was pacing again, frowning and fidgety, avoiding his eyes. "Listen, I keep telling you, you don't need to stay here for me. You go on home. I'll just stay here and wait for the—"

He snaked out a hand and caught her by the arm. She sucked in air as her head snapped around and her eyes burned at him like a tiger's in the night.

"Hey," he said softly, "come 'ere."

"What?" she demanded in a hushed voice as he drew her slowly toward him. Her eyes were wary...still those of a tiger, but a frightened one now, ears flattened and fangs showing, ready to flee.

What do you want from me?

With pounding heart, deceptively relaxed, he guided her between his outstretched legs as he leaned, half-sitting, against the dresser. "Just come 'ere for a minute, and look at me."

Look at me. Last night's fear burned like old embers in her eyes, whispered like ashes in her voice. "What do you want?"

"What do I want..." Troy looked away for a moment, then heaved a sigh and brought his gaze back to her pale, tense face. "Look, you s'pose we could manage to spend a night makin' love and still look one another in the eye in the mornin'? Think we could do that? Jeez Louise, woman, what are you, some kind of shrinking maiden or somethin'?"

"That's me," said Charly with a dry laugh. "Definitely."

He brushed her chin with his thumb, then leaned his body forward and gently, gently kissed her.

"Look," he murmured, pulling back just enough so he could see her eyes—eyes that now held the warm, unfocused glow of confusion. Whiskey eyes. "I don't know about you, but my feelings don't crawl into a coffin come daylight. Nothin' here's changed. Yesterday I was your friend, last night I was your lover, this morning I'm still the same guy—friend *and* lover. Ease up, okay?" He brought his mouth to hers again, brushing his lips across the abashed beginnings of her smile. "And let's get some-

thin' straight. I'm not goin' anywhere until you've got those issues of yours resolved.''

"Issues…" She laughed and leaned against him, and he could
feel her body trembling slightly. He wrapped his arms and his
body protectively around her, wishing he could protect her heart
the same way.

"You know what's really bothering you, don't you?" he murmured, combing his fingers through her hair. Her head moved
affirmatively against his hand. Then she turned her face into his
chest in a quick little movement of denial, like a mouse looking
for a place to hide.

"Dobrina's right," he went on, his voice growing husky. "You
need to show your son that diary. He needs to know the truth."
She pulled herself slowly back, one hand flat against his chest as
if, he thought, by pushing him away she would keep the words
away, as well. He held her gently by the shoulders, denying her
escape. "He wants to understand, can't you see that? He wants
to understand the reason why his daddy killed himself." Her
mouth popped open, letting a strangled sound escape. He touched
her lips with a finger and finished softly, "Honey, he needs to
know it wasn't your fault."

Her eyes turned liquid and spilled over. He felt his own eyes
burning as he took her face between his two hands and brushed
away the moisture with his thumbs. "You made a promise," he
said thickly. "And you never broke it. You didn't, not even in
that diary of yours, not on purpose. But Dobrina knew the truth
soon as she read it, and so did I. Cutter's gonna know it, too.
Maybe not right away, but he'll figure it out…that his daddy killed
himself to spare you both from a lifetime of livin' a lie."

There was no answer, save for a long, quivering breath. And
then she closed her eyes, and her face seemed to crumple in his
hands. Nothing for him to do then but fold her in and hold her
close and keep her safe while she sobbed.

"He's not here," Charly said as she opened the door of the
Cherokee and climbed in. She sounded a lot more out of breath

than she should have been, just from running down the steps of her father's house. "Dobie says he went for a drive."

"What do you want to do?" Troy asked, staring through the windshield, watching a squirrel scamper across the brick-paved driveway. "You wanna wait for him?"

His peripheral vision caught her headshake; he heard her seat belt click. "She says she thinks he might be up at the spring. She says he likes to go there sometimes."

When he's hurtin'. Troy could understand that. Sometimes a man just needed a quiet place to be alone in. A place...and time...to heal himself.

"Okay, then," he said, reaching for the gearshift, "you wanna go for a drive?"

"Might as well," Charly said grimly. "Before I lose my nerve."

He glanced at her as he aimed the Cherokee between the gateposts and into the quiet street, but didn't say anything. All the way through town and out on the highway and up the winding grade to the mountains, he drove in silence, listening to the pounding of his heart. Even Bubba was quieter than usual, maybe picking up the tension vibes the way dogs do, lying on the middle seat behind them, alert but still.

How must it be for her? he wondered. What was she thinking of now—the tiny baby she'd held for such a brief time in her arms, or all the years she'd missed, the first smile, the first steps, the lost teeth and skinned knees she hadn't been there to comfort him through? Or was she only thinking of the tall, good-looking young man with the anger and hurt in his eyes? Troy couldn't even imagine it. He'd never been a mother—hell, he'd never even been a father—so how could he begin to know what it must be like to have a child taken away from you?

He knew it had been a long time since he'd felt like this—adrenaline pumping, heart pounding, tension vibrating through his muscles and nerves like charges of electricity. He found himself preparing himself, focusing all his energy and concentration on what lay ahead, the way he once had before an important mission. And in a way, he thought, this might be the most important mission of his life; surely it was one of the most dangerous, this business of committing another human being's heart, soul and happiness into his own keeping.

"I'm scared," Charly whispered as they turned into the clearing at Mourning Spring Park. There was one other car there, a blue Mustang a dozen or so years old. Troy pulled in beside it and turned off the motor, then reached over and put his hand over hers.

"I know," he said in a gravelly voice. So am I. "But it's gonna be okay. You understand me? No matter what happens."

But he didn't think she heard him, or would have believed him if she had.

Cutter was sitting on a picnic table, the same one he and Charly had been sitting on that morning, when she'd told him about Colin, and how all this had come about. He had his back to them, although Troy knew very well he'd already marked their arrival.

Charly reached for the door handle and yanked it open. Bubba was already on his feet, whining and chompin' at the bit to get to that water, so Troy got out and opened up his door and let him go. The pup went galloping by Charly, who was making her way across the sun-dappled gravel with the diary hugged to her chest. Troy got Bubba's leash out of the back of the Cherokee and then followed, hanging back far enough to give her room, but close enough so she'd know he was there if she needed him.

The dog went galumphing by Cutter and splashed his way into the stream, making it pretty hard for the kid to go on pretending he didn't know they were there. He turned to look over his shoulder, impatiently frowning, and muttered, "What do you want?"

From where he stood, Troy could see Charly's shoulders lift, and he knew she must be trying to pull in a breath, one that probably felt like shards of broken glass. When she spoke, though, her voice was steady and strong, and he felt an unheralded glow of pride.

"I'm glad I found you—Dobie told me you might be here. Look, I just wanted to tell you I'm going to be leaving soon. They're bringing me a car either tonight or in the morning."

Cutter grunted something Troy couldn't make out and turned his back to her again. She took a step closer.

"Cutter, listen." Her voice was so low, so vibrant with emotion that it seemed to Troy he could feel it in his bones rather than hear it. "I understand my coming here was a shock to you." She gave a soft huff of laughter. "Finding you here was a shock to me. Look, I don't want to upset you—that's the last thing I ever wanted. I understand you don't care to have me be a part of your life right now. But maybe someday—" she took a deep, unsteady breath "—maybe someday you'll have...questions." She held out the diary, a quick, jerking motion. "Dobrina wanted me to give you this. It's, um, it's my diary. I kept it the year...the year everything happened. The year before you were born. I thought— she thought maybe you should read it."

Cutter twisted toward her, tense and shaking. "What do I have to say to you to make you understand? I'm not interested in anything you've got to say. If Pop and Dobie want you back in their lives, that's their business. I don't want you in mine, okay? Can I make myself any clearer? And you can take that book with you—there's nothin' in there I need to see, nothing you can say I want to hear." The young voice cracked. He hauled in a breath and pulled himself up, clutching desperately at his pride. "Now, I'd be obliged if you'd leave me alone."

Listening to that, Troy felt a strange sensation, like a cold wind blowing through him, chilling his body, drowning thought. He had no real sense of how long it was before Charly finally turned around and started back toward him, walking as though the ground underneath her feet were rocky. He didn't hear anything except for the rushing in his ears as he guided her to the truck with one hand on her elbow. He whistled for Bubba, opened up the door for him when he came running, and it never even occurred to him to mind the mud and water he was bringing in with him. Something primitive in him was wanting to kill the kid for doing this to the woman he loved, even while the reasoning part of him was telling him nobody in this world was hurtin' any worse than that boy was right then.

Except, of course, for Charly.

Troy helped her into the passenger's side of the Cherokee the way he would have if she'd been old, or disabled. He shut her door and went around to his side and got in and started up the engine and backed slowly out of the clearing. And all the while she didn't say a word, didn't make a sound.

He waited until he'd pulled out onto the highway, then cleared his throat and said, "Well, we probably should've expected somethin' like this. It's awful early yet. He'll come around."

She shook her head. "No," she said softly, "he won't. You saw his face." Troy was getting ready to argue with her when she suddenly gave a sharp little laugh. "He's got too much of me in him. Lord, it took me twenty years to forgive my father. And I'm expecting him to do it in two days?"

She looked down at the book in her hands, slowly shaking her head, her voice going soft again, tired and sad. "Look, I tried, okay? It's no use beating my head against the wall. All I'm doing is hurting myself. I don't need this. *I don't need it.*" She caught herself, then went on in a whisper, "At least...I know now. I know he's okay. And he's with people who love him. That's all I wanted...."

"Well," said Troy, easing his own aching chest with a breath, "maybe what you should do is leave the diary with Dobrina. If anybody can bring that boy around, she— Hey, what are you doing?"

What Charly was doing was rolling her window down. And before he could even think about stopping her, she'd already done it. She'd thrown the diary out of the car.

Troy gasped as he watched the little green book go arcing through the air, over the side of the embankment, to land somewhere in the underbrush below.

"What'd you do that for?" he yelled as he tromped reflexively on the brake, looking wildly around for a place to pull over.

"Just...get me out of here," she said tersely, rocking herself with her arms folded across her waist, as if she had a bad bellyache. She sounded like her jaws were wired together. "Just...get me away from this town. *God...*" She leaned back suddenly, lifting her hands to push her hair away from her face in a gesture that was becoming familiar to him, then gave her head that little shake that settled everything back into its proper place. He couldn't help but think how symbolic that was. "I can't wait," she said in a voice that was rough with passion, "to get back to L.A. Back to *civilization*."

"Lady," Troy growled, "you've got a pretty peculiar idea of civilization." He wasn't sure whether he was mad at her for what she'd done—throwing her diary away—although he was still jangling from the shock of that, for sure. Or the people—the fates— that had hurt her so badly. Or whether it was just the accumulation of everything he'd had to deal with over the past few days. Either way, it had finally happened. He'd reached the end of his rope.

And Charly knew it. She felt the sudden coldness of fear—not of *him,* not of Troy, she knew he'd never hurt her, not in a million years—but of losing something she hadn't known was hers until that moment.

"Okay, maybe that was a bad choice of words," she said, glancing at him uneasily. "I just meant—you know, some place where life is a bit more sophisticated. All this soap-opera stuff is getting to me."

"Sophisticated." He said the word, then snorted. "You know, Mirabella says that about you—'Charly's so confident, so funny and smart. So cool and sophisticated'—like it was a compliment. Well, hell, lady—let me ask you this—What does that mean, anyway? Can you tell me that?" He threw her a look, but she didn't reply, and he went back to watching the road while she sat hunched and cold, watching a muscle work in the side of his jaw.

After a while he went on, in the slow, measured way people do when they aren't used to making speeches. "All I know is, folks who live in small towns, particularly Southern small towns, are supposed to be *un*sophisticated. And folks who live in big cities supposed to be *sophisticated*. So, what is it? Huh? You tell me. Some kind of dress thing? Knowin' what wine to order? Bein' in on who's hip, who's hot and who's not? Does it mean big-city folks know more'n small-town folks?"

He gave a short, harsh laugh. "I'll tell you somethin', lady— when you live in a small town you learn more about human nature and the dirty little secrets people carry around with them, and what makes for good and evil, than anybody. You oughta know that.''

She opened her mouth to say something, but changed her mind when she saw he was only thinking, and hadn't finished yet. She swallowed instead, and it sounded loud in the silence.

''Maybe,'' he said after a moment, tilting his head a little to one side, ''that's what sophistication means. Not how much you know, but whether or not you give a rip. Tell me somethin'—in L.A. when you hear a siren, what do you think about? Do you even notice? Does anybody? In a small town, when folks hear a siren, let me tell you, they *notice*. They stop what they're doin' and they listen, and they're tryin' to figure out what kind of siren it is, and where it's going. And if it comes down their street, they run out on their porches and front lawns to see it, and their hearts are pounding, and they're wonderin' who it's for, which one of their neighbors is in trouble. And after it goes by, five minutes later they're on the phone to their neighbors, askin' who is it? What's wrong? Is everybody okay? Can I help? And if it's anybody they're connected to even a little bit, the next day they're goin' up the walk with a covered casserole dish in their hands. And come Sunday, you can bet they're gonna be mentioning those people in their prayers.

''Do they make mistakes sometimes? Do they rush to judgment? Do they gossip and find fault? Act mean and petty sometimes? You bet they do. But they care. Maybe that's not very sophisticated, but you know what? *I* don't care. Because that's the kind of place I want to live in, where people care about one another, warts and all. And that's the kind of place I want my kids to grow up in. You can go on back to your sophisticated city folks, lady. Tell you somethin'—people live like that because they don't want the burdens that come from caring, and that's the truth. And to make themselves feel better about it, less lonely, maybe, they call themselves *sophisticated*.''

On the last word the Cherokee jerked to a stop. Charly looked up, surprised to see that they were back at the Mourning Springs

Motel, parked in front of room 10. Her vision blurred and shimmered.

"Here's the key," Troy said in a harsh and gravel-filled voice. "You're paid up for tonight, if you need it."

She could only stare at him, cold inside with fear and shock, unable to believe she could have blown it so badly. So suddenly.

His eyes...his beautiful eyes gazed back at her, dark with disappointment and pain. *What do you want from me?* She knew the answer to that question now—maybe she always had. Something she hadn't been able to give him, then. Maybe she still couldn't. But, dear God—had she lost any chance she might have had to try?

"You're leaving already?" she mumbled. Her lips felt stiff and numb. *Please, Troy...please don't give up on me.*

"Time I headed on back." He was mumbling, too. "Need to get at that nursery job for Mirabella."

"What about your bag? It's inside."

"You can bring it to me when you come. I expect we'll be seein' each other. At the wedding..."

"Yeah," she whispered. "Okay...sure, I'll do that." He was holding out his hand, giving her the room key. What could she do but take it? And after that...

She groped blindly for the door handle. *Jeez,* she was thinking, *all I've done since I got to this damn town is cry.* She found it finally and pulled it open. "Well," she said, "thanks for everything. I really do appreciate all your help."

"No problem," said Troy abruptly. "Glad to do it. Listen—" she turned to look at him, and he nodded at her "—I hope everything works out for you. And you let me know how your daddy's doin', y'hear?"

"Yeah...sure. I'll do that." She felt numb.

She was about to slide out of the seat when Bubba suddenly stuck his head over the back of it and gave her face a worried lick. It was almost more than she could take. She wrapped her arms around the dog's neck and buried her face briefly in his silky coat, then choked out a strangled "Bye—thank you," and hopped out of the car, slamming the door behind her. She hadn't

even turned around before she heard the Cherokee's engine roar
as Troy backed out of the parking space and drove away.

"Well, Charly," she whispered as she fumbled to put the key
in the lock and tears dripped from the end of her nose and
splashed onto the backs of her hands, "you are really somethin'
else, you know that? Cool, capable, *sophisticated* Charly... So if
you're so damn *smart*," she growled furiously as the lock finally
gave and she pushed the door open, "how come, when it comes
to human relationships, you...don't...know...*jack!*"

Troy drove like a bat outta hell. It did enter his mind, as he
headed up the curving mountain road, that if the right trooper
happened along, Charly might wind up bailing *him* out of jail.
But he didn't let it slow him down.

Just before he got to the fork where the road to Mourning
Spring Park branched off the main highway, he pulled over onto
the grassy verge, turned on his flashers and stopped. He had
nerves jumping around in his belly like fleas on a hot rock, and
thoughts and emotions chasing one another around inside his
head. He knew if he could ever manage to pin one of them down
he probably wouldn't be doing what he was doing, so he didn't
even try.

He got out of the car and slammed the door, then went around
to the back and got Bubba's leash. He gave the pup a hug and
rumpled his neck fur as he clipped the leash onto his collar. Then
he said, "Okay, boy, let's go find Charly!" and stood back out
of his way.

Of course, ol' Bubba was just happy to be out of the car, happy
to have some new territory to investigate and mark in his usual
way. Down the bank he went, Troy slippin' and slidin' along after
him, just trying not to lose his feet. When they got to the bottom,
he let the dog snuffle around some, then gave his leash a yank
and said it again, "Come on boy—find Charly. Where's Charly?
Go get her—go on!"

What was he thinking of? The dog wasn't even a tracker to
begin with, and nothin' but a pup besides. And there were enough
interesting, good-smelling distractions in those woods to keep him

busy all afternoon, what with squirrels and turtles, mushrooms and deer sign and no telling what all. So Troy wasn't expecting much.

They'd been at it maybe fifteen minutes and had gone about fifty yards from where they'd started, Troy thinking it was about time to call it quits on this crazy fool idea, Bubba plowing his way into a little thicket of cedar and holly where last winter's leaves still lay rotting in knee-deep drifts. Troy was about to call him back when the pup, instead of snuffling on to the next excitement, sat abruptly back on his haunches and turned to look at him over his shoulder.

"What is it, boy? What'd you find?"

Bubba just looked at him, tongue hangin' out, pleased with himself. So Troy went on over and dug around in the piles of leaves, and there it was. Impossible to see because of its color—without the dog he'd never have found it in a million years.

"Good boy—good ol' Bubba..." Troy crooned, hugging and petting the dog for all he was worth. His heart was pounding in his chest and those thoughts and emotions were still running around in his head, and he still didn't care to try to pin any of 'em down.

Instead he tucked the little green book inside the waistband of his jeans, and he and the dog scrambled back up the bank and loped down the road to where the Cherokee was parked with its flashers still blinking away. He opened up the door, and Bubba jumped in ahead of him and wallowed across to the passenger's side. Troy got in and started up the truck and off they went, burnin' rubber, heading up the mountain toward the spring.

Troy was banking on the kid still being there, and he was—not sitting on the picnic table any longer, but standing over by the granite memorial, sort of leaning against it, with his arms folded on his chest, staring down at his feet and brooding. And there's nobody does that better, Troy thought, than a twenty-year-old kid.

Cutter straightened up like a shot, though, when he saw the Cherokee, his face looking like a thundercloud, eyes shootin' sparks. He seemed a little less sure of himself when he saw Troy was alone.

"I was just leavin'," the boy muttered, starting past Troy with his head down.

Troy stopped him with a hand on his shoulder. "Not yet, you're not." He walked him backward until he was up against the granite monument again. "I got somethin' to say to you first. And make no mistake, this isn't your mama talkin' to you now. You *will* do me the courtesy of listenin'. You got that?"

Only a fool or a very stupid man would care to argue with Troy Starr when he used that tone of voice. Cutter was neither. He nodded.

Troy let out a breath. "That's better." He held up the diary, and the boy's eyes fastened on it, blazing with helpless fury.

"A little while ago, your mother tried to give this to you," Troy said in a quiet voice. "You refused to take it, and that's your choice. I can understand you being afraid—"

"I'm not afraid!"

"Yeah, you are. And like I said, I can understand that. Sometimes it takes a lot more courage to face up to a brand-new truth than it does to hang on to a good ol' familiar lie. Look, I can't force you to read this. But what I am gonna do is read just one little bit of it to you, and unless you know of a way to turn off your hearing, you're gonna listen to it. And after that…well, the rest is up to you."

He let go of the boy's shoulder and opened the diary. He cleared his throat. "Okay. This is what your mother wrote on April 12, 1978—that date sound familiar to you? That's your birthday, right? Okay, you just shut up and listen…

And then he started to read. "'Today I held my son in my arms….'"

Chapter 15

April 12, 1978

Dear Diary,

Today I held my son in my arms. I'm naming him Colin
Stewart, after his daddy. I just wish his daddy could be
here to see how beautiful he is. Aunt Dobie says he is here,
looking down on us from Heaven, and that he will always
be with us. I don't know if I believe that—about Heaven,
I mean—but if it's true, then Colin, would you please look
after our baby? Keep him safe, and see he grows up happy
and strong, and make him be a good and sweet person, like
you were. Because I won't be able to. They won't let me
keep him. They let me hold him for just a little while, and
then they came and took him away. They took him right
out of my arms. It felt like my heart was being torn out of
my chest. I've never hurt this bad—not even when he was
being born, not even when Colin died. I don't know what
I'm going to do. I don't think I can stand to live here
anymore.

Thought for the Day: Sometimes I think Colin is the lucky one.

April 13, 1978

Dear Diary,

Today I am leaving this God Forsaken place forever....

Troy closed the diary and thrust it against Cutter's chest, pinning it there with his hand. "It's yours now," he said hoarsely. "It's up to you."

He didn't wait to see if the kid was gonna take the book or not, or even look at his face; his own vision was blurring, and after all, he had a certain image to protect. He just turned around and walked back to his truck and got in it and drove away.

He drove down the highway to the fork in the road, where he turned right instead of left, heading south out of the Alabama hills, heading home to Georgia. He didn't look for a radio station playing golden oldies this time, or pop in one of his favorite tapes to keep him company. He drove all the way home with his own song playing inside his head. A song with only one lyric: "Charly...Charly...Charly..."

"I'm the one supposed to be doin' that for you," Troy said, scowling down at the yellow rosebud his brother was pinning to his lapel.

"Aw, you'd just go an' stick yourself," said Jimmy Joe, smiling his slow, sweet smile.

Troy snorted. "Yeah? Well, what's the matter with you, anyway, little brother? You're the one gettin' married. How come you're not nervous?"

Jimmy Joe tilted his head to admire his handiwork. "Got nothin' to be nervous about. This is the smartest and best thing I ever did. When you know you've found the right one..."

"Yeah..." Troy said on an exhalation as he turned away to check himself in the full-length mirror on the door.

They were in their old room at his mother's house, the room four Starr brothers had once shared. His mama had turned it into some kind of den, maybe partly an office, with a big desk and a computer, and a couch with a pull-out bed in it for company. But there were still a lot of memories there in that room. He could see some of them in the mirror, the team photos and graduation portraits on the walls, and the shelves full of sports trophies. His little brother's face, looking at him over his shoulder.

"You're a lucky man," he said softly.

"Don't I know it."

There was a silence then, the kind that falls between brothers who are also friends, but who wouldn't know how to put that into words if their lives depended on it. The door opened, and the minister from the Methodist church down the road stuck his head in.

"It's time," he said, pointing at his watch. "You boys about ready?"

"Will be in a minute," said Jimmy Joe. The minister nodded and closed the door. Jimmy Joe turned and picked up his suit jacket from the arm of the couch, and Troy took it from him and held it for him while he shrugged himself into it. He felt like he oughta pinch himself—he was having a hard time getting used to the sight of his truck-driver brother in a suit and tie.

"These jitters of yours," Jimmy Joe said, checking out his tie in the mirror one last time. "They wouldn't have anything to do with the fact that you're about to come face-to-face with a certain good-lookin' maid-of-honor, would they?"

Troy let out a breath in a short laugh. "You know somethin'? Findin' the right woman, that's one thing. Gettin' her to realize it—now, that's somethin' else."

"Oh, yeah," Jimmy Joe said with a chuckle, "Mirabella, now...she took a *lotta* convincing."

Troy gave him a curious look. "That right? How'd you do it?"

His brother's smile would have been smug on anybody else but him. "Refused to take no for an answer."

"Yeah, well...it's not always that easy," Troy said, frowning.

"Hey, I never knew you to give up on a fight."

"It's not a case of giving up. It's more like...the ball's in her court, now, you know? I've done about all I can do." Troy paused with his hand on the doorknob, thinking about it, looking for the words. Finally he cleared his throat. "She's got...some issues."

"Yeah," said Jimmy Joe, putting his arm across his brother's shoulders, "Marybell mentioned that."

"I think she'd like to say yes," said Troy gruffly. "But she doesn't think she deserves to." He gave his brother a hard, intent look. "You know what I mean?"

Jimmy Joe gave his back a slap. "Yeah, man...I believe I do."

Troy opened the door, and they went through it together. They could see the minister waiting for them at the bottom of the stairs. Just as they started down, Jimmy Joe nudged him in the ribs and whispered, "Don't give up on her."

Then the minister had him by the arm and was hustling them both through the French doors and out into the backyard, down the aisle between rows of folding chairs that had been borrowed from the Methodist church and set up last evening on the lawn. When he got to the rose arbor at the far end, the minister turned and faced the congregation, Jimmy Joe on his left and Troy right behind him.

It was a beautiful day. The line of thunderstorms had moved on, so the humidity was about normal for June in Georgia, the sky a pale, hazy blue and a hum of bees and the smell of flowers in the air. The friends and relations gathered in the folding chairs were fanning themselves, the ones unlucky enough to be in the sunny patches turning red in the face anyway, but nobody getting too unhappy about it, since it was pretty much to be expected, that time of year.

Troy stood beside his brother, drowning in his own sweat and his heart going like a freight train, and watched his family and Mirabella's come down the aisle—the kids first, Jimmy Joe's boy, J.J., pushing Amy in her stroller, his cousin Sammi June beside him, the two of 'em nudging and poking one another with their elbows. Then Mirabella's sister Summer holding her two kids by the hands, and after that, the other sister, the older one—

Eve, her name was—the globe-trotting TV producer, both of them tall, blond California girls, real knockouts. And then all the rest of his and Jimmy Joe's brothers and sisters: Roy and Jessica, Calvin and Rhonda, and Joy Lynn, who'd already done this twice herself and hadn't managed to figure out how to get it right yet.

So there they all were, gathered around the minister and Jimmy Joe, and all laughing and smiling just like it was a family picnic or something. And then they all watched as their parents came down the aisle, Mirabella's dad with her mom on his arm, Jimmy Joe's mama helping *her* mama, Granny Calhoun, along. It was the way Mirabella had wanted it, all the families together, and Troy thought it was just the way it oughta be. He was already starting to get a lump in his throat and a crowded feeling in his chest he thought could have been happiness, if there hadn't been something important missing. As it was, it just felt like loneliness.

The parents and Granny Calhoun took their seats in the front row of chairs. The organist from the Methodist church struck some chords on the old upright piano—which Troy and his brothers had hauled out onto the patio last night—and then launched right into "Here Comes the Bride." A rustle of anticipation ran through the crowd, and Troy felt the same shiver in his insides. Everybody turned to look. Troy was looking, too, but his vision was starting to go shimmery on him.

And then here she came. *Charly.*

She came down the aisle toward him, looking straight ahead, walking with assurance in spite of the grass and the high-heeled shoes, with those incredible legs of hers going on forever. He thought she seemed thinner than when he'd seen her last, but it could have been the dress, which was the soft green of new leaves, with a skirt that stopped just above her knees, and a top that left her throat and arms bare. Her skin was pale as wax, and she had her hair slicked back and up in that way that reminded him of Audrey Hepburn, or maybe a prima ballerina, and topped with yellow roses. She was holding a yellow rose, too—he happened to know they'd been picked this morning from this very garden.

Troy thought she was the most beautiful sight he'd ever seen in his life.

But that wasn't what had his throat swelling up and his eyes misting over. What did him in was the way she carried herself—head high, shoulders back, and a "Go ahead, make my day!" look to her chin—that took him straight back to the first time he'd ever set eyes on her, that night he'd watched her come toward him down that hallway in the Mourning Spring jail. Bravado. Sheer bravado.

As the maid of honor took her place on the minister's right, Troy could hear Bubba barking out in front of the house, where he'd been tied to a tree to keep him from getting in the way. At least, he thought, he's not howling.

And then the organist started the wedding march all over again, and it was Mirabella's turn to make that long walk down the aisle. Troy knew he should be watching her along with his brother and everyone else, but he couldn't seem to take his eyes off Charly.

Don't give up on her.

Troy could hear his brother's voice as clear as if he'd just spoken the words aloud. And right then and there he vowed he never would, no matter how long it took.

He wasn't sure when he'd stopped worrying and thinking about what he was going to do with himself now that he'd retired from the navy. He just knew it didn't matter anymore *what* he did with the rest of his life; the only thing that mattered was *whom* he did it with. And he knew, beyond any shadow of a doubt, that the *who* for him was the woman standing across from him, the woman with the pain of unresolved issues in her whiskey eyes. It didn't matter to him that she was an L.A. lawyer with some peculiar notions about what sophistication was, or that she'd made up her mind to hate everything about the South. He didn't care that she had no real idea what it was like to be part of a family—he figured he had family enough for the both of 'em, and he couldn't wait to make her a part of it. All he knew was, in her he'd found his soul's compass, his life's magnetic north. All the rest, as he'd heard it said somewhere, was details.

For the first time in his life he thought maybe he understood why it is that people cry at weddings.

"Dearly beloved," the minister began, "we are gathered here in the sight of God and this congregation to join this man and this woman in holy matrimony...."

When he got to the part that usually goes "Who gives this woman to be married..." and so on, what he said instead was, "Who stands with this man and this woman?" That had been another one of Mirabella's ideas.

Then all the family that was gathered around shouted out in joyful chorus, "We do!" And they scattered and took their seats, all but Charly and Troy, while Mirabella and Jimmy Joe came together face-to-face in front of the minister, and took hold of each other's hands.

It was then, in the humming, rustling quiet, while everyone was getting settled again, that Troy heard Charly make a sound. A soft, choking sound.

Her face looked frozen, pale as marble. In it, her eyes seemed to glow like liquid fire. But she was gazing, not at him, not at the bride and groom, not at anyone in the seated congregation, but beyond them. At someone who was standing there, all alone. A young man, hardly more than a boy, with dark gold hair, a sensitive face and a certain proud jut to his chin.

Cutter.

He was holding something in his hands. A small book, bound in dark green leather.

My diary. Charly stared at it, uncomprehending. *But...that's impossible.*

Then slowly, wonderingly, she turned to Troy. She knew that tears were streaming down her face, but she didn't care. Through them she saw sunshine...rainbows. And she could see his face, more clearly than she'd ever seen anything in her life before.

"...and do you take this man...to have and to hold...to love and to cherish...from this day forward, as long as you both shall live?"

She heard the words, but they seemed to come from the sky and the air, the sunshine and breezes, from the grass and the flowers and trees. From deep inside her, from her heart...from her soul.

With her eyes clinging to his...to the most beautiful, incredible, miraculous pair of eyes she'd ever seen...she felt her own lips moving, forming the words as Jimmy Joe and Mirabella spoke them aloud.

And through the golden shimmer of her tears she could see Troy's lips saying them, too, at the very same moment:

Yes! Yes...I do.

I love you.

Epilogue

From the diary of Charlene Elizabeth Phelps
Final Entry

(So much has happened between my last entry and this one, it would take a book to tell it all. Maybe I will do that someday—write a book about it—who knows? Stranger things have happened!)

October 5, 1998

Dear Diary: (Okay, it still seems hokey to me, this business of writing to an inanimate object as if it were a living, breathing person, but I suppose customs must be adhered to.)

I came home today. Home to—are you ready for this?—Mourning Spring, Alabama. That's right, the very same place I ran away from over twenty years ago, swearing never to return.

Home. What an amazing thing. How could I not have

known that home isn't a place at all? But a state of mind—
or perhaps I should say, of the heart—a safe haven created
by the people we love, and that love us. Yes—love us. I,
Charly Phelps, am loved! Is that incredible, or what? Even
more amazing, I am loved even though I have done nothing
whatsoever to deserve it! I am loved in spite of myself.
This is a truly incredible and humbling thing, and I am
having trouble even now believing that it is true.

But it is true, Dear Diary. Today, a few hours ago now,
right down there in the backyard of the house where I grew
up, where Colin and I used to play, I officially became
something I never in a million years ever thought I'd be.
Yup, I am now the wife of an honest-to-God Southerner.
Who'd a' thought, huh? Wow.

My wedding day. Could it possibly have been more
beautiful? The sky was so blue and the sun so warm, and
for a backdrop, the woods where Colin and I once hid notes
to each other, looking as though they were on fire. (Poor
Bubba just about had a fit because he couldn't get loose
and chase after the squirrels!)

It was a very simple ceremony. Naturally, we had Bella
and Jimmy Joe stand up with us, although I sort of hated
to impose on Bella, what with all the trouble and worry
she's having over her sisters (especially Summer with that
no-good ex-husband of hers still missing—and if you ask
me he's probably dead by now—and Evie off somewhere
in South America filming giant reptiles or who knows
what.) But you know Mirabella. Not only was she my maid
of honor, but she insisted on planning the entire wedding,
down to the nth detail! All I can say is, it's a good thing
Jimmy Joe is a patient man.

I can't believe how many people were there. All of
Troy's kinfolk came up from Georgia, which is a good-size
bunch right there! And most of the town of Mourning
Spring, it seemed like. (Kelly Grace bawled her eyes out,
wouldn't you know.) Anyway, I guess the town's forgiven
me, especially since the judge came through his bypass

surgery and is out of the hospital and doing so well. He—my dad—was right there in the front row, and he looked pretty impressive, if you ask me, even without his robes. (Troy had the idea of having him marry us, but Dobie wouldn't hear of it, and insisted on a preacher.) Anyway, he sat there the whole time holding Dobie's hand, right in front of everybody. ('Brina, he calls her—my stepmom. Wow.)

He looked proud. PROUD. Of me. Can you believe it?

And right next to him was Cutter. Cutter, my beautiful, miraculous, grown-up son. Still very much a stranger to me, but then I can't expect to make up for the twenty years I've missed overnight. At least we're talking, getting to know one another little by little. Who knows? Maybe one day we'll get to be friends. It's getting easier, these days, to believe in miracles.

I walked my own self down the aisle. Hey—what did you expect? I've been on my own most of my life, it wouldn't make much sense to have somebody "give me away" at this late date, would it? Anyway, I did it, walked down the aisle—which by the way was an actual white carpet, Mirabella's idea, which she says she learned the hard way after trying to walk on grass in high heels at her wedding!—and down there at the other end, there was Troy, waiting for me.

Oh boy. I'm not sure I can find the words to tell what I felt then. What I still and will always feel, for as long as I live. I remember that I couldn't feel my feet touching the ground. I remember that I felt as if I were flying, and at the same time like I wanted very much to cry. I'm still not sure I deserve to be so happy. But you know what? Dobie said all those years ago that God had something important for me to do, and I know now that she was right. It was this and only this: to love and be loved by this man.

Troy says that I am his compass, his magnetic north. I understand, now, what he means by that, because today I found out that he is mine as well. It was at that moment when I put my hand in his that I knew I had found my way home.

Well, Dear Diary, I guess this is it. It's time to say good-bye. Troy is waiting for me to finish this so we can begin our life together. (Yes, he, too, is a patient man!) We're going to the South Pacific for our honeymoon, can you believe that? We are such a cliché! When we come back—and we are in no hurry, believe me!—we are going to be hanging out our shingles in downtown Atlanta (I forget the name of the street, something with Peachtree in it, probably) not far from the capitol building. That's right, I said "shingles"—plural. Troy's decided to go into the investigations business. He's going to specialize in finding missing children and reuniting broken families, isn't that cool? And one of his first clients is for sure going to be the law firm of Charlene Phelps-Starr, right next door.

We're not going to live in the city, though. No way. We've bought a place north of town near a lake, about halfway between Troy's folks and mine, with enough room for Bubba to swim and roam and chase all the squirrels he wants. Room for kids, too. Lots of them.

Funny how things happen, isn't it, the twists and turns in life's pathways that bring us full circle back to where we began? Maybe Dobie was right, and everything that's happened is, if not the Will of God, at least just part of some complicated structure called My Life, each part necessary in bringing me here, to this:

Home.

Oh yeah—almost forgot—Thought for the Day: I was wrong about knights. Yes, there are still a few around. Well, at least one.

And you know what? He doesn't look anything at all like...you know who.

* * * * *

Take 2 bestselling love stories FREE

Plus get a FREE surprise gift!